That Moment When

That Moment When

George K. Jordan

URBAN BOOKS

www.urbanbooks.net

URBAN SOUL is published by

Urban Books
10 Brennan Place
Deer Park, NY 11729

ISBN-13: 978-1-59983-019-3
ISBN-10: 1-59983-019-1

First Printing: April 2007

10 9 8 7 6 5 4 3 2 1

Printed in the United States of America

Chapter I

"Get out of the car," a voice boomed against the windowpane. The man said some other things, but my eyes focused on the long black gun barrel pointing at my head through the windowpane. My hands were trembling so badly I dropped my car keys. They bounced against the cup holder and thumped on the passenger floor.

"Bitch, get out of the car!" *I'm trying*! I screamed in my head, but my body wouldn't cooperate. I tried to will my fingers to curl around the door handle, but they froze on the armrest like gargoyles, petrified on a rooftop. My eyes darted from the gun to the man's face.

He wore a black cap that covered the top of his head, but when he looked over the top of the car for one brief second, I got a clear view of his face. Proud cheekbones held it together like chiseled marble. But when you looked into his eyes, set deep under bushy eyebrows, his youthfulness gave him away. He was a baby. Probably somebody's prom date just last summer.

You watch the nightly news and see the mug shots of so-called killers, rapists, and thugs. They almost snarl for the camera. Almost always their perms or braids need a touch-up and they look like the photo was taken just as they got out of bed. But this boy/man was unnervingly handsome. How many situations had he taken advantage of because of this fact? How many women had fallen prey to his pretty face? Was I next?

Suddenly the man cocked his arm back and slammed the gun into the window. Glass shattered everywhere, pelting my face and arms. After the flash of pain, the glass felt almost like hard raindrops. They splashed across the dashboard, and I watched as they rolled all the way to the passenger side.

I heard some rustling on the inside of my car and watched as the door swung open. A strong arm grabbed mine. I could feel each finger pressing hard against my flesh. I tried to resist, gripping the armrest to anchor myself. But the man was too strong. In a twisted tango, he swung me out of the door and tossed me to the concrete. I made a last-ditch effort to land on my butt.

The man attempted a passing glance, but stopped in his tracks and looked at me for a long second. I watched his eyes zero in on my big belly. He must have realized I was pregnant. His eyes seemed to sink for a moment and then he hopped into the driver's seat. He leaned over in the seat, and for a brief moment my purse entered my mind. I didn't need my wallet or credit cards. But I definitely needed my BlackBerry.

It had client numbers, private e-mail addresses of celebrities I would never be able to obtain again. It was my career, my life trapped on an LCD screen. I leaned against the curb and pushed myself up to a parking meter. Balancing on its pole I pulled myself upright. The man was still fumbling in the front seat. I knew when he unlatched my door he had unlocked all the doors. I quietly tried to open the back door, maneuvered it a few inches, and stuck my hand inside. I clutched the BlackBerry and slowly attempted to pull my hand out. I almost got to the door when I heard the engine roar.

The truck bucked back, carrying me along with it. I lost my grip on the BlackBerry, and the car jerked forward. The seat belt caught my arm, and I was pulled down God knows how many blocks. My head tilted back so far, I only saw the bright sky watching the entire event. The car veered to the right and I tumbled to the ground and rolled until I skidded on my back to a halt.

The sky was the kind of blue that encourages picnics and long walks through open fields. Only the occasional cotton-ball-shaped cloud coasted through the sea of blue. The sun toasted my face. I could feel the streams of sweat as they dripped from my soaked hair and plopped into my ear canals. I focused on the sky and counted four passing puffballs before I heard a man's voice.

"Ma'am," the man said, his face dropping to just a few inches from mine. "Can you hear me, ma'am?"

His head lifted away from me and I wanted to grab him and scream, "Don't go! Don't leave me here!"

"We have another victim behind the bank." His hand touched my belly. "She's pregnant. We need an ambulance now!"

His hands pushed back my hair. "I'm so sorry, ma'am. I can't believe . . ." I squinted to protect my eyes as the sun's glare reflected off the man's badge.

"I have to go get this guy now, ma'am." His soft hands caressed my face. I could hear an ambulance wailing behind us. Several doors slammed and then there were voices and hands everywhere.

"Hey, sweetie," a female voice said. "I know you are tired of this hard ground." It wasn't until she said the words that I could feel the glass and gravel that ripped my skin and embedded themselves in my back. I nodded and tried to smile, but only tears came out.

"We got her now, Officer. She's going to be all right."

"I gotta go," the officer said. He leaned down again. "It was a pleasure meeting you, ma'am."

I smiled. He was gone.

"All right, y'all, let's go," the woman said. I saw a hulking form at my feet. "One, two, three." I was lifted onto a stretcher. Needles poked through my arm. A cool soothing feeling traveled through my arm, and then there was only black.

A sharp jutting pain brought me back. As my eyes adjusted to the blinding light I could make out a few shapes. A beige door stood in the corner of a room. Azure-colored walls framed the door and a small window dressed in venetian blinds. The pain subsided and a glazed heat covered my body. I watched as white outfits moved quickly in and out of my room. This worried me. People only moved quickly when there was something serious. But then my eyes fixed on the familiar hand that palmed mine. I traced it back to my husband.

"David," I mouthed. I could barely make out what I said.

"Hey, baby girl." His eyes were puffy and his face was shiny and wet. "How ya feeling?"

"Like someone put me into the trash compactor by mistake."

"You were definitely bounced around."

"What happened?"

"You were carjacked."

"Are you serious?" Another pain stabbed my leg, but I realized I had a morphine drip and its clicker in my hand. I pushed the button until the hurt subsided.

"Yeah, babe, what do you remember?"

"His face. The gun."

"Jesus." David's hand gripped mine harder.

"I remember trying to get my BlackBerry out of the backseat."

"What?" David's voice rose into his nose, and had that whiny tone he used whenever he wanted to lecture me. "Why would you do that?"

"I had five years of connections on that thing."

"He could have killed you, J.C."

"I would have killed myself if I let him drive off with it."

He leaned in, shaking his head.

"Why me? Why then?"

"The police said he robbed a bank just down the street from you and needed a ride to escape."

"This is Atlanta. He could have bought a getaway car without so much as a credit check."

David offered me a pity laugh, but his hand gripped mine tighter.

"Six years I have lived here, never even had my car broken into. Then, on the greatest day of my life, I get carjacked, robbed." I felt the bitterness gather in the back of my mouth as I spoke. Indeed, before that moment it had been the perfect day.

Thanks to some persistent calls and heavy prayer, I had finally landed a meeting with Carlos Vega, the biggest thing to happen to R&B since Usher. He moved to Atlanta after a major shuffle at his record label left him without a contract. Monumental Records quickly snatched him up and moved him down here to work with Daddy Brown, the hottest producer around.

As I sat in the lobby of Monumental Records' corporate office, I clamped my hands over my knees in a sad attempt to calm my bladder. I was so close to landing the client of my life, I didn't want to go pee and miss Carlos as he walked out of his office. He said he only had a few moments.

"Ms. West." The receptionist finally stopped jabbering on the other line long enough to acknowledge my presence. She swiveled her chair around to face me. Her nails were painted the kind of red you only see on girls on late night phone line commercials or porn ads. The word LEXUS was embroidered in tacky gold, à la Carrie from *Sex in the City*, and hung around her neck.

"Mr. Vega is on an important phone call and won't be able to see you today." I held my smile in place as this little girl lied to my face. "He said if you leave your card he'll be sure to get back to you next week."

The corners of the girl's mouth crinkled deep, revealing a shameless smirk, and I pondered if my purse was heavy enough to knock her unconscious. I couldn't leave now. Next week, some PR shark would pounce on him at an after-party. Or worse, he'd promote some heffa he slept with to the coveted spot, and I'd be back representing children's hospitals. This was my one shot to make it to the big leagues. I had to think fast. I was desperate. Suddenly it hit me. I relaxed my muscles and let the Avian water I had drunk earlier that morning trickle down my leg.

"Oh my God." I clenched my stomach.

"What is it?" The woman jumped to her feet.

"My water just broke." I stepped back to reveal the small puddle on the carpet."

"Oh my God, should I call 911?" The woman scrambled to dial the phone.

"I got them on my cell." I placed the phone to my ear. "Could you just get me a towel, some napkins or something?"

"Sure, I'll be right back." The girl scooted to the bathroom. I watched until the tattoo on the small of her back disappeared around the corner, and then headed down the hallway her desk was guarding. I passed a couple of empty offices until I reached a door with a red light lit above it. I peeked inside the window and saw several brothers bobbing their heads in front of a mixing board. I took a deep breath and made my entrance.

It took a second for one of them to look up, but then a small guy in a chair toward the end of the board looked up and muttered, "What the hell?" From the way everyone looked at him before they glanced my way, I knew he was the center of the show. He was Carlos.

"Look, I have about two minutes before your brilliant receptionist discovers I didn't melt into the floor and calls security."

"Who the hell are you?" The guy punching the buttons on the boards swung around to face me too. It was Daddy

Brown; I would recognize those long locks twisted into tight braids anywhere.

"My name is J.C. West and I am your publicist." I tried my best to saunter with six months of baby riding low in the front. "I am smart, hungry, and willing to do anything for my clients."

"How did you get in here?" Carlos asked. He folded his arms. He was interested.

"I told the receptionist I was having my baby now and pretended that my water broke." I smiled. "By the way, you will have to replace your carpet." The entire room cringed as I stepped closer to Carlos.

"You are at a critical point in your career." I tapped one of the men next to Carlos and he rose to his feet. I plopped into the chair. "You have two great albums and a mediocre one. That's the one that got you dropped. That is why you are here. Everything has to go right. The beats, the songs, and your presentation—I can help with that."

"He's already using my PR people," Daddy interjected.

"You mean the people who let your cocaine bust land you on the eleven o'clock news?"

"I told everyone that was not cocaine, it was protein supplement."

"I don't care if it was crack rock freshly cooked off a hooker's ass. No one would have found out if I was on the job."

The room fell silent and everyone began to look at each other. I could tell their minds were churning. I had them.

"Look, you can keep on hiring your cousins and groupies to do the job of a professional and see how far your career gets you. Or you can hire someone who was born to make you look good. That's all I got, boys." I pulled out a few business cards and placed them on the plush cushioning that wrapped around the equipment.

"You have my card. Call me when you want to stop playing music and be moguls." I hobbled out and let the door close behind me. As I suspected, Lexus and her henchmen were waiting in the hall for me. I had taken a few steps toward them when Carlos ran out to me.

"Hey, Ms. West." He wrapped his arm over my shoulder.

"Call me J.C."

"Yeah, J.C., um, give me your phone." I passed him my phone.

He punched at the keys and passed it back. "That's my private number. I like your style. You crazy like my little sister. Maybe we can do something."

We walked past the receptionist and I smirked at her as I passed. Carlos opened the door for me to leave.

"You will not regret this. Trust me. I will make you infamous. Like Michael Jackson before the courts got hold of him."

"Look forward to working with you," Carlos whispered as I shook his hand.

"Hey, is it a boy or girl?" Carlos asked as I turned toward the street.

I patted my belly. "It's a girl."

Suddenly, a rush of reality brought me back to the present. I could hear my heart pumping in my ears as my hands eased onto my stomach. The roundness was gone and only a soft, small hump remained. I pressed hard, searching for a kick or any movement.

I shot up and screamed, "David!" David caught me with his arms and held me. I could feel the tears hitting my bare shoulders.

"The baby didn't make it, J.C."

I didn't know if anyone could hear the sound I let out, but it rang in my ears like a bell. Then the nurses ran into the room and surrounded my bed.

"What's going on?" A nurse checked all the machines stirring softly next to my bed.

"I was just telling her about the baby." David rubbed my hand.

The woman's mouth drooped down slightly as her eyes fell on me. Her bottom lip pouted a bit. "Oh, honey. I know it seems like the end right now, but you will get past this. God never gives us more than we can handle." She moved into my space. "God will see you through this."

I wanted to ask, "Do we know the same God? 'Cause never in our conversations did he mention swiping my first child from me." In fact, I didn't recall getting any memos about being carjacked, thrown from a moving vehicle, or being in so much mind-numbing pain that even crying hurt.

"Thank you," I whispered. The nurse smiled and continued her checks. I wanted to cuss her out. Cut her throat for even pretending to understand the pain inside and outside my body. But why let her have it? Let her think she helped me. She'd go the cafeteria, order her pork chops and mashed potatoes, and tell the other nurses on duty how this poor girl lost everything in the blink of an eye. She'd breathe deep and sigh a little as her big breasts settled back into their casual pose. They would all shake their heads and think to themselves, *What a shame*. But it was okay because she told me God was on my side. They'd nod and moan, maybe even blurt out a quick prayer on my behalf. Then it'd be back to devouring their dead animals and ingesting ridiculous amounts of cholesterol while I lay in this bed unable to fathom leaving this place without my baby.

"Can I see her?" I asked David.

He gave me a bewildered expression. "Her, you mean . . ."

"Sonja."

David looked to the nurse who was on her way out, but the request stopped her in her tracks.

"Ms. West." The nurse cleared her throat. Her smile uncurled, forming a pseudo-serious grimace. "We had to dispose of the fetus. She is gone. I am sorry."

"I want to say good-bye."

"Baby, you can't," David said.

"I want to say good-bye."

"Baby—"

"I want to say I'm sorry."

"For what?"

"I told her I was tired of carrying her last month. I was sore, you were at work, and I couldn't get comfortable in the bed. I cursed her out. I said I wished she were out of me."

"J.C., that's just talk."

"I meant it, David," I screamed. "I wanted her gone, and now . . ."

"This is not your fault," he belted. "That mothafucka robbed you and left you for dead on the street. He killed our baby, not you." His eyes swam in tears. "He took away our baby girl. He is not going to make you blame yourself." The nurse backed out of the room and eased the door closed behind her.

"I want my baby." I wanted to scream, but only a whimper escaped my mouth.

"We are gonna have lots of kids," David said. "And Sonja will be in heaven watching over all of them."

"Do you think she will forgive me?"

"If she was anything like you, I'm sure she already has."

"What are we gonna do?"

David wrapped his arms around me. I could feel his steady heartbeat beating against my chest. "Whatever we have to do, baby," David said, and rocked me until my eyes closed and there was black again.

Chapter II

"Good morning. How can I help you?" Monica mumbled to a man, using that monotone voice Christopher hated so much. His eyes faced Eric, his bank manager, who waxed on about some issue he knew Christopher didn't care about, while Christopher kept attuned to Monica's movements. She was smart and a hard worker when encouraged. But one thing Christopher wouldn't stand for was attitude behind his teller counter. That was why he interviewed every teller personally.

HR and Eric hated that. "It's not proper for a VP to be interviewing tellers," Eric tried to scold him, in his typical passive-aggressive tone. But it was Christopher's job to ensure that his people were on point, especially *his* people. His bank was the only downtown branch with a predominantly black staff. And it was the most successful branch in the region. Other Southern National Bank managers came down to see why it was so successful.

"We have labored to build lasting relationships with the major businesses in the area," Eric boasted to them every time the question arose. The truth was that the moment you walked in the door you were greeted with smiles and friendly faces. Every point of entry and exit had greeter's who threw a smile before you could clearly focus in on their gold-plated nameplates.

Every teller offered a "How are you today?" or a "Have a fantastic afternoon."

Monica's body language was all wrong. Her arms pressed against the counter as she stretched her left heel out of the sling-backs she knew were against bank regulation. Christopher threw a dismissive finger in Eric's face to stifle his droning and headed toward Monica. He was halfway there when he realized that her body had jerked to attention. She nodded vigorously at the man. As he stepped closer, Christopher noticed her hands trembling as her right hand rubbed underneath the counter.

Was she . . . Christopher's stomach buckled when he thought of what Monica might be attempting to do. After a second she eased her hand behind her back and spread her fingers out in a V symbol. Fuck! She was being robbed. V was a hand signal Eric had devised in case tellers were unable to reach the silent alarm safely. Christopher casually slanted his direction so that he would reach one of the back tables and tap the silent alarm.

"Oh my God," Eric blurted, obviously catching Monica's signal. He attempted to run to his office.

"Hey, white boy, yo' teller here needs your help," the man called out to Eric over Monica's head. People started shifting their attention to booth eight, and Eric stood frozen. All the tellers slammed their drawers shut and moved toward the back. Customers started whispering. Where was security? He shot his best mean mug at Eric and quickly walked to Monica's station.

"How can I assist you, sir?" Christopher practically shoved Monica, who was visibly shaking, out of the way with his shoulder.

"I asked for the white boy." The man looked more like an art student than a bank robber. Splotches of paint covered almost an entire baggy pant leg. Christopher stifled a laugh looking at his *Bush is a Criminal* T-shirt.

"Well, I'm the bank vice president. I'm in charge."

"Yeah, right, you just some rent-a-cop playing games."

"No, he ain't," Monica yelled. "He is the VP."

"Bitch, ain't nobody talking to you." His hand moved to the small of his back.

"How can I help you?"

"Nigga, you know what this is."

"Oh my God!" a woman screamed from behind the man. "He's got a gun!" That was it. People broke in all directions, screaming and cursing. Some just dropped to the floor. Suddenly the fire alarm blared overhead and the man presented his weapon to Christopher.

"I want everything you got in all the drawers." The robber's hand quaked a bit. He twisted his arm, so that he looked like all the brothers trying to be badasses in the movies. But as Christopher looked into his eyes, he thought he couldn't have been more than twenty-three. His eyes still held the light of youthful arrogance and abject stupidity. At thirty-two, Christopher realized any light left in his eyes was diluted by vodka binges, Prozac, and the disappointing years that were his twenties.

"There betta not be no ink on this money or I am shooting as many niggas as I can."

Christopher reached in the drawers and pulled out the cash. He could hear the footsteps of the security guards finally scrambling out of the stairwell from their hiding place in the basement of the bank. He made a mental note to fire every last one of them as he pulled the last stack of hundreds from the last open station.

"If you don't hurt anyone in here, I will personally walk outside with you."

The man grabbed the bag from Christopher and gazed into his eyes. "You for real?"

"You have 230,000 dollars. I can replace that," Christopher said. "But if you harm one person in here my career will be finished, and those men behind you will kill you." The man stared for a second and finally looked back at the four armed men pointing guns at his chest.

"Climb over," the man demanded as Christopher hopped onto the counter and dropped to the floor. "Move slow." The man led Christopher across the marble floor. Each square seemed to stretch for miles until they finally reached the gold-trimmed double doors. Christopher pulled one door back and walked forward. *Thank God no cops*, Christopher thought. The man could run off and get caught down the street. Maybe they might even recover the money. No casualties, very little press.

The man peered down the street in both directions. "That fucking bitch!" he yelled out. "Bitch! Bitch! Bitch!" He moved a few steps back from Christopher and stomped on the ground. He kicked the brick wall behind him. Christopher prayed he was having a seizure and would possibly fall to the ground.

"Do not move." A deep voice disrupted Christopher's escape fantasy. An officer peered from behind a garbage bin. He wore a safety helmet, sunglasses, and shorts. A bicycle cop was going to ruin his life.

"Don't get buck, nigga, or I will shoot this buppie mothafucka."

"You will be dead before he hits the ground."

Christopher's mouth dropped in amazement. These two idiots were having a cockfight to see who had the biggest gun.

"Officer, we were handling this just fine," Christopher interjected.

"Shut up," the officer yelled. "Drop your weapon. There are like eight cops running this way who have been itching for a gunfight since they got out of the academy."

"I will shoot him."

"No, you won't. You're not that dumb."

"The hell I ain't."

The officer and Christopher simultaneously shook their

heads. But the officer quickly whipped off his glasses. "Damon?" he questioned.

"Huh?" The man's body, which was pressed against Christopher's, suddenly tensed.

"Damon Harvey, please tell me that ain't you, kid." The officer raised an eyebrow as silence filled the space between them.

"Naw, son, you got the wrong cat," the man said.

"Nigga, I was your mentor at the Boys and Girls Club," the officer said. "I practically changed your diapers. Don't you lie to me."

"We a long way from them days in the West End, man."

"Man, do you think yo' mama wants to see you on the news?"

"She'd be watching from heaven."

"That's even worse." The officer inched closer as he talked.

"Nigga, you been out of the hood since you went off to college," Damon yelled. "You don't know me or my life."

"I did," the officer said. "I didn't used to be just 'nigga.' I was yo boy Oscar. Man, you used to follow me around everywhere."

"And you left like all the rest." Damon stuck the gun harder into Christopher's back. "Well, while you was gone I had to handle mine."

"This is handling yours?" Oscar rolled into a fit of laughter. "Messing up a bank job in broad daylight? Not even having the decency to wear a mask? You might as well have left your business card."

"If you weren't here I would have been gone by now."

Christopher chuckled to himself. The kid was right.

"Well, I am here, and I am your only hope."

Oscar was just a few feet away from Christopher, whose feet were soaked from sweat. His legs were numb from standing so stiffly. He contemplated doing a drop and roll like he saw in the movies. But the man's hand grasped the back of his shirt.

"Look, Damon." Oscar extended his hand. "If you come with me, I can say you turned yourself in. I can personally attest to the real person you are."

"It's too late." Damon edged backward, pulling Christopher along with him. A low siren moaned in the distance.

"Those are for you." Oscar stepped toward the two men.

"I'm sorry, man, but I can't leave without this money."

"And I can't let you go."

"I will shoot you."

"I will kill you." Oscar pointed his gun at Damon.

"You ain't got time."

"Why?"

"You got a man down."

A shot crackled, and Christopher fell with a thud. He watched as Oscar dove to the ground, his gun firing at Damon. Smoke filled the air as bullets dug into the wall behind him. From the ground Christopher watched the back of the boy shrink down the street.

"Fuck!" Oscar fell to Christopher's side. "Man, you all right? Let me see." Oscar ripped off Christopher's shirt, tracing the line of blood to his chest.

"Man down," Oscar shouted into his radio. "Man down on the corner of Peachtree and Lexington Circle. Ambulance requested." Oscar turned to Christopher lying on the ground. "What's your name, man?"

"Chris." Oscar leaned in close so he could hear Christopher's whispers. "I think I'm shot."

"Chris, you know you will be fine, right?"

The people from inside the bank ran out to Christopher's aid. "Christopher," Monica screamed.

"Give him your jacket," Oscar said. "Put it over him." Monica obeyed and draped her suit jacket over Christopher's bleeding frame. Eric fell to the ground and placed Christopher's head against his knees. He blotted Christopher's forehead with his tie.

"Can y'all take care of this gentleman?" Oscar asked.

"We got him," Monica blurted out. "Our Father who art in heaven . . ."

Christopher felt hot tears dribble on his face as Monica prayed over him. He fought to keep his eyes from rolling up in his head. A chill rustled in his toes and rode up his leg with a shot. Soon his entire body was shivering.

"I'm cold," Christopher mumbled.

Eric whipped his jacket off and tucked it around him, making sure every inch of his torso was covered. "Go see if there are blankets in the back," he yelled to no one in particular.

"The ambulance will be here in a minute," Oscar said. "I have to go."

"Christopher watched the officer dart down the street and turned to his staff. He was so happy no one else in the bank had gotten hurt. He could survive getting shot, but he wondered if his career would survive such a PR nightmare.

Chapter III

Maria hunched over the steering wheel, her forehead pressed against the hard plastic. G-Unit drowned out her screams. She banged her head against the steering wheel until hot liquid ran down her face. She put her hand in the center of the pain and came away with blood.

"Stupid, stupid." She leaned behind the back of her seat and rummaged on the floor until she found an old towel. She cleaned her face and sat up straight. Cars whizzed by the darkened alley where her car rested. She checked her watch. If she hurried she could still find Damon and they could drive out on I-75 to Florida like they planned. They could have his mother catch a Greyhound with Qoundrus and they would be a happy family for real this time. With a house set far back against the street. And checks that didn't bounce like basketballs in the playoffs.

All she had to do was wait across the street until Damon hopped back in the car."

"Mami, it's gonna work okay." Damon kissed her eyes.

She fought the smile that wanted to explode from within.

"You believe me, right?"

"Yeah," Maria whispered. She wanted to say, "Let's go

back home. Try something else—maybe something legal for a change."

"No more schemes after this," Damon continued. "No more selling dimes to get by, no more bootlegging, no more third-shift bullshit-ass jobs."

"They weren't so bad," Maria countered. She had landed a job as night auditor at a swanky but sleazy downtown hotel. She loved gossiping with the other girls, eating all that good food. And she got paid every week.

"You fucking crazy," Damon said. "Paying for them babysitters almost broke us." Was it the babysitters or the fact that someone didn't want to stay at home with little Q even though someone didn't have a job? Just so someone could screw all them hoes that didn't have enough money for a rock, Maria thought.

"It wasn't that bad." Maria's whisper was quieter than the last, but quite stern in her opinion.

"Well, this is gonna be way better than being some loser with a day job." He looked out at the bank, which stood quietly under the shade of two magnolias posted on either side of the entrance.

"I got the hookup." He smiled his famous toothy smile. She melted every time. "I paid this cat five heads to tell me all about the bank."

"He does security and said he would keep everyone downstairs." Maria watched as her husband pulled a long 9mm out of his jacket. He bent forward and stuffed it in the small of his back.

"Only person to watch out for is some faggot who runs the joint." He opened the glove compartment and pulled out two clips and slipped them in his front pocket. "Says everyone else is either a bitch or a cracker."

He put his hand on the nape of her neck and drew her into him. Their kiss was long and soft. She didn't want to let go.

Eventually, he pecked her lips one last time and broke away. "I'll be out in five minutes. Do not fucking move!"

"I'm not." She leaned back in to kiss him.

He grabbed her face with his hand and crushed her skin together. "I'm fucking serious."

"I know, damn." Maria pulled free and adjusted herself in the mirror. "Just hurry up."

Damon winked at Maria and climbed out of the car.

"Say a prayer for us," Damon said and then slammed the door. It took twenty-seven seconds for him to reach the door and walk inside. She sat there trying to think of a prayer, but couldn't find one that covered armed robbery. She thought of maybe saying just a prayer for God's protection, but looking at the unused gun clips piled in the glove compartment, she was short on scripture.

"Lord, please help me," she said out loud. "Tell me what to do." A knock on her window caused Maria to jump out of her seat. A cop on a bike was leaning against her Kia.

Her hands trembled as she rolled down the tinted window. "Yeah."

"You're illegally parked." The officer pointed to the fire hydrant hiding in some bushes just a foot away from them.

"I didn't see it."

"You gotta move."

"I'll just be a minute. I'm waiting for someone."

"Wait at a metered parking space."

"There are no open spaces around here." Maria tossed her hair back and curled her lips into her sexiest smile. "Can I please wait here for like five more minutes?"

"Hell naw." The officer pulled out his ticket book. "Move!"

Maria shifted the car into drive and pulled out slowly. She stuck her head out the window. "Why don't you find a murder or something, ya bike-riding rent-a-cop?"

"I bet my bike moves faster than your Kia," the cop retorted. "Hit it!"

"Maria sped off and hit a corner, hoping to circle back around. But as she drove, her mind closed in on her haphazard prayer. *Tell me what to do. Was that a sign?* Did God want her to get away from the bank? She turned another corner and was a few yards from the other turn that would put her back in front of the bank. She suddenly hit the brakes. She sat frozen in her seat, looking at the two streets. Surely Damon would be done by now. All she had to do was make a quick stop in front of the bank and they would be gone. She got to the four-way stop and stopped again.

Damon was gonna kill her if he walked outside and she had disappeared. But her little prayer kept swirling in her brain. She let a car pass her at the stop. She searched for a quarter to flip. After rummaging through the cigarette-infested ashtray she said, "Fuck it" and pressed the gas.

A garbage truck honked at her as it crossed in front of her, stopping at the corner. The truck blocked the one-way street she was supposed to turn down. Maria pressed the gas and sped down the long street leading to the highway.

Her heart thumped in her ears as she whipped onto the highway on-ramp and drove until the yellow gas light blinked at her. She pulled into a vacant alley hidden from the street and let the fear of her actions conquer her body. Tears flew from her eyes and she rocked slowly in her seat.

"What did I do?" she yelled. "Stupid, stupid." She imagined Damon's crunched-up face staring at the empty parking space that was their pickup point. He'd kill her. No doubt. She would have two bullets planted in her head. No crime of passion, either. He would devour her like an antelope caught away from the safety of the herd and snatched by a lion.

She knew her boundaries with Damon. She never joked too much or spat too much sarcastic venom. She remembered how his knuckles felt whacked against her face. She heard the snap of her forearm when she refused one of his requests before. She always forgave him, because she knew no else would touch her like Damon. His kisses brushed her lips like soft magnolia petals. His arms could house her body against his chest, and the world could not penetrate his human fence. And when he entered her and whispered, "I'll always love you" in her ear, she would have to curb herself from bursting into tears.

But all that would be over now once he saw that she was gone. In his eyes, she was a goner. She snapped the stick into first gear and pressed the gas till she reached the entrance to the street. What was she going to do? It was the first time she actually thought of her plan outside of reacting to Damon's anger.

Little Q popped into her head. What was he going to do? Would he be mad when his daddy didn't come home to pick him up like he did almost every night? If Damon managed to get back home would he be waiting for her? Would he get to Q, hurt him? She hit the accelerator, and the car lurched onto the graveled pavement and raced down the street.

The road leading to Damon's mother's house was bare except for a mail truck that rested on the opposite side. A postal carrier strutted down the street, jamming to his iPod. Maria eased out of the car and maneuvered to the front door. She could barely breathe, leaning on the banister that lined the front steps. She rang the doorbell and prayed.

"Lord, please don't let this man be here," she whispered to herself as the door swung open.

"Mama." Q jumped into her arms. "Mommy, I am learning Spanish, see? *Uno, dos, tres, cuatro, cinco, seis . . .*" He pressed his thumb on his fingers as he counted. "Five . . . two hundred, see?" She would have corrected him, but his smile penetrated her teacher facade. Q wrapped his arms around her neck, and Maria held him for as long as she could before he squirmed out of her grasp.

"Where is Damon?"

"Maria looked up to find Damon's mother holding up one

side of the front door. "Hey, baby, why don't you go to the car? You feel like ice cream?" Maria asked Q.

"Yeah," Q screamed and danced to the car. Maria turned back around.

Candace Whitlow was the kind of woman who invoked fear with just a look. Her deep-set eyes were hardened by sketched-in eyebrows that took the shape of a frown on her forehead. Her thin lips lay in a straight line, squashing any hope of a smile.

"Hello." Candace shrugged her shoulders.

"Huh?"

"My son," she snarled. "Where the hell is he?"

"He went to take care of some more business."

"Well, he owe me three dollars and thirty-eight cents 'cause I have to feed his child and I know your broke ass ain't got no money."

"Um, I think I got that." Maria dug deep in her pocket and pulled out a ten-dollar bill. "Oh, it's the smallest bill I have."

"Well, you owe me for other shit too." Candace snatched the bill from Maria's hand and forced it down the back pocket of her stretched-out capri pants. "What's wrong with you?"

"Nothing," Maria lied. "I'm just worn out from looking for a job today."

"You need to watch your damn child and let Damon be the man he needs to be." Candace rolled her eyes. "That's why him and his nappy-headed chile are both so spoiled."

Maria wanted to remind Candace of who supplied her son with an allowance until he was twenty-five. But she had to get out of there before Damon came through or worse.

"Well, I gotta go cook dinner," Maria said, backing away from the stoop and turning toward the car.

"Cook?" Candace chuckled. "Taco Bell is not cooking. Them boys ain't ate a decent meal since last Thanksgiving."

"I am trying my best, Mama Whitlow." Maria offered a half smile as Candace backed up two steps and slammed the door in her face. Maria turned, ran to the car, and hopped in the front seat.

"Where's Daddy?" Q asked.

"We'll see him soon." Maria smiled. "How about that ice cream and maybe some McDonald's?"

"Are we going to see the doctor?" Q asked, his face filling with fear.

"What?"

"Every time we go to the doctor's, you take me to McDonald's," Q protested. "I don't want to go if I have to see the doctor."

"No doctors today." Maria rubbed his hand. "We're just going to go 'cause I want us to spend some time together. Just the two of us."

"Is Daddy coming?"

"I have a feeling your Daddy may already be waiting for us." Maria looked around one last time and spun off down the street.

Chapter IV

Oscar darted down the street looking for Damon. When he reached the corner he looked around for any sign. The street was lined with cars parked for blocks in single file. There were no vacant spaces. Maybe that meant he hadn't stolen a car. He ran down the street, until his eyes caught the long one-way street that intersected Lexington. His stomach churned as he looked down the quiet street. He had to go with his gut.

He hit full speed about halfway down the block, conking out when he reached the sidewalk on the other side. He looked around but saw nobody, heard nothing. Was he hallucinating? Could this kid he helped raise actually have shot a man, and be getting away with maybe thousands of dollars on his beat? He turned back toward the injured man when he heard a car screech and a woman screaming.

"Lord, please give me strength." Oscar tracked a black Range Rover speeding away from a side street with what looked like a body dangling behind. He ran toward the car as the body bounced on the concrete and rolled to a stop. The SUV almost tipped over as it maneuvered a curb. It was gone, but the body lay lifeless on the steamy ground.

Oscar blew out a long breath, prayed another silent prayer, and ran toward the figure.

* * *

That was an hour ago. Now police cars scoured the area where the robbery had taken place. Oscar could hear the sirens all the way in the West End where he rode his bike. He told his sergeant that he would file his report when he got back from lunch. But he had some leads of his own to investigate.

When he reached his old neighborhood, he was shocked. Several houses stood like gleaming castles. New paint washed over restored wood. Manicured lawns rolled out to thick picket fences that guarded their homes. But as he rode farther he was reminded of the past he had grown to call home.

Dilapidated houses, with caved-in roofs and boarded windows, were sprinkled between the immaculate houses. Crackheads bounced across the street as old men sat on their front porches, looking out at the Atlanta skyline that rose behind the neighborhood. White men directed several brown men carrying long ropes as they pried a wall from its foundation. The cement and wood landed with a crash as Oscar reached Damon's old home.

The redbrick Colonial stood so close to the street, from the side it looked as if you had to pass through it to get to the other side. He parked his bike against a tree stump that jutted out from the uncut grass. Though the grass was wild, the place looked lived in. Windows were scrubbed clean, the porch clear of dust and dirt. Maybe someone else had moved in, Oscar thought. This was the last house Damon listed as his address. Maybe the new owner could help him get a forwarding address.

Oscar leaned in and pressed the doorbell. Before he could straighten up the door opened to a familiar face.

"Yes?" Ms. Whitlow peered through the half-opened door. Oscar's mouth fell. Damon's mother stood before him, her eyes crunched into low slits. According to Damon, she was supposed to be dead. He wondered if Damon's ploy for sympathy had saved him from a bullet. If Oscar hadn't felt a little sorry, he knew he would have shot him point-blank in the head. But he had hesitated. Now this lying criminal could have killed two people and injured countless others.

"Wiener?" Ms. Whitlow's lips curled into a smile. "Wiener Parks, is that you?" Oscar hadn't heard that nickname in years. After all, nobody ate Oscar Mayer Wieners anymore. He knew he was free of that nickname once he was grown. Wrong again.

"Yes, ma'am, it's me, Oscar." He held the syllables of his name as if he were teaching an English course. Ms. Whitlow grabbed him in her meaty arms and held him just long enough to make Oscar feel uncomfortable.

She licked her lips. "Boy, you turned out to be a nice-looking man." He watched her eyes scan down and linger just below his belt buckle.

"You married?"

"Yes, ma'am. Four kids too."

"Candace." She had a sparkling white smile except for a gold plate that covered a canine.

"Yes, ma'am." Oscar stepped back slowly, retrieving the personal space that had been robbed from him. She followed, her lips inches away from him.

"So what?" She rubbed his arm while feeling his blue cotton shirt. "You a security guard now?"

"No, ma'am." Oscar stiffened. Enough play. He had already been molested. He was damned if he was going to be insulted too. "I am an Atlanta police officer."

"Oh." Candace's face froze. Her smile flat-lined as she stepped back to the door. She leaned against the frame and muttered, "I suppose you're looking for Damon?"

"Yes. I want to talk to him about—"

She tossed her hand to his face before he could complete his sentence. "I don't want to hear this shit." Hot spit fired from her mouth and landed on his face. "I don't know anything about him or that heffa he's screwing. They on drugs if you ask me."

"What girl?" Oscar whipped out his pen and pad.

"Her name is Maria," she yelled. "And she has been getting my son in trouble since he knocked her up."

"Does she have a last name?"

"Sadu, Badu, something like that."

"Does he live with her?"

"I told you I don't know nothing about Damon no more."

"But you know he dates this Maria?"

"I wouldn't call it dating." She pulled a cigarette and matches from her pocket and lit up. "She got pregnant, said it was his, and has been following him around ever since."

"Um-hmm." Oscar scribbled on his pad.

"Before her, Damon promised me he would go to technical school, pick up a trade. Web designing."

"Do they live together?"

"He could have been a cop like you. Hell, he could have been a sergeant like Danny Glover in that movie with that cute white boy."

"Do they live together?"

"You remember that movie with the white boy acting crazy and Danny had all those children, all light-skinned as black as he was, ridiculous."

"Ms. Whitlow." Oscar locked in on her eyes. She jumped at the sound of his voice. "I was asking if they lived together."

"And I told you I didn't know, damn."

"Do you have an address for the girl?"

"Maybe it's lost somewhere in my house—could take days to find." Ms. Whitlow's smirk could be seen from down the street. And it was more than life-sized to Oscar.

"Can I give you a card in case you find it?" He extended his hand, the card fixed between his fingertips.

Ms. Whitlow grabbed the card and held his hand. "You sure I can't get you anything in the back?"

"No, thank you, my wife will fix me something when I get home." He beamed as he turned around and walked off.

"Have a great one," he offered her as he walked down the steep steps. He felt a gush of wind and heard a boom as the door slammed shut behind him.

Oscar pulled out his cell phone to call the station and give up his information. He couldn't wait to kiss his wife and battle his sons for some time with the Xbox. After all, he took the bike beat so he could stay safe for his family. Five years with the DEA and Homicide had taught him the value of KFC and movie nights in front of the television. He gave it all up for his career once. Not again.

But Damon was a different story. For two years out of their lives they were inseparable. It started off with his after-school job at the Boys and Girls Club. At sixteen, Oscar was undisputedly the most popular boy in school. Though he enjoyed watching sports, rather than playing them, he was good enough to start on both the football and baseball teams. Colleges were calling his junior year, hoping to whisk him away as their token black player at some country college on the outskirts of civilization.

Oscar had found peace at the B&Gs Club, partly to help others, but mostly so he wouldn't have to deal with all the adult decisions that banged on his door. He usually pumped weights, flirted with girls, and shot hoops with the kids. The first time he met Damon, he knew the young boy offered him the distraction from his own life he desperately needed. A slight child drowning in his oversized T-shirt, Damon walked up to Oscar as he stood in the back office.

"Hey, you go to Turner High School, right?" the boy asked.

"Yeah," Oscar answered. "You go there?"

"Naw, man. I'm only ten." Damon laughed. "But I saw you playing against Central High a few months ago."

"Yeah, I really stunk that game up." Oscar laughed.

"They whopped y'all's asses."

"It was seven to three," Oscar replied, trying to hold his defensive tone against a kid.

"Yeah, but they scored the first seven in, like, three innings." Damon's smile resonated across the room.

Everyone seemed to be watching the kid, Oscar noticed. "We got a few runs on them."

"You pitched pretty good."

"I appreciate it."

"But I'm better." Damon's eyes fixed on Oscar, like he was challenging him.

"You play?"

"Yeah, I was in Little League, and now I play varsity for my middle school."

"You in middle school already?"

"I took some crazy tests in third grade and they bumped me up two grades because of the scores."

"Wow, pretty impressive. You'll have to show me some of your skills one day."

"I got a ball now," Damon offered and then walked around him and headed for the door. He pushed the door open and then turned around and said, "You coming? The center is only open till nine."

"Smart-ass." Oscar pushed the boy out the door and their friendship was cemented. He wouldn't admit it then, but Damon was his best friend for his last two years of high school. While most people were concerned with his future, Damon only dealt with Oscar's present.

But as his high school career drew to a close, decisions had to be made. And his biggest decision cost him Damon's friendship. He knew the conversation would come up but he kept avoiding it, until Damon finally asked him during one of their early-morning runs.

"So, did you get accepted to Georgia Tech?" Damon always ran a pace ahead and turned his head back when he spoke. He had grown from a lanky ten-year-old to a muscular twelve-year-old. He looked as old as Oscar.

"Yeah," Oscar said between huffs. "Got my package last week."

"Last week? Man, I been asking you about that for a month straight and you just now telling me about that?"

Damon's scolding tone sometimes made Oscar feel like he was the one tagging along. "I had to consider all my options."

"There are no other options. Georgia Tech is the bomb. And they're paying for everything. You know I'm going there. And if I study real hard in school I can be out of high school in three years. We can both be in the same school together. That would be the bomb."

"Damon." Oscar took in one final long breath. "I am going to UCLA."

"What? Why?" Damon jerked to a stop and Oscar ran into him. Damon pushed him off hard.

"Hey!" Oscar yelled.

"What the fuck are you going there for?"

"I got an academic scholarship there too. They have a great political science department."

"I thought we were going to play baseball."

"You are ten times better than me. Man, that was just something to do for me. I gotta think about my future. I'd like to be a lawyer one day."

"So us going to Georgia Tech, that was all bullshit."

"No, Damon." Oscar put his arm on Damon's shoulder. "It wasn't bullshit. I just had to think about what was best for me. You know what I'm saying?"

"Whatever, man." Damon turned and walked off.

"Hey, man, don't be that way. I still want you to go there and play ball and get that million-dollar contract."

"Man, that was just something to do to kill time," Damon said. "I gotta go cook breakfast before my mom gets up."

"Hey, we still got one more mile to go."

"I'll make it up tomorrow." Damon darted off down the street.

That was the last time the two had a real conversation. Oscar tried to call and visit Damon during the summer, but he could never catch up with him. When he got to UCLA, he got a letter from Damon's mom saying he was hanging around the wrong crowd. She pleaded for Oscar to call him. After reading the letter, Oscar intended to call but he overslept from a night of drinking and studying. One day melted into months, then years, and he never saw Damon again until that moment at the bank.

That is why his finger hesitated at the trigger. He owed him more than a bullet to the forehead. He owed him a chance to make up for the friendship he had walked away from so many years ago. He owed him a future.

Chapter V

Crisscross ran out shaking his head and hands violently, before the black Range Rover even pulled into the garage.

"Hell naw, son." He rapped on the hood of the car with his palm. "Get this shit out of here."

Damon climbed out of the driver's seat, offering the wide-toothed smile he knew got results.

"Calm down, man." He stretched his arm around Crisscross's massive shoulder blades. At six foot one and 450 pounds, his girth was upstaged only by his eyes, set so far inward they seemed to merge into one giant optical orb. "You need to be easy."

"Nigga, you need to be aware!" Crisscross yelled back. "Your shit is on blast all across the news."

"Then you know why I'm here, Criss," Damon whispered. "I gotta break this car down."

"Brother, I don't know what you talking about. This is a detail shop." Crisscross threw his hands up and pointed to the dingy yellow sign that bore CHRIS'S DETAIL STATION in crimson block letters.

Damon looked at the sign, then at his friend, and burst out laughing. "Nigga, is you crazy?" Damon walked back to the car and pulled out a dark brown bag. "This is a mothafuckin' chop shop." He drew a small stack of bills from the bag.

"D, man, I can't do it." Crisscross backed up slow, his stomach bouncing with every step. "You on *Five Alive News*, man. I ain't doing time for yo messed-up shit."

"Chris, don't make me go back on you." Damon retracted his smile. "I helped finance this place. I helped flip the cars until you found them grimy niggas back there to work for you." There was a long silence that held the two in their stubborn stances. Both stared each other down.

"I can get you another ride, but I am not fucking with this one." Crisscross mounted his folded arms onto his stomach. He looked like a defiant Buddha.

"Fuck," Damon yelled and climbed back in the car. "Fuck all that. Just give me some more plates."

"What you gone do with the Range?"

"What the fuck you care, Mr. Car Detail?"

"Man, you still my boy. But I got a family."

"Nigga, I got a son and a bitch-ass girlfriend I don't know if the po-po got on lockdown or what."

"Here, man," Crisscross handed Damon a small roll of bills. "You betta not use that cash."

"True."

"I'll be right back." Crisscross bounced off into his shop and came back with two white plates. "Be careful, man. These are for a Ford Taurus."

"Jesus." Damon jumped out of the car and helped his boy switch plates on the car. He was back in the Rover in under five minutes.

"I better get out of here, man," Damon said, offering his hand to Crisscross, who shook it vigorously.

"Hey, Damon." Crisscross moved in close to Damon. "Did you know that chick was pregnant?" Damon took a moment to consider his friend's question. He had been so busy pushing the morning out of his mind, he had not thought about the woman he had shoved onto the ground. He could see her face as she looked at him in abject terror. He wanted to take in the incident, but now was not the time. He turned up the radio and skidded away from his friend in reverse. He hit the street hard and headed north.

Damon carefully navigated the side streets as he sped toward Buckhead. He knew he had to get rid of the car and his clothes before the police started doing spot checks on all brothers in luxury vehicles. He decided the best place to get rid of the vehicle was the one place black men could roll in luxury cars and not get harassed. Lenox Mall. He looked at the crowded underground parking garage located across the massive lot, and decided to take a risk and park in the valet parking. He got up to the door and had just pressed the driver's window button when he realized he had broken the window earlier that morning. Bits of glass still pricked out of the rubber lining. He brushed away what he could before the valet driver hopped to his side.

"Good afternoon." The young man beamed, his blond buzz cut seeming to amplify the sun's rays."

"Yeah." Damon cast out his smile again. "My car just got broken into at the restaurant down the street. Can you park it near a corner so people can't see I got a busted-out window?"

The boy cocked an eye until Damon pressed a hundred-dollar bill into his palm. When the boy saw the one accompanied by the two zeros his smile resurfaced. "Right away, sir."

Damon stuffed the money bag into his backpack and headed into the mall as the valet squeezed the vehicle between two other Rovers. He threw the ticket the boy gave him into the nearest trash can. He had to make a 360 on his appearance before pictures started circulating. He dipped into several shops, handpicking items for his transformation: a new shirt and some slacks, dress shoes, new underwear, socks, Gucci sunglasses, a luggage bag, and a pair of barber clippers from Sharper Image.

He scanned the mall for the biggest store and walked in and went to the nearest bathroom. He took the handicapped stall and sat until the last remaining person left the room. He guesstimated how long before the next ten people came through. About ten minutes. He stripped down and put on his new outfit. Then he plopped back down on the seat and waited a few minutes until another person came in and funked the room to hell. As soon as that person left, Damon let out a long sigh. He quickly hooked up the clippers to the wall mount and began shearing his midsized Afro until one side was almost bald. When he heard the outside door creak, he pulled the cord from the socket and recaptured his spot in the big stall. After the person left he resumed his makeshift cut until he was completely bald.

He dabbed some water over the top of his skull to dampen the sporadic dry patches. He looked like a completely different person. At least different from the man he knew this morning. He threw everything but the clippers in the trash, grabbed the rolling suitcase he bought at the luggage store, and headed out the door.

Damon felt way more comfortable walking in the mall with his buppie gear appropriately assembled. He looked like every other brother in a Banana Republic ad. He strolled into the hotel anchoring the north side of the mall. He walked through the glass double doors and scanned the front desk. He had enough cash for a room, but they were going to ask for a credit card for incidentals and he would be stuck. He locked on a pretty sister at the corner of the desk and moved in for the scam.

"Hello." Damon tried to mimic his whitest of white voices.

"Hey," the girl said in a southern drawl that relieved Damon. If the girl was all stuck-up his job would be hard. But the girl's voice felt warm and cozy like the southern peach Atlanta women were often compared to.

"I need to get a room for a couple of nights."

"Okay." The girl paused, her eyes scanning his face. Shit,

had she made him already? He placed his hand in his front pocket, resting his fingers on his gun.

"You look just like that rapper, um . . ."

"I get that a lot." Damon pounced on the mistaken identity. "Okay, uh, can I make a confession? I'm not a rapper. I'm an actor. You've seen me in that movie with Jamie Foxx."

"Oh, I didn't see that one but I knew I saw you somewhere."

"Yeah, that's me. Anyway, I need your help." Damon leaned in close, using his finger to pull her into him. "I need to get a room, but under an alias."

"Oh, we do that all the time." The girl smiled. "Nelly actually stayed here a few weeks ago."

"For real?"

"Yeah." The girl smiled a sly grin. "He had to change his name and room like three times."

"Well, you can understand why I need to use a false name, and why I can only pay cash."

"We usually need a card for incidentals."

Damon placed three hundred-dollar bills in her hand. "Will this cover your incidentals?"

"For me?"

"Yeah, girl, you need to buy some new shoes for my movie premiere party next week."

"Yeah?"

"It's real hush-hush. What's your name, sweetheart?"

"LaToya." The girl beamed from ear to ear.

"Well, LaToya, you are going on the VIP list and I am personally going to leave you an invitation before I check out."

"That's straight." The girl blushed. "What name do you want to use?"

"I'll let you choose."

LaToya stared at Damon again. Her eyebrows scrunched in the middle. "You look like a David or Damon."

Damon pulled back. He wanted to grab his gun until he saw the girl giggle. "How about Mr. Magoo?"

"Mr. Magoo?" The girl burst out laughing. She shot to attention when she eyed a man coming around the corner.

"Let me get your room, sir." She clicked at the keyboard, and placed a key card on the marble counter.

"We'll just use the card you gave me for incidentals."

She winked as she passed the key to Damon.

"Thank you." Damon winked back.

The walk to the elevator seemed like an eternity. He watched every person through his shades. He had almost made it to the elevator bank when he heard his name from the bar. He slowly turned his head to see his face planted on a plasma television in the bar. The camera flashed back to a sister with a short bob.

"The robbery happened earlier today and police are still trying to identify this man. Once again, if you have any information regarding this crime please contact the Atlanta Police Department at . . ."

Damon forced his jaw to stop from dropping. He hurried to the elevator and almost hopped in when the gold doors opened. He stepped to his room and shot through the door. He surveyed the room and shook the drapes for hidden police. He checked the bathroom and the balcony, which looked over northern Atlanta. The moon was rising slowly into the darkening sky. Damon locked the door to his suite and crumpled to the floor.

Had he ruined everything? Would he ever see his family again? Was he going to go to jail? Words tried to fill his mouth, but nothing came to fruition. The fear of losing the very family he was trying to protect was too much to handle. His body shivered from the cool air filtering in from the air conditioner. Only the heavy heaves of air filling his chest covered the room as he rocked and cried himself to sleep.

Chapter VI

Despite losing the baby, all my other injuries were pretty minor. So after a couple of days I was back at home and going crazy. I had never been the type of girl who sat around the house watching flowers grow and wondering if my husband missed me at work. I was trying to be a mogul. And one crazy Negro with a checkered past was not going to stop me from living my dream. I had too much work to do.

Somewhere between downing my second carton of Ben & Jerry's Cherry Garcia ice cream and watching my third episode of *Judge Judy*, I had reached my domestic stopgap. So despite David's complaining, which I never listened to anyway, I returned to work after a measly two weeks of bed rest. In corporate America if you're gone for two weeks, it's called sick leave. If you're missing in the entertainment industry, people assume there's a hooker, heroin, and a motel that charges by the hour involved. So, to prove I was still the queen bee of the PR world, I started planning Carlos's album release party. I could tell Carlos was a little nervous when I called him on the phone to confirm a date.

"So are you okay? I heard what happened."

"Hey, I am a survivor."

"I see. Look, I don't want to do anything that will upset

you. If it's too much work we can work with someone else."
There was genuine concern resonating in his voice, such a
rarity in the music business. But I could not afford to rest on
my butt and let some twenty-two-year-old, big-breasted
model/publicist take my one shot at glory.

"I'll be fine, trust me. Your party is going to be sick."

"I hope so," he said. His soft baritone belied the bellowing
tenor that I heard on his albums.

"Trust me." I hung up the phone and took several deep
breaths. It was time to trust myself.

But right now, priorities came first. I needed to find something to wear to this bash.

Since my incident I was a little nervous about driving. And
since now there was only one car between the two of us, I resigned myself to staying in the house. That was until last week
when David pulled into the driveway with a baby-blue Mercedes convertible.

"You need something new to drive." He smiled and kissed
me as I beamed from ear to ear.

"How can we afford this? Don't we still owe on the
Range?" I questioned. I mean, hell, I was gonna drive it, but
I didn't want to seem like my personal happiness should
break the family bank.

"They cashed out the policy and I had enough for a down
payment for this beauty right here."

A new party, a new car, of course I needed new outfits and
shoes to make the theme complete. At first I headed down the
long road that led to the freeway. I figured the best place to
shop would be Phipps Plaza in Buckhead. Their mix of
anchor stores and boutiques would provide the best selection.
But halfway down the freeway, my neck started sweating and
my stomach churned until I had to pull off the road. I knew I
would have to go back to the city sooner or later, but I wasn't
ready yet. I got off the freeway at the next exit and headed

toward a little strip mall just outside Atlanta. I was staying outside the perimeter for now.

I snagged a parking space just a few steps away from my favorite store, Angie's. I didn't hear the automatic doors of my car click before a nasally voice crushed my good spirits.

"J.C." Nicole Stevens sauntered over to my car, an armful of clothes hiding the skin her too-short mini failed to cover. "How are you, girl?"

She moved in close and patted my back as if I were a newborn. Her cheek rubbed slightly against mine. "I heard all about your accident. I am so sorry for your loss."

"Thank you." I forced my lips to smile.

"How is David taking it?"

And here we go. This heffa had been trying to sleep with my husband since we were roommates at Spelman. Since I trusted David, and frankly was too busy at the school paper to worry whether my boyfriend would be seduced by a fashion merchandising major, I barely paid her any attention. She hated me, and was probably dancing at home when word circulated about my carjacking.

"I would die if I lost Thomas or Abigail." She pressed her hand on mine, and I placed my free hand over hers to return the favor. Not out of any form of endearment, but to prevent myself from clocking this chick. First of all, she should be lucky if she could give away her ugly bucktoothed children. Which just goes to show, just 'cause you marry a gorgeous football player does not mean your children will inherit the cute gene.

"Well, it has been hard, but we're making it through," I managed to say. Then I leaned back and let out a sigh to let her know I was ready to go.

"You really should come to church," Nicole offered. "My wedding ministry has been praying for you since this happened. You are still a member, right?"

"Yes," I countered. It had been a few weeks since I had

been to church, but I was pretty busy with being hospitalized, losing a baby, and little stuff like that.

"Hmm. . . ." Nicole's eyes tightened into little slits. "Well, you know what they say about faith without works."

"No, what do they say?"

"Well . . . it's in the Bible, J.C., you should read that passage."

And you should stop quoting verses you ain't got memorized. I was already bored with this conversation, and now she was crossing the line. I sidestepped her and began walking. "Well, maybe I'll see you at church. Do you attend the seven a.m. service?" I asked.

"Usually nine a.m."

The 7:00 a.m. service it'd be, then.

"So rumor has it you're throwing Carlos's album release party in a few weeks," Nicole said.

"It's just a small gathering for some industry folks, the press, and some clients. No big deal."

"Well, I thought my husband was one of your clients."

Oh no, she didn't! Technically he was. But this was for *paying* clients. After three months of begging from Mr. Two-Time MVP, I wrote some press releases and tried to organize a fund-raiser for Nicole's cheap-ass husband. He tried to nickel-and-dime me on everything from the invitations to the catering, which I had to pay for with my Amex card. And then he strolled into the affair an hour late with a diamond-studded cross the size of my head. He had bought it the night before for the occasion. But it took him six months to pay off my invoice. Screw him and this crazy cow.

"It's for new clients," I lied.

"Well, I called David, and he said he couldn't wait to catch up on old times."

To-do list item one: Cuss out big-mouth husband. "I guess I'll see you there," I said. *At least until security taps you on the shoulder.* "Well, I gotta find an outfit, so . . ."

"I'm sorry for keeping you, honey." She giggled. "I have to pick up the kids from day care."

I never really understood the concept of a woman with no career, job, or hobby for that matter putting her kids in day care, but who was I to judge?

"I have been so busy trying to design my high-end clothing line for next fall," she said.

Though I was half interested in discovering how an ex-stripper defined high end, I had enough with reminiscing.

"Gotta go, sweetie. Call me, though." I walked off knowing that I had changed all my numbers after I was robbed.

After a cleansing mocha coffee, I was devoid of any animosity I had toward Nicole. Bottom line: She was a ho looking for a sponsor and self-esteem, in that order. I wasn't surprised she would try to attack me when she thought I was down. But J.C. does not get down. I always keep fighting. And I was about to don some boxing gloves when I came out of my semiprivate dressing room at Angie's Boutique and was confronted by waves of flashes and microphones in my face.

"Ms. West, Carmen Walker of *Channel Eight News*. Can I ask you some questions?" The plump newscaster flung her bob and smiled.

I dove back in the dressing room, and scrambling to put on my clothes.

"You better not use any of those photos or footage or you will be sued," I jabbed with a sharp, hard threat, hoping to at least get the chance to use some of my head shots instead of the paparazzi stalker shots I'm sure they captured.

"How do you feel after your brutal carjacking?"

"You have the wrong woman." I blocked the punch. *Take that!*

"A source confirmed that you were involved in that incident downtown, and that we could find you here."

That skinny heffa Nicole had set me up. *Okay, just regain*

your composure. I had done such a good job avoiding the press at the hospital and denying so much, I assumed they had just dropped that angle.

"Are you scared that your assailant is still uncaptured at this point?" A tall man needled his way past the chunky girl and had his tape recorder three inches from my face.

"No comment," I politely stated. In addition to avoiding all phone calls, I also ignored the news. What had happened was over; I made peace with it. Why discuss and cry over it all day? Besides, I would have thought the police had have caught that guy by now. It upset me more knowing he was getting all this mileage out of my ride. But that man was not going to kill me like he did my baby. I was going to go on; I had too much living to do.

I tried to grab a dress from a chair next to me. I watched a reporter pull the chair to his side with his foot.

"We aren't leaving with just 'no comment.'" His smile was devilish. It was too bad these poor fools were going to have to experience a full-blown A.B.W.—Angry Black Woman.

"Move the hell out of my way, white boy." I pushed the cameraman so hard that he fell into another and they all fell back like dominos. I swiped a sweater from the stack of clothes on the chair. The sweater fell below my thighs. It wasn't a DKNY dress, but it would have to do.

"Now you listen to me. I have worked for, worked with, fired, or fucked all your bosses. I know them by name and number. And I have more dirt on them than you could ever muster in your puny, midlevel careers. So you are going to back up and call my office for a statement, schedule a sound bite and photo, or you will all be covering dog shows and *Sesame Street Live* for the next three years. And if you think I'm bullshitting, call your bosses and tell them you're bothering J.C. West." I swung around and pushed some skinny girl who had snuck up behind me. I saw her crooked teeth hanging out of her mouth as she stood with her jaw dropped.

"And for God's sake," I said to the poor girl. "You're a cute girl. Just get your grill fixed and you could probably be an anchorwoman." The woman slapped her hand over her mouth and ran toward the hall. The crowd stood stunned and silent. I slammed the dressing room door behind me. I heard mumbling and cell phones dialing. And then a silence covered the hallway outside, and then some cursing and a soft rap on my door.

"Ms. West, can we call to set up an appointment soon?"

"Just leave a message," I sang through the door. These young bucks had to learn that they might have cameras, but I ran these streets."

When all the hounds left, I had the sales associate pull out three more dresses. The last one was a red number that settled snugly on my hips. The soft silk material caressed my skin as it moved; it was girly, sexy, and seven hundred dollars. I plopped my card on the counter and walked out without any shame. I figured the dress was my prize for single-handedly knocking out six Atlanta reporters. Oscar De la Hoya would be proud.

Chapter VII

"If ever anyone needs to go to church and testify, it would be you," Dr. Evers said to Christopher, as he held an X-ray chart out in front of him. "Seriously, a few more inches and we would have been planning your funeral."

"Thank you, Jesus." Deborah Roberts stood over her son, arms tucked under each other as if she were hugging herself for comfort. "So when can we take him home?"

"I would say in a few days. I just want to make sure those stitches heal properly," Dr. Evers said. He moved toward Christopher, who stared at the ceiling. "How do you feel?"

"All right, I guess," Christopher managed. "A little tired."

"That's natural." Dr. Evers smiled. "You'll be running five-K marathons in no time."

"You must have switched my heart with someone else's while I was in surgery. I hate to walk from my parking deck to my office."

"Well, you will have to begin some type of exercise program when you're healed, 'cause you'll be bedridden for four weeks."

"Four weeks?" Christopher jolted up, and then lay back down when his head started spinning. "Are you serious?"

"Yessir," Dr. Evers said. "Don't worry, it will go by faster than you realize."

"Yeah, right," Deborah chimed in. "That boy has never taken a day off of work since he was fifteen years old."

"Are you serious?" Dr. Evers's laugh filled the room. He piped down when he saw the monotone expression on Christopher's and his mom's face.

"Well, I suggest you catch up on your reading 'cause you are not going back to work for a while."

"God," Christopher muttered to himself.

"Well, I'll leave you two alone." Dr. Evers headed for the door. "Cheer up, Christopher. You are a living miracle. Take some time to take that in." Dr. Evers gently closed the door behind him as Deborah moved toward the window.

"Well, are you going to move back home or are we going to have to argue this point too?"

"Mom." Christopher paused to select his words. "I don't want to be an inconvenience."

"Christopher, you're my son. You're a nuisance, an arrogant son of a gun, a reminder of my old age, but never an inconvenience." They both laughed. "Seriously, sweetie, you need to just stay for a little while. Till you get better."

"Mom, I will be okay at home," Christopher said.

"Well, I won't be," Deborah argued. "I'll be sitting up worrying all day about whether you are okay or not."

"Well, let me be blunt." Christopher paused for a moment. "I am not going anywhere in Mississippi."

"Boy, I am only six hours away from Atlanta."

"That's six hours too far away from my plasma TV," Christopher whined.

"We can get you another TV at my house."

"Yeah, but I'll miss my bed. And I am not driving my car on those horrible dirt roads."

"Okay. I'm getting the feeling that you don't want to leave

your precious city." Deborah slumped down on the edge of the bed.

"I totally get you getting tired of the city life, retiring to a quiet spot. But I'm a city boy. I would die out there in the country."

"Don't play, boy. You almost died yesterday."

"Put me in the middle of nowhere in the Bible Belt and I will die."

"Okay, Mr. Dramatic. I'll move in with you."

"Mom, that's not necessary." Christopher shook his head. "I'll hire a nurse and Vince will probably stay with me."

"Oh God." Deborah sighed violently. "You are not going to get my goat when you are lying in a hospital bed."

"Good."

"But do you think your *friend* will really take care of you like your mother could?" Christopher hated how she said friend, laced with sarcasm and contempt. Her eyes rolled every time she said it.

"I doubt it. But I am thirty-two, Mom," Christopher said as he tried to sit up against the wall of pillows. "And he is my—"

"Don't say it."

"—boyfriend."

"Didn't I say not to say it?"

"Well, we've been seeing each other for six months, and you need to realize he may be around for a while."

"Seriously, you look too good to waste it all on some man. I could name three beautiful women who would kill to marry you right now."

"Tell them to call Dr. Evers. He's single."

"Oh, please, who cares about him?" Deborah spat. "Besides, he was looking at you so much I think he's suspect too."

"Suspect?"

"Yes, suspect. A candidate on the fruit train."

"God."

"Am I ever going to have a grandchild before I die?"

"You could have had more children."

"Please, I could barely stand to talk to your father, let alone let him climb on top of me."

"Mom," Christopher blurted out as his mother bunched over in laughter.

"Did I miss the joke?" Vince poked his head in through the door. Deborah rolled her eyes as Christopher managed a smile for the first time all day.

"Hey, man," Christopher said.

"What's up, buddy?" Vince's straight white teeth glowed as he came near Christopher. He slowly reached his arms around Christopher and held him tight. Deborah straightened out her cardigan with her hands.

Vince eased back and looked at Deborah. "How are you, Ms. Roberts?"

"Living." Deborah smirked until she caught Christopher's eye. Then she smiled and offered her hand. "I'm doing fine, Vincent."

"Good." Vince turned back to Christopher. "And how 'bout you, buddy? You all right?"

"I'm bitter that I have a scar on my chest, but other than that, I'm okay."

Deborah gathered her purse from a lone chair across the room and headed for the door. "Well, I'm gonna head out. My offer still stands, baby." She winked at her son. "Take care, Vincent."

"Good-bye, Ms. Roberts." They both watched as the door slammed behind her. "Boy, she really hates me, doesn't she?"

"Don't take it personally." Christopher smiled. "I am probably the only person with a penis that she can stand. And even then it gets dicey."

"So, how are you feeling, really?" Vince rested his hand over Christopher's kneecap.

"Pissed," Christopher finally let out. "I have to be laid up for four weeks, and do you know the bank hasn't sent so much as a sympathy card? Only Monica, that one teller, sent me a card. Can you believe it?"

"Sorry."

"Ten years of kissing ass and taking bullets figuratively and now literally for this shit! And do you know that white boy is acting VP? I stay gone and he will keep my job for sure."

"You sound like you need this time to rest and get that job off your mind anyway."

"Easier said than done. Oh, speaking of which, I have to ask you a question."

"Ask."

Vince's smile always had a tendency to melt Christopher's stone-cold demeanor. A fact Christopher admired and hated at the same time.

"I will be getting a nurse and stuff, but my mother suggested that someone needs to stay with me, and she volunteered, but I didn't want my mom taking care of me and I wouldn't need that much help, and I know we have only been seeing each other for six months, but . . ."

"Yes," Vince said softly.

"Yes what?"

"I will move in with you."

"Seriously?" Christopher smiled. "Look, you don't have to stay once I am better. I don't want to force a live-in situation out of necessity."

"It was going to happen eventually, right?"

Christopher hesitated. He had to really analyze if he was asking Vince because he loved him or because he needed to be taken care of and was too afraid to admit the truth.

"Yeah, sooner or later," Christopher said.

"And you know I love you, right?"

"Yeah."

"And you love me."

"Most times." Christopher laughed as Vince grimaced.

"Then let's at least try it."

"Are you sure?"

"The question is: are you sure?" Vince said.

"Yeah." Christopher wanted to say so much more, but Vince just leaned in and kissed him, soft and quick, and he knew his opportunity had passed.

"Cool. Well, if I'm going to move in, I need to stock up on the frozen pizzas, and you have got to get TIVO."

"Whatever." Christopher laughed. "All I need is my CNN and the *Wall Street Journal*, thank you."

"There is no life without HBO and reruns of *The Cosby Show* and *Voltron*."

"Oh, dang, I forgot the cartoon fetish."

"That's not the only fetish I'll be exploring." Vince was moving in for the kill when a knock at the door interrupted them.

"Sorry," a man said as he edged his way inside. "I was looking for Christopher Roberts."

Christopher scrunched his eyes to focus in on the man's face, and then his own face went white.

"Dad?" Christopher mumbled.

"Oh, good," the man said. "I'm glad you at least remembered my face."

Vince shot up and moved toward the man. He threw his right arm out. "Vince Peterson."

The man took Vincent's hand and pumped it firmly. "Alonzo Roberts." He studied Vince's face. "But everyone calls me Al."

"Hey, Al, I'm Christopher's . . ."

"Man," Al said. "I caught ya smooching in the corner. I lived through the sixties and I've seen it all. Where have I seen your face before?"

"I used to run track."

"Wasn't you on the Olympic team in ninety-six?"

"Yep."

"I lost a lot of money on you."

"Yeah, and the ol' self-esteem takes another blow." Vince pretended to jab himself in the face and chest.

"I done seen you somewhere else."

"He's an anchor on CNN."

"You on that political show *Viewpoint*?"

"Yep."

"I knew you was a liberal, but damn."

"Okay, cool." Vince turned to Christopher. "Hey, man, I'm packing but I'll visit you later tonight to discuss details and my pay arrangements."

"Yeah, well, my car needs washing." Christopher tried to laugh. "We can always discuss payment later."

Vince left, leaving the two Roberts men alone.

"You're awful quiet, son, even for you," Al said as he inched his way toward the bed.

"I'm speechless."

"You ain't speechless. You was talking to your boyfriend. So you're like a VP of a bank and he is on TV. What y'all make between the two of you, like five hundred K?"

"I don't know."

"No wonder y'all gays stick together. Hell, I'd be gay too if I didn't like them sugar walls so much. You really should at least try it once in your life, son. You can't beat it."

"I haven't seen you in what, ten years, and now you want to teach me about the birds and the sugar walls?"

"I was just passing through town and saw what happened to you on the news, son. I am truly sorry."

"I'm all right."

"Have they even caught that guy?"

"Not to my knowledge."

"Figures." Al plopped on the bed. "Cops will take you to jail for pissing on the street, but when a real crime is happening they're stuffing their faces at Krispy Kreme."

"Why are you here, Dad?" Christopher felt a tinge of pain encroach on the back of his head.

"Look, I ain't here to bother you or ask for money, which is what your mama got you trained into thinking."

"I never said that."

"I can see it in your eyes," Al said. He rubbed his fingers across the rubber that covered the bedpost. "But I wanted to make sure you was all right."

"I am. Thanks."

"Look, I got my own apartment now. It's an efficiency, but at least it's a stable address. And I got a job, driving a truck. Guess all those years of running from place to place paid off, huh?" Al released a restless chuckle.

"Um, here." He handed Christopher a crumpled piece of napkin. "Here is my cell number. Call me if you ever want to talk, or yell at me, or just to make sure your old man ain't put a bullet to his head."

Christopher winced. "Dad."

"Sorry." Al placed his hands on his son's leg, and then quickly removed them. "Sorry, bad choice of words. Just call me if you get a chance. I am . . . I am trying to change my life, son. And, well . . . well, just call if you want."

As he walked out, Christopher took a hard look at his father. Once tall and muscular, he was thin and hunched over. The only hint of his old father was his bright hazel eyes, which still sparkled whenever he told a joke. Christopher wanted to stop and ask him for a hug or strangle him. Both ideas gave Christopher pleasure.

"Hey, Chris," Al said as he reached the door. "It just hit me, but I really missed you." He smiled and walked out.

Christopher fell back in his bed. His hands gripped the napkin his father gave him. He wanted to yell or throw something, but he just maneuvered into the fetal position and closed his eyes until sleep washed over him like a rolling tide.

Chapter VIII

"You have to go to the police," Leia said, swirling the merlot in her wineglass. "It's your only option."

"Leia." Maria peeked around the corner to check where Q was positioned. She zeroed in on him, leaning into his Harry Potter book. "You know it's not that simple."

"The hell it ain't," Leia said. Small drops of wine fell into the thick shag carpet. Leia wet her napkin with her tongue and bent over to rub the stain out. "That nigga is going to jail. You cannot afford to play devoted wife in this situation."

"True—but what about Q? That is his dad."

"And you're his mother. You both can't afford to desert him."

"But I drove the car. I'm an accomplice."

"Honey, one look at your arms and back, and you can see there is some serious manipulation going on here. He forced you to help him." Maria covered the bruises on her arms with her hands.

"But what if they arrest me too?"

"That's why you have to turn yourself in and cooperate. They will understand your story the way you'll explain it. But if they find you, it will be his word against yours, girl, and . . ."

"And what?"

"Look, I never liked Damon. You know that. But . . ." Leia

rolled her eyes and sighed. "He's like this real charming dude. He got hella game, and if he cleans himself up . . ."

"So what you're trying to say is I'm a troll, heffa?" Maria let out the first laugh she could remember in several weeks.

"No, baby." Leia cupped Maria's chin in her hand. "But let's just face it, the reason you're in this mess right now is because of his charm."

"That is not true." Maria pulled away. "I loved . . . love him for who he is, not what he looks like."

"Girl, I'm just saying a jury could get caught up in them eyes like you did, and him with an expensive suit and a good lawyer, you could be blamed for this whole thing."

"That's crazy. Besides, Damon wouldn't do that to the mother of his child."

"You left him at a crime scene, Maria. He is not going to be concerned about your well-being."

"But what about Q?" Maria glanced at her son again. "What if they want to keep me for a while?"

"A few days in jail are better than six years away from your son." Leia knelt down in front of her younger sister. "I'll watch him till you get back. We can visit Mother in Milwaukee."

"God, that is worse than prison." They both laughed as Maria got up from her seat and began pacing.

"I really don't have a choice, do I?" Maria stared into her sister's eyes, hoping for a glimpse of hope. Leia ran her fingers though her short-cropped hair. It fell perfectly back into place as she rose to her feet and adjusted her poncho.

"Afraid not." Leia braced Maria by the shoulders. "Look, if anyone can get through this it's you. And if anyone deserves some happiness in their lives, it's you and Q."

"Yeah, I know he is a great kid."

"And he needs his mother."

"What about his father? Q is crazy about Damon."

"Hey, I cannot predict the future. All I know is right now

that child needs someone who will make him a priority. I'd do it, but I have a really active book club."

Maria busted out into a fit of laughter, climaxing in a crying fit. Leia stepped in and hugged her sister with all the strength she could muster in her tiny frame. They held each other for what seemed like the entire night, until Q tugged at his mother's shirt.

"I am ready for my bedtime story," he announced and moved swiftly to his makeshift room in Leia's home office.

"You heard the man." Leia smiled, wiping her eyes. "The boy wants a story."

Maria sighed and gathered herself. She walked slowly into her son's room. He lay silently in a mountain of blankets that formed a palette on the floor.

"So, what story do you want to hear?"

"Is Daddy gonna tell me a story?"

"Daddy is on his business trip, remember?" Maria clenched her teeth. She hated lying to her son.

"When is he coming back?"

"When he is done."

"When will that be?"

"It's hard to say."

"Why?"

"Sweetie, there are a lot of different things he has to do."

"Like what?"

"Grown-up things."

"Like what?"

Maria tried not to change her tone, but she wanted to slap her child. Didn't he understand his deadbeat daddy was running from the law as usual and didn't care about anyone but himself?

"What stories does Daddy tell you?"

"He sometimes reads from my Harry Potter books, but mostly he makes things up."

"Really?" Maria smiled. She always wondered why she

was never allowed in the room when Damon read to Q. It was such a secretive thing. But she knew it was okay because she could hear Q giggling every five minutes.

"Well, I don't know how to make up stories."

"It's easy, Mama, just make up anything."

"Okay, there was a little girl . . ." Maria sidled up next to Q under the blankets.

"Uh, Mama." Q tapped her on the shoulder. "It's always a little boy."

"Excuse me, Mr. Chauvinist." Maria laughed.

"What is a shoveist?"

"Never mind. Why does it have to be a little boy?"

"'Cause the story is always about me."

"Oh." Maria rolled her eyes at her little egomaniac. "I didn't know. Okay, let me think, then."

"Mama, you're taking too long, I'm already tired. Let me tell the story."

Her mouth dropped at her son. He was so smart and forceful, just like Damon. And you could see the resemblance all over him, from the deep-set eyes to the full lips. She wanted to break down again, but she didn't want to upset Q.

"Go on, tell your story."

Q pushed her shoulders to the blanket. "You have to lie down."

"Okay."

"There once was a little boy who lived in a tall castle. He had a horse and a sword, and a Benz on twenty-inch rims."

"Rims." Maria jerked up. "What do you know about rims?"

"Lie down, Mama," Q giggled. "So, the boy lived with the queen and the king in the castle. But one day all their gold disappeared. So the king went out to get more gold and left the boy to watch the queen and the horse and the car and the dog."

"Where did the dog come from?"

"They have a dog too."

"Since when?"

"Daddy doesn't ask all these questions."

Maria lay back down and stifled a laugh. "Continue."

"The boy watched the castle, and all kinds of dragons tried to take them away. But just when the dragons were about to come inside the castle, the king came back and killed all the dragons with his sword. He had lots of gold, and they lived happily ever after."

"Wow, that was a good story."

"Daddy tells them better."

"I thought your story was great."

"Mama?" Q snuggled close to his mother.

"Yep."

"I miss Daddy."

"Me too, baby. Me too."

Before the sun rose above the trees. Before the mist rolled back into the trees. Before the animals scurried off into the forest. Before hot water washed away the dirt and funk off her body, Maria was outside. A cup of coffee was her only companion as she braved the chilled night air and leaned against the banister on her sister's porch.

She looked up at the stars and inhaled the thick smell of pinecones and the freshly lacquered birch floors on the porch. The moon, though only a sliver, lit the sky enough to see the Atlanta skyline from her sister's home in Hampton.

She quietly sipped her coffee till it was gone and then just held the cup for warmth. She placed the cup on the banister and let out a "Lord."

Suddenly, as if a weight forced her to the ground, she fell to her knees. She tried to get back up, but her body resisted. "Lord, do you hear me?" She laughed to herself for a second. But then she took in one more loud breath and let her heart guide her actions.

"Lord, I know I have sinned like a million times, but I don't want to lose my baby. I know what I have to do, but I don't want to lose Q. He is the only good thing I have done in my life, and I can't lose that. Lord, please, I can't lose him." Maria prayed until the words and the tears stopped. She lay on the deck and closed her eyes until the sun battled the dark for space on the horizon.

She got up and walked back into the house. She was showered, dressed, and on the freeway within forty-five minutes. There was no talking herself out of her decision, no game-playing. She had to do the right thing. But as she turned onto her exit she was free of her fears. In fact, she had a calmness she hadn't felt in years."

The car rolled into the Atlanta Police Station parking lot, and Maria placed the car in park. She combed her hair more out of routine than any real maintenance. It didn't matter at this point. She pushed the door open and attempted to get out, but fell back like she forgot something. She looked at her wedding ring.

The small gold band wrapped on her finger had been the only proof that her relationship was real, through the beat-ings, arguments, poverty, and pain. She pulled the ring off her finger. It offered no resistance at this point. Neither did she. Maria placed it in the ashtray and slammed the car door behind her.

She entered the almost vacant station and scanned the room for an officer or a receptionist. No one was at the front counter, but a few men stood in a far corner laughing and slapping five.

"Hello," Maria said as the men all focused on her. Their laughs resigned to sly smiles. A man in a dress shirt and slacks pimped toward the counter. His eyes scanned Maria from top to bottom.

"Yes, ma'am?"

"I would like to turn myself in."

"I would be happy to help you with that." The man

smiled. "Kind of early for a confession statement, but I got a little time."

Maria stared at the man, as he cracked his gum between his teeth. He slouched over the counter as if he were a cashier at McDonald's.

"Okay, so what is it you did this early?" His lips curled at the edges. "Hit and run? Ya beat some girl for giving your man head at the club? Oh, I know, you cut him for cheating with your best girlfriend?"

"Is this my confession or yours?" Maria questioned.

The men in the back had eased to the front and were chuckling and elbowing themselves at the conversation. Just then the door behind Maria swung open and another man entered the station. He was dressed in a police uniform, only he had shorts on.

"It's biker boy." The guy at the counter laughed, and the crowd of men fell out. "Catch any murderers on the bicycle beat?"

"No, but I think when I was over at your mama's house I caught crabs," the man said as the gang in back hit the floor. He turned to Maria.

"You'll have to excuse us. It gets a little rowdy this early in the morning. Can I help you with something?"

"I was trying to turn myself in," Maria said, shifting her focus to the new officer.

"Okay, for what?"

"I was an accomplice in the robbery shooting at the bank last week." Silence fell hard on the room. Maria glanced at the bucked eyes and open mouths.

"Do you know Damon Harvey?" the man whispered.

"How do you know him?"

"You need to come with me to the back." The man gently grabbed Maria's arm and led her behind a glass door. The group of men watched in silence until the door slammed and left them alone.

Chapter IX

"Have you been watching the news?" Oscar asked Maria from across the long white table. She sat, arms folded, watching the glass of water he had put in front of her minutes before. He closed the manila folder he was holding in his hands and plopped it on the table.

"For you." Oscar slid the folder across the table. Maria opened the folder and fingered through the photos. She grabbed her mouth.

"You must have found the picture of your husband's first victim," Oscar said. "His name is Christopher Roberts. The bullet missed his heart by a few inches. He just got out of the hospital. That picture is before they ripped open his chest, pulled the bullet out, and stitched him up again."

Maria's hands still cupped her mouth and chin as she blinked back tears.

"Pretty, huh?" Oscar rose and walked over to her. "Let me show you my favorite." He stood behind her and arched over Maria's shoulder. His hand slid over hers as he ruffled through the various photos until he found the one he wanted.

"Oh my God," Maria screamed and tried to jump up. Oscar held her down with his arms.

"Yeah, this one is your husband's second victim, Jean

Catherine West." Oscar could feel Maria trembling under him. "She's just twenty-seven. That was her first baby. See all that blood around her? After your sweetie threw her to the street, she began hemorrhaging. The baby was gone before she made it to the hospital. Do you have any children, Ms. Adee?"

"Yes," Maria whispered. She sniffed in between sighs.

"I'm sorry. I didn't hear you."

"Yes," Maria moaned.

"The doctors told me that because of all the damage she might never have kids again. How many kids do you have?"

"One."

"Boy or girl?"

"Boy. His name is Qoundrus."

"Cute name."

"We call him Q."

"Well, Lil' Q should be so proud of his mom and dad, the baby killers."

"I didn't know." Maria broke down. She quaked in a spasm of tears and cries. "I didn't know all this would happen."

"You were robbing a bank, what did you think would happen?" Oscar moved around Maria and sat in the seat next to her. "This is not good."

"No shit," Maria countered, wiping her eyes.

"All I want to know is where you dropped him off."

"I am here to turn myself in. I don't know anything about him."

Oscar stood and walked around her. "Are you crazy?" He pulled out a pack of cigarettes from his back pocket. He tapped the end until a single white tube poked out. He placed it in his mouth. "You smoke?"

"No." Maria stared at her lap. Her tangled curly hair hung across her face like brown question marks.

"Shame," Oscar mumbled. "Without him, it's just you. With no one else to blame you won't get out of jail till menopause."

"I wasn't even there, I drove off." Maria jumped up.

"Sit your ass down." Oscar pointed at her with his cigarette. "This is not the time to get buck."

"Officer . . ." Maria hesitated as Oscar smiled.

"Parks," Oscar said. "Oscar Parks, but if you're gonna make it through this, we'll have to be friends. And if we're going to be friends you better call me Oscar."

"Oscar." Maria combed through her hair with her fingers. She was rather pretty, with thick lips and angled cheekbones. Her soft eyes caught the light in the room and seemed to shimmer. *In another life, she could have been a model,* Oscar thought.

"I was not involved in the robbery."

Oscar grimaced. "Attempted murder."

"Murder?" Maria sighed. "I drove off and left Damon there. I don't know what happened to him after that, and frankly I do not want to run into him."

"Afraid he'll add more marks on your arms than he already has?"

Maria covered her arms with her hands. "I just want to cooperate so I can take care of my baby." Her voice trembled.

"I'm gonna need more information if you expect to go home to your kid." Oscar laughed. "You are an accomplice to attempted murder."

"What do you want from me?" Maria yelled. "I told you I was planning on going through with it, but I just couldn't—"

"Well, tell me more about the plan," Oscar interrupted. "What were you planning on doing with the money?"

"Go to Florida."

"What part?"

"Miami."

"Makes sense," Oscar blurted. "You rob and almost kill two people and then go vacation in Miami."

"We just wanted to start over."

"At what cost?"

"I don't know." Maria bowed her head as a knock at the door startled them. Oscar got up and opened the steel entranceway.

"Adrienne Bates. I am Ms. Adee's attorney." The woman maneuvered past Oscar and sat down next to Maria.

"Uh, Ms. Bates, can I talk to you over here for a second?" Oscar tried to control the anger threatening to ooze between his words.

"Do not say another word," Adrienne said to Maria and walked over to the corner Oscar was huddled in.

"Uh, baby, what are you doing?" Oscar asked.

"Hey, I got a call this morning from Ms. Adee's sister. She said they couldn't afford a lawyer and found my number online."

"You cannot represent her," Oscar said.

"Why?" Adrienne moved in closer.

"You're my wife, for starters!"

"There is no conflict. I represent Ms. Adee and you are not opposing counsel, just an officer investigating the case."

"What if I talked about the case at home?"

"That's no problem since we haven't held a real conversation in, like, eight months."

"You want to do this now?"

"There is no conflict, no issue unless you want to make one." Adrienne pressed her hand on Oscar's hand. "She needs proper representation."

Oscar rolled his eyes. "Where are the kids?"

"In school. It's like nine thirty a.m. already. Which means you've had my client alone for what, like almost four hours?"

"It hasn't been that long," Oscar said as Adrienne smirked and walked over to her client."

"Ms. Adee, I represent Legal Aid and I want to help, but I have to disclose a couple things to you."

"Now what?" Maria rolled her eyes.

"I am married to Officer Parks over there." She smiled.

"And while that doesn't pose a legal dilemma, it may pose some discomfort to you."

"Can you keep me out of jail so I can be with my baby?" Maria pleaded.

"I will try my best." Adrienne smiled and gripped her hand. "Then you're hired."

"Officer Parks," Adrienne said. "Ms. Adee won't be answering any more questions right now, and since the real person you want is still out there she will be going home now."

By the time Oscar finished typing all his reports it was way past dark. The moon stood high, like a badge the sky bore nightly. He spotted Adrienne's SUV sitting in the driveway and clicked the garage door open. He heard the washing machine humming in the distance as he walked through the door to the house.

"Daddy," a chorus of voices shouted as four children ran up to Oscar.

"Hey." Oscar stretched his arms around his children and closed in tight.

"Daddy, you're crushing us." Joy squirmed out of the embrace. "This is a new dress."

"Well, excuse me." Oscar grabbed his daughter and threw her in the air. She screamed as he caught her fall.

"Do me next, Daddy," Tre begged. Before long Oscar was spinning and throwing his children like piñatas for fifteen minutes, until his arms grew tired. "Where is your mommy?"

"She's at the computer," Tiffany whispered. "She said not to be 'sturbed while she was working."

"Really?" Oscar smirked.

"She even let us watch *Spongebob* till nine as long as we didn't laugh loud." Terrence pushed his huge glasses back up on top of his nose.

"Well, you know what time it is now, right?" Oscar said. "Bath and bed time."

The children moaned in unison as Oscar scooted them toward the children's bathroom. "I don't want to hear none of that. You have already been up an hour past your bedtime."

"Can we say good night to Mommy?" Tre asked. A certified mama's boy, he wouldn't last a night without kissing his mom.

"After you take a bath and brush your teeth."

The children ran down the hallway to their bathroom, as Oscar eased into the kitchen where Adrienne sat fixed in front of her laptop. He snuck behind her and kissed her head.

"Hey, babe," Oscar said as Adrienne jumped up.

"Oh, hey, sweetie." She kissed his lips and they shared a brief embrace before she broke and planted herself in front of her computer.

"What you working on?" Oscar leaned over her shoulder and tried to read. But Adrienne placed her hand on his face, covering his eyes.

"Case stuff." Adrienne laughed.

"Must be stuff I can't read."

"Exactly." Adrienne clicked at her computer.

"So you're really going to defend that dumb girl?"

"Okay, ground rules." Adrienne swung around and rested her hands on Oscar's arms. "No calling my clients names."

"She is just so stupid, letting that trifling nigga beat her down and then making her rob a bank."

"You don't know her."

"I know him."

"Damon." Adrienne smiled. "You knew him and you used to love him, if I recall."

"We were kids." Oscar turned toward the refrigerator and pulled out a Coke. "That was years ago."

"You told me he was like your little brother back then."

"He was." Oscar flipped the soda top open and took a long swig of caffeine. "Things change."

"True, so it's safe to say you don't know him or her or what they went through."

"He shot a guy in front of my face," Oscar yelled. "A woman lost her kid 'cause of him. Could you imagine losing one of our kids?"

"It is not my job to imagine that. It's my job to defend my client." Adrienne grabbed the soda from Oscar's hands and took a sip. "And it's your job to get facts on the case and make an arrest based on those facts."

"Those two are just a waste," Oscar said.

"A waste of what?"

"Space, breath, life," Oscar said as Adrienne shot up.

"What the hell is wrong with you?" Adrienne said. "We are dealing with issues bigger than two kids who made huge mistakes. We're talking about years of brainwashing, racism, and self-hatred."

"I am just a little tired of that being used as an excuse," Oscar said. "They are two adults responsible enough to drink, vote, and screw. They know the difference between right and wrong."

"Since when did you become so judgmental?" Adrienne yelled.

"Since the guy I had in my sight got away," Oscar said. "And he destroyed two lives in the process."

"You did the best you could," Adrienne said.

"No, I didn't," Oscar yelled. "I could have shot him dead and saved a whole lot of people some hurt and suffering."

"You are not God, you're a police officer," Adrienne said. She moved in close to her husband and wrapped herself around him. "You don't know what God has in store for him or anyone else."

"All I know is because of me, he got away," Oscar said.

"He had a gun on someone," Adrienne said.

"Yeah, but I had a clear shot," Oscar said.

"Maybe there was a reason."

"Yeah, I had a moment of emotion for the boy I used to play baseball with, go fishing with," Oscar said. "You know, he told me his mother died."

"Oh," Adrienne said. "That is so sad."

"What's sad is I believed that crap," Oscar said. "She's still alive in the same neighborhood we grew up in, wearing baby tees and high heels."

"Sounds like a classy lady."

"You know, she is still protecting him." Oscar banged his hand on the table. "I think she is secretly proud of her son for being a dope dealer and criminal."

"Don't worry, you'll find him," Adrienne said.

"I know I will." Oscar finished his drink and crushed the can between his palms. "And if the situation happens again, I will pull the trigger."

Chapter X

After the alcohol was gulped down, the snack food devoured, the room service menu exhausted, the fly buzzing around the room killed, the genitals molested, the money counted, recounted, and counted again, the nervous breakdown subsided, Damon decided it was time to leave his hotel room.

Save fleeing to a darkened stairwell for a couple of hours every morning so the maids could clean his room without fixating on his all-too-familiar face, thanks to the local news, he hadn't left his floor. He managed to survive the first couple of weeks fine until he clicked on Cartoon Network and saw Samurai Jack slicing villains with his sword on the TV screen.

"Q," Damon muttered. He could feel the empty space at his side where his son was usually planted himself every night as their favorite cartoon aired. The sound of squeaky giggles filled the air as he imagined his son jumping back into his arms in bouts of laughter. He thought about all the books they read each night and the wild stories he made up to make his son fall asleep.

Worst of all, he missed her. He didn't even want to utter her name in the back recesses of his mind, for fear he might call

her up and cuss her out. How could she have betrayed him
when he did nothing but love and protect her for seven years?
Sure, he would wil' out sometimes and things got a little ugly,
but she knew he loved her. Hell, he cared for her more than
any of those other punks she was used to dating.

But try as he could to imagine his semiautomatic pressed
against her temple, his mind wandered a little south of her
head. He thought of her soft round breasts pressed against his
chest, arms stretched out, and tears rolling back on her face
when he was inside her. He caught himself staring at the
phone too long and jumped from his bed.

"Fuck that bitch," Damon mumbled and slammed the door
behind him. He reached the elevator and pressed the UP
button. By the time he reached the roof and walked outside,
cool air was brushing over the deserted swimming pool, sending Damon into a bout of shivers. He walked over to the iron
fence that surrounded the roof.

The Atlanta skyline sparkled as the sun set behind steel
buildings dotted with lights. Cars began to swarm like bees
along Peachtree Street and Highway I-85. The cold air broke
the clouds, so moonlight tangoed with man-made lights to
form a city illuminated in blue and white.

Damon felt like a king trapped in his modern steel castle.
All the amenities of royalty were his, as long as he never left
his safe haven. But how long could he stay huddled in a hotel
room? Certainly the staff was wondering how a black man,
no matter what his perceived celebrity, could stay in a five-
star hotel suite for three weeks. Surely the envelopes of
money he sent down with the concierge were strange enough.
Add black to eccentric behavior and it is always read as crazy
and/or illegal. It was only a matter of time before hotel security, or worse, the police, would pound in his door and either
kill him or take him to jail. Either way his life was over.

All for $230,000. He had counted the money and had al-
ready spent more than seven thousand of it on the stupid hotel

with wimpy pillows and hard water. He wanted to leave and head for Miami, but he was sure she had blabbed his business to the cops, so the airports and train stations would be flooded with pigs.

His only hope was to hitch a ride with someone, but the idea of carjacking another person left an aching pain in his stomach. Besides, he would walk all the way to Miami if he could see Q one more time. He had to explain to him why his daddy had to go away for a while. But he couldn't abandon his son like his father did him. He made a pact to care for his son and be a part of his life. Yeah, he made mistakes, but he was always there, except now.

Damon turned back in toward the door when he spotted the figure standing under the tan canopy, blocking the door. He couldn't see the man's face, but he spotted the shiny badge on the man's chest and the gun holstered at his side.

"Pool area's closed, sir," the man said, edging toward Damon. The man's hand slid back on his holster.

"Sorry, I just thought you couldn't swim." Damon presented his smile and the man crept closer to him.

"You a guest here?"

Damon could make out the man's blue security suit that merged onto his dark skin. "Yes."

"What room?" The man was only a few feet away, and his eyes were fixed on Damon's bag, which rested on the ground.

"Fourteen twenty-three" Damon bent toward the bag. If something popped off he would need his gun and his money. "Let me show you my key."

"Hold it," the man shouted. His thumb flicked the safety latch off the holster. "Throw the bag to me. I'll find it."

"It's a little heavy." Damon smiled. "And I got all kinds of stuff in there. You'll never find it. Just let me—"

The man swiped the gun from its cradle and pointed it toward Damon. "Put your hands up," the man said. "You think I don't know who you are?"

It was over. Damon slowly raised his hands to the sky, tossing options in his head. "What you talking about, man?" Damon's smile disappeared, but his voice still bounced in his higher register.

"You ain't no celebrity," the man explained. "I been watching you for weeks trying to put your face to the picture in my mind. Then I saw you on TV."

Damon shook his head. He knew he was made, and would possibly have to hurt or kill this man. For a second he contemplated falling to his knees and surrendering, but looking at the guard with his angry face and shaky hands he knew he couldn't settle without a chance of seeing Q again.

"Nobody believed me," the man said. "Now when I get that reward money all them haters gone look stupid when I ride up in my Escalade."

Damon walked toward him. "That's great, man. Just one problem."

"Don't move." The man's hand trembled against the weapon in his hand. "I will shoot you."

"Not today." Damon lunged forward and grabbed the gun as the two men struggled. Damon lost his footing and looked back at the cold water as the pair fell into the pool. Though the water slowed his punches, he managed to plant several blows to the guard's head and stomach. It was a quick battle. He dragged the barely conscious man to the edge of the pool and jumped out. He grabbed his bag and dashed to the door. When he reached the elevator doors he stopped cold. He could ride down and face cops in the lobby, or take the stairs and face getting trapped between floors. He opted for the stairs, hoping to dry his clothes by the time he reached the ground floor. He had reached the second-floor doors when he heard doors busting open below him.

"Code 234," a radio echoed in the stairwell. "Suspect is armed and dangerous. Please be advised police are en route." Damon shot through the second-floor door and walked into the busy hotel restaurant. He moved through the thicket of people looking for the front entrance, but spotted some security guards running past the restaurant.

"Excuse me, sir." A waiter with a huge plate of food on his shoulders whizzed past him. Damon looked back at the swinging kitchen doors, and eased through them. He followed the exit signs to a back door that led out to a long narrow alley. Damon's heart drowned out all sound. He raced to the front of the alley and peeked out. One direction led to a cluster of small shops. The other led to his saving grace— a MARTA train station sign.

Damon inhaled long and slow and hit the pavement. When he reached the entrance to the station, he slowed his trot to an easy pimp. He scrambled for change, looking at the crowd through the corner of his eye. He placed a twenty-dollar bill in the machine and heard a rain shower of tokens and change fall into the tray below. He grabbed a handful of tokens and walked toward the entrance.

"Sir." Damon turned to face an old woman pointing at him. "You left your money," she said.

"Keep it," Damon whispered, trying not to draw the attention of the MARTA officers gathered in a corner laughing.

"What?" the woman shouted. She rushed past Damon and scraped the rest of the change from the tray. "Thank you."

He dropped his fare in the slot and managed to board a train unmolested. He rode the train back and forth from the airport to the North Springs suburbs. As he watched trees and trains zip past his window in a flurry of color and light, he knew he had to leave Atlanta. He knew he had to leave everything behind, including his son.

Damon tried to imagine Q sitting next to him, his small head nestled against Damon's arm. He slowly blinked and fell asleep.

"Daddy, tell me a story," Q said.

"What do you want to hear?" Damon asked, his arms trying to hug his imaginary son.

"Tell me a happy story." Q smiled.

Damon always dissolved when he thought of his son's toothy smile. His bright brown eyes, as big as saucers, searched his father's eyes for direction, love, and life.

"Okay. There once was a young king who left his family for a while to give his family a better life."

"Why did he have to go away?" Q questioned.

"I don't know," Damon pondered. "I guess he felt that was his only option. So the prince was in charge."

"Did he ever come back?" Q asked.

"Of course he did." Damon smiled at his son.

"I wouldn't want you to go, Daddy," Q said, his words piercing Damon's heart.

"Sometimes daddies have to do hard things to make their families happy."

"Sometimes the hardest thing is the right thing, Daddy," Q said.

"What do you know about hard times?" Damon yelled. "You're a kid."

"I know you left me." The child's words vibrated in Damon's skull. Suddenly, Damon turned to see Maria standing over him. Her arms were crossed.

"You left all of us," she said. "How could you desert us like this?"

"You drove off and left me here alone," Damon screamed. "What the fuck was I supposed to do?"

"Be a man," Maria said.

"I am a man," Damon yelled.

"Then do what you know you have to do." Maria began shaking violently. Her skin evaporated under an intense light that seemed to glow from inside her. Soon she was just an orb of white-hot heat burning Damon's face.

"This is not who you are," the voice said, though it was no

longer Maria's. It was deeper and came from Damon's head, not the figure before him.

"Daddy, I need you," Q said, and he was sucked into the object like a dust ball in a vacuum.

"Q," Damon screamed. "Where is my son?"

"He is with your destiny. Catch them if you dare."

Suddenly the light expanded like a sunrise and spread beyond the skies, and Damon awoke with a jerk.

"Attention, MARTA customers." A stale voice ran through the air. "This is your last train on MARTA's East Line. Please be advised all passengers must exit the train." Damon got off the train and walked along dimly lit streets until dawn.

After walking for hours, he caught the attention of an idle taxicab on the corner across the street. He displayed his cash and hopped in the car. There was only one place left he had to go.

"Do you go out to Hampton, Georgia?"

Chapter XI

"I missed you," David whispered in my ear, in that please-sex-me tone. I didn't hear him come into the room, but I jumped when his big arms wrapped around my shoulders. I turned and pecked him on the lips, hoping to get back to my to-do list for my party. There was still so much to get done. Hotel reservations for the industry types had to be booked. The VIP list had to be jotted down. Three security companies were vying for the opportunity to keep the regular folks away from the celebrities. I was so proud of all the RSVPs I had received.

Not only was my small cache of clients ready to attend, but there was a gang of wannabes and up-and-comers all willing to smooze, booze, and ultimately trash me behind my back. But I didn't care. I was sure to at least snag three or four medium-sized clients, and who knows, maybe Tom Cruise or Will Smith would drop by and give me an opportunity to work with him. Either way, I was too busy planning to indulge in any distracting, albeit pleasant, hanky-panky.

"I miss you too." I kissed David a little longer this time. "But I'm working on something."

"So am I." David grabbed my hand and placed it on his pleasure principle.

I was once again facing the ultimate quandary in marital

negotiations. I could refuse service, inciting an attitudinal tidal wave, and be forced to watch my husband pouting around the house for days. Or I could concede and make him feel good, thus making him more accommodating to the ridiculous requests and journeys I would no doubt send him on before this party thing was over.

And unlike friends I talk to who say their husbands slam them into the bedposts like slabs of beef, not paying attention to the women underneath them, David was a very good lover. He didn't mind kissing me all over my body until I was quivering, ready for him to take me home. He whispered things like "You are so beautiful" and "Why are you so sexy?" while he held me in his arms. I never heard "I'm gone stab them guts" or any other crude variation. I was always appreciative of that.

But the aftereffects of the accident were slowly taking their toll. I could barely feel my own legs some days, let alone accept the loving motions of my husband. My job was the only thing that cluttered my mind enough not to rehash that moment when my life had vanished.

Most days only anger carried me through. I was furious at that crazy Negro for killing my child. I was pissed that I was scared to drive anywhere I used to freely roam. I was indignant at the millions of times I recounted the incident in my head. How many times I winced at the thought of the glass ripping my skin apart. How many times I frowned when, from the corner of my eye, I saw a brother stare a little too hard at me. I was terrified of my men, my city, my life, and most importantly, my future. Nothing held any weight anymore. Not even my handsome husband who just wanted to be intimate with his wife. So I bowed gracefully, and turned into him as he lifted me out of my chair and carried me to the bed.

My body felt like it was asleep as David rediscovered it. His once-soft lips felt coarse on my skin. His callus-free hands burned as he rubbed my breasts. When he finally was inside me, I blinked back tears, not because it was awful, but because I couldn't recapture how good it had been. I opened my eyes to tell him to stop, but my husband was gone.

The deep brown eyes of the man/child who had left me for dead on the street searched my face, like they had done that day. I swung my arms out to belt him.

"Get off me," I screamed. I pushed my arms against his chest to get him off me, my eyes fixated on his soft eyes. But a different voice came out of his mouth.

"Baby, what's wrong?" David's hushed voice pierced through my scattered imagination. I fell back into him and burst into tears. David moved behind me and gripped me like Velcro. He kissed my neck, and said, "It's all right, baby, it's just me."

He repeated the words more than a hundred times before the vision of the one man who ruined my life was replaced with the reality of the man who allowed me to keep living. After our helter-skelter attempt at love, David turned to his gym for comfort and companionship, and I dug even harder into my only relief, my job.

But for one night my distraction seemed to pay off. The album release party was, for all intended purposes, a smash hit. When David and I arrived at the abandoned car garage, it had been transformed into a piece of art. Dirty brick was painted a blue deeper than the ocean at Tybee Island. Small birch trees lined the front courtyard leading to my favorite part of any party, the red carpet.

My biggest client, Terrain, a self-made entrepreneur, indie filmmaker, and media hog, was already waving for flashing cameras and pulling along some model-turned-permanent showpiece behind him.

"I owe all the success of my first film *Pimp Like Me*— which won first prize at the Atlanta Film Festival, by the way—to the PR magic of J.C. West." Terrain smiled as he caught my eye. "And here is the woman of the hour. My girl! Come here."

I smiled at all of Terrain's lies. In fact, he owed most of the success of his film to the off-screen romance he had with the leading lady. Honestly, it was surprising to see him here. He hated popular music almost as much as he hated dating black women.

He motioned me over, but I gripped David's hand tightly. This was my first time in the city, and though I had envisioned this party for weeks, walking those few feet to Terrain seemed like the most frightening thing I ever had to do. I felt my legs stiffen under the weight of my body. I couldn't move. David squeezed my hand and said, "Go get 'em, baby."

I had all the encouragement I needed. I released David's hand and sauntered into the spotlight to reclaim my life.

"Ms. West," a reporter shouted as I hugged Terrain. "Are you happy with the turnout tonight?"

"I am ecstatic." I beamed. "I have to thank so many people for coming out and supporting Carlos's album release party. He will be the next king of pop and R & B. Believe that. And West World PR, Incorporated, is proud to represent him." I was floating. I scanned the crowd, looking at all of the beautiful people caught behind the red rope, all trying to attend my event. When I got inside, it was even more packed. Men in expensive suits floated across the room, occasionally stopping long enough to check out the ladies in short dresses with exposed backs. The strobe light flickered staccato against the hip-hop beats that shook the floor. I was spellbound by the pack of dancers that gyrated in unison. I was headed to the VIP room to mingle with all the potential clients when I spotted some eyes locked in on me.

I turned to face a guy I had never seen before. He smiled and waved and I moved on. But as I moved through the dark passageways that led to the VIP lounge I noticed some more eyes staring at me. They looked just like his eyes, and I dashed toward the restroom. Carlos caught me at the door.

"There you are." Rumormongers speculated that Carlos had paid forty grand to have his teeth fixed. Worth every dime, if you ask me. Each tooth seem to shimmer on its own. But when set against his beautiful full lips, they seemed to sparkle like white diamonds.

"Hey there." I managed to grin. "Are you enjoying your party?"

"I love it, it's so . . . what is the name for it? Elegant."

"Well, thank you."

"I guess I should have expected nothing less from a woman as elegant as you."

I tried not to raise my eyebrows, which was my usual response when I detected a pickup line. Was Carlos hitting on me, or just feeding me the same manure he shoveled at everyone?

"Well, thank you. When are you set to perform?" I asked, already knowing the answer. But I hoped to jar him back to business.

"Oh yeah, I am set in like thirty minutes." He moved in closer. "I got a seat for you right in the front row."

"Thank you, but me and my husband always choose a spot in the back so we can drink and ridicule in private."

He cocked his head back and giggled. "I understand. Well, make sure to take some time to talk to me before the night ends."

"I will," I said and leaned one hand against the bathroom door. "Bathroom."

"Oh, sorry." Carlos turned purple. "Sorry for keeping you. Um, I'll talk to you later." He turned around and faced a barrage of fans and press as he headed back to the stage. And I felt a rumbling in my stomach, and ran inside the bathroom.

I found an empty stall and plopped down on the seat.

My stomach churned as I tried to focus in on my present surroundings.

"That bitch thinks she's on point because she got some little no-name singer to throw a party," a familiar voice said. "The only reason people are here is 'cause they felt sorry for the poor little black girl who got beat down."

"I think she rigged the whole thing to get publicity for her little makeshift company," another woman said.

I could hear water splashing and then a blow-dryer.

"The only reason I'm here is 'cause I heard Usher might be here."

"You didn't see him?"

"He's here?"

"Sweetie, they're all in VIP."

"You think we can sneak in?" the other girl said as my stomach quaked.

Suddenly something wet snaked down leg. My hands pulled away blood. I felt faint. I wanted to jump up and find David, but I didn't want those hoes to have another opportunity to belittle me.

"Well, even though I have been told I look like Beyonce, I don't think you could pass for Kelly," the girl giggled.

"The only way you could pass for Beyonce is if she developed an addiction to Krispy Kreme and gained forty pounds," the other woman yelled. "And even then it would be shaky."

"Cow."

"Hater."

"Tramp."

"You thirsty?"

"Hell yeah," the girl said. "Let's find some niggas who ain't cheap to at least get us a glass of wine or something."

As soon as I heard the door slam I buckled over in pain. The blood was pouring instead of dripping and I could barely stand. I fumbled through my purse, hoping to find something to stop the bleeding. But now the pain was so acute my head throbbed in conjunction with my heartbeat. My hands quivered as I unlatched the bathroom door. I braced myself

against a steel railing and hoisted my body to a standing position. I toppled to the row of silver sinks and ran the water. I
used a wet towel to cool my aching forehead, and then pulled
out my cell phone.

I dialed David's number and prayed he hadn't turned his
phone off.

"Where are you?" he screamed through the phone. "I got
press and all your people trying to talk to you. You know I
don't know about any of this stuff."

"David . . ." I could barely move one way or the other,
scared I would fall on my face.

"What's wrong?" he said, his voice shaking to match mine.
"Are you okay? Where are you?"

"Your wife is in trouble again." The same voice from inside
the bathroom now blared through my cell phone.

"Who is that?"

"Where are you? I'll come get you," David said.

"I'm in the bathroom. David, I'm bleeding kind of bad."

"You're what?" David yelled. "Which bathroom are you
in—the front or back?"

"I don't know." My head burned, but all I could focus on
now was the voice at the other end of my husband's phone.
"The same bathroom where that heffa standing next to you
was in."

"I'm just standing next to Nicole," David said. "Nicole, did
you just come from the bathroom?"

"Yeah."

"Which one?"

"That one over there."

I heard the phone click off and within seconds the door
swung open and smacked against the wall. David ran to me
and lifted me up.

"Baby, what happened?"

"I don't know. I . . ." I was determined for this man not to have
to carry my unconscious body through a crowd of my peers.

"Can you just sneak us out of the back door, please?" I begged.

"We gotta get you to a hospital."

"And I will jump into an ambulance down the street, but can we please not make a scene in here?"

"J.C., are you all right?" Nicole inched her way toward me. Her six-inch heels made her tower over my already-slumping body. I wanted to slam her head against the sink, but in my weakened state it was all I could do to stay alert. So I had to give up the ghost and ask for this woman's help.

"Can I please use your shawl?" I asked.

"Sure, but it hardly goes with that color scheme you got going."

I wrapped it over my head. "If you could just help David carry me out the back as quickly and discreetly as possible."

"Of course." Nicole put her meaty arm around my back and dropped my lifeless arms over her shoulder. She and David lifted me up and quickly raced through the kitchen entrance to the alley out back. From there David called an ambulance, and I was soon lying in a hospital bed right back where had I started. I asked Nicole not to tell anyone what had happened to me. Little did I know she would do much worse.

Chapter XII

In between swallowing painkillers and inching to the bathroom Christopher had spent the last three days watching the phone. He marveled at the gray and black cellular device. He rubbed his fingers along the blue LCD screen. When he was really desperate he flipped the top and scanned through the numbers, searching for the last time Vince had called: July 9, two days after Christopher arrived home from the hospital. It was a brief conversation. Final arrangements about moving his furniture, adding another connection for the DSL line in the attic, which would be Vince's office, and a couple of "Love yous" spat out just as they said good-bye.

That was several days ago. Eight days, in fact, since the day Vince was officially supposed to move in with Christopher. When he didn't receive a call all night, Christopher got worried, then angry. But bedridden he couldn't take his anger out on the weights and punching bag in the basement. He could barely maneuver the remote control. The only human contact he had since he got home was his housekeeper, Gloria, who only smiled at the floor and muttered "Hello" when she came and "Have a good day" when she left. She knew—or at least pretended to know—very little English. But it wasn't her job to fix vodka tonics and dissect his love life. So he clicked on the phone and dialed the number 5, hoping to have an emergency relationship intervention.

The phone only rang twice before Armando answered the phone.

"*Hola*, amigo."

"*Hola, papi*," Christopher responded.

"*Como esta bien?*"

"Now, you know that is all I can say." Christopher managed to laugh. "I know about as much Spanish as Gloria knows English."

"Are you still too lazy to clean your own house?" Armando laughed.

"Why, when I can hire one of you to do my work?" Christopher smiled through the phone.

"You niggers kill me," Armando retorted. "You get a little money and forget you were riding the back of the bus like two years ago."

"Since the Hispanics jumped the border and stole all the jobs, we had to come up somehow." Christopher let out a long-needed laugh.

"Keep laughing," Armando said. "Ol' Gloria is just sizing up your house so she can rob you blind."

"I've already been shot. A little robbery would be relaxing," Christopher countered.

"Is Vince over there spoiling you yet?"

"Humph," Christopher grunted.

"Y'all didn't have your first fight already, did you?"

"One would have to be living together for that to happen."

There was a soft pause and Armando whispered, "I don't understand. Where is Vince?"

"Haven't heard from him in a week." Christopher could feel the venom in his tone, but he didn't care.

"But I thought . . ." Armando started and then caught himself.

"Me too."

"So, has he called you?"

"Nope."

"For real? Man, I'm sorry," Armando said. "So, you're all alone in that huge house."

"Pretty much. Unless you count Gloria, my nurse, and satellite television."

"I'm coming down to stay with you," Armando said.

"Absolutely not," Christopher said. Even if he did want the company, he was not going to guilt his friend into flying across the country to get Christopher's Ben & Jerry's ice cream out of the freezer. "I'm fine. All I am doing is resting anyway."

"You mean obsessing."

"When you're used to working seventy-five hours a week, lying in the bed obsessing about trifling niggas is resting. Hell, it's almost a vacation."

"Have you called him?" Armando said.

"Hell no."

"Why? He could be dead," Armando countered.

"Oh, that's what they always want you to think," Christopher said. "Then you call and they're sitting right there, and then you get even more pissed. And they're all like, 'What? I'm just cute and dumb. Why are you mad at me?'"

"You owe it to yourself to make sure he is okay," Armando offered. "Then, if he is alive, you hire a hit man to take him out."

Christopher tried not to laugh, but he couldn't help busting into a fit of heaving laughter.

"Just call him, and then call me back so I can tell you when my plane arrives."

"You don't have to come here."

"Please, it's the summer," Armando said. "Do you have any idea how boring the summer is for a professor?"

"Don't you do lesson plans or something?"

"I am an econ professor," Armando added. "The economy is shit. End of story."

"I don't want to impose."

"You have been imposing since we were in college, nigga."
Armando chuckled. "Plus, if you get on my nerves, I'll just
make you overdose on your medication."

"Thank you," Christopher mumbled.

"Just have junk food and alcohol available, none of that
healthy shit," Armando said. "We Mexicans like our fatty
acids."

"Uh, have you heard of fried chicken?" Christopher countered. "We do too."

"Touché. Call."

"I am. Right now."

"Peace," Armando said.

"One."

Armando clicked off, and Christopher threw the phone on
the floor. He hoped he'd drift back to sleep and tomorrow
forget about Vince and the aching that had pinched his heart
for the last several days. But as soon as the phone slammed
against the carpet it began ringing.

Christopher hugged his bandaged chest with his left hand
and pulled himself to the corner of the bed with his free arm.
He stretched his arm to the floor, searching for his phone. He
finally grabbed it and clicked it on.

"Hello?"

"There ain't no bus that goes to your house." Christopher's
dad boomed through the phone.

"Huh?"

"There is no bus or train to your house," Alonzo said.
"What, they fly you in every night from that bank?"

"It's only Hampton, Dad," Christopher said. "And you
could get here if you had a car."

"Well, I would have, but I lost my little trucking gig and I
am on MARTA," Alonzo said. "I have some soup for you."

"What?"

"Soup, soup," Alonzo said. "What, you hard of hearing too? It's to help you get better."

"Dad, I was shot, I don't have the flu," Christopher said. He looked at the clock on the wall: 6:30 p.m. It was now officially eight days since the alleged move-in date.

"I know you were shot, boy," Alonzo said. "I should have known you would be gay with that flip-ass mouth."

"Well, I got soup here, Dad, so you don't have to come all the way out here."

"You don't have my soup," Alonzo said. "How much would a cab cost me?"

Christopher blew into the phone, realizing this was a losing battle. When his dad had his mind made up, a stampeding bull couldn't detain him. Just like when he decided to leave Christopher and his mother to pursue his jazz career. Alonzo had stood right at the door of their one-bedroom apartment, saxophone case in one hand, backpack slung high over his shoulders.

"You watch over your mother," Alonzo had said as Christopher wiped away the ten-year-old tears already soaking his cheeks. "Daddy has to go make us some money."

"I want to go with you." Christopher clamped on to his father's leg.

"Who is going to take care of Mommy?" his father asked. It seemed like a logical question at the time. He was too young to conclude it was, in fact, his father's responsibility to take care of both him and Mommy.

"I'll call as soon as I get settled in New York." Alonzo hugged his son tight. "Be good." Christopher took the instructions to heart. He got straight As, graduating with honors from high school, college, and grad school. He got a job at eighteen and never took another penny from his mother. Instead, he sent money to her as often as he could. Though his father never came back for more than a few days at a time,

Alonzo's instructions had helped Christopher to be the man he was, whether he could admit it to himself or not.

"Where are you, Dad?"

"In the West End."

"God," Christopher sighed.

"What, you bourgeois Negroes don't come down to the city?"

"I'll come get you."

"I am a grown man. I can take a cab."

"Dad, a cab will cost you like a hundred dollars." Christopher edged up off the bed. "I'm bored here anyway. I'll come scoop you up and we can grab something to eat."

"What about the soup?"

"I'll take it back with me."

"I haven't made it yet."

Christopher slapped his hand against his head. This man would probably drive him back to the bottle. "What, are you just holding a can of soup?"

"No, nosy," Alonzo yelled. "I just got back from the farmers' market and I have all these great ingredients to make the best soup you ever tasted."

"Okay, okay," Christopher conceded. "I'll come get you and bring you back here to make the soup. But you'll have to spend the night 'cause I won't feel like driving all the way back to the West End."

"That's fine." Alonzo laughed. "You gone love my soup."

"Yeah, yeah, can I call you back on this number?"

"Yep."

"I'll call you when I'm on my way." Christopher hung up the phone and fell back on his bed. Not only was he missing a boyfriend, but he was facing a sneaky father creeping his way back into his life. He could feel the anger rising through his chest and wetting his eyelids with tears. He dialed Vince's number.

"Hey, what's up, man? Why haven't you called me?" Vince said, immediately defusing Christopher's anger with confusion.

"What?"

"You ain't called me in days."

"I know." Christopher sucked his teeth. "Do you remember what we had planned for last Monday?"

"Yeah. I don't think that whole living together thing is going to work out."

"Apparently."

"It's just my career." Vince stumbled over the words. "I am an anchor. I can't let everyone know my business."

"What about all the people who see you in the clubs and the bars?" Christopher checked himself from screaming. "Hell, what about the bookstores and parks we saw each other in?"

"Yeah, but those punks and sissies ain't my demographic."

"So sucking dick through a hole is okay, but having a shot at a real relationship would hurt your career."

"Honestly, I just kind of thought this whole messing-around thing was kind of a phase."

"You're thirty-three."

"Yeah. I mean, I love you, but I never thought I would be in love with a man. You know what I mean?"

"But just to be clear you do love me, 'cause this is not really what I thought people who loved each other did." Christopher felt hot tears, but he let them slide down his face. He refused to sniffle or sigh and let on to his emotional breakdown.

"Yeah, but love and life are very different sometimes."

"So now you're Dr. Phil." Christopher laughed at the pseudo-philosophical theory.

"I just hope we can still hang out, be friends."

"You mean fuck buddies?"

"How's the chest, by the way?"

"By the way?" Christopher burst into tears. "Jesus. I was shot, almost killed in fact, laid up in a hospital bed for two weeks, and the only thing that kept me going was knowing you were by my side."

"This was a hard decision for me to make too."

"But I wouldn't have known about it if I hadn't called you."

"I would have called you, it's just work was hectic and you know my schedule."

"Vince, I am getting off the phone now. Not 'cause I want to, but because I have to. I did something with you I hadn't done in years. You had me open. But once again I understand exactly why I live for my job and don't let my guard down. Now I have to heal my heart along with my chest, and I really don't think it's fair."

"What can I do to make it up to you?"

"You can make sure you continue not to call, and if I slip up and call you, ignore it."

"Don't act like that."

"Like what?" Christopher asked. "Hurt, broken, numb, sick, angry? Tell me which one to delete, 'cause they're all there."

"Just don't be mad at me."

"Fine, I'm not mad at you."

"You know I don't believe you."

"I guess that's my fault too, 'cause I believed you." Christopher hung up the phone and walked to the bathroom. He buckled over the toilet and threw up till his insides were raw. Then he walked back to his phone and deleted Vince's number. Purged just like his stomach."

Chapter XIII

Hot water pressed into Maria's back like a well-oiled masseuse's hand as she sat crunched in a ball in the porcelain tub. Steam billowed to the ceiling. Cool air kissed the small of her back as the hot water kneaded her shoulders. She couldn't remember how long she had been in the shower, but her skin felt rubbery to the touch. Her eyes pointed straight ahead, fixed on a ladybug crawling on the grout between the tiles.

Maria watched as the bug maneuvered across the tiles, inching its way to the steel faucet. She stretched her finger to touch the red and black pattern on its back. Her mind traveled to the same pattern that rested on the dining table in her grandmother's kitchen. The scent of apples and brown sugar wafted in the air. Her grandmother, who everyone called Mama, hunched over the table, pushing a rolling pin over a glob of dough.

"Baby, can you get me some Coke out of the fridge?" Mama asked seven-year-old Maria, who was lying on the kitchen floor doodling in her coloring book. Maria ran to the small yellow box and pulled out a Coca-Cola bottle and ran it back to her grandmother. Mama grabbed the bottle and in one quick action twisted the bottle cap on her apron.

"Mama, how long before the pie is done?" Maria asked as she leaned over the table. She put her hand in the bowl of freshly sliced apples, and drew back a prize.

"Girl, you got one more time to stick that dirty hand in my bowl and I am gone cut it right off," Mama said between sips of soda. Maria glanced at her granddaughter as she munched on her apple slice. "It will be ready when it's ready."

Maria frowned at her grandmother's typical nonanswer. She squeezed her eyelids closed so her mama wouldn't see her pupils draw high up in her head. Maria's lips poked out just enough for her grandmother to add, "Don't be pouting at me."

"I'm not pouting, I'm chewing." Maria mashed her teeth together to exaggerate her chewing.

"Why don't you do something useful and measure me a cup of sugar to go into the pot with the apples?"

Maria smiled and giggled as she slid across the kitchen and slammed against the cabinet. She pulled a drawer open and grabbed the measuring cup. She placed the left leg, which was an inch longer the other one, on the linoleum counter and gripped the top cabinets with her tiny hands to pry herself up. She fumbled through the soup cans and condensed milk until she reached the bag of sugar that leaned against the corner of the cabinet.

"Girl, get your little butt down off my counter," Mama yelled from across the kitchen. She flattened little strips of dough and lined them up on the table.

"You said measure the sugar, Mama." Maria landed with a thud on the floor.

"Girl, is you crazy?" Mama threw a piece of dough and watched it thump against Maria's head. "I already got the sugar down here."

Maria let out a sigh and walked to her grandmother. Her lips poked out a little as she sidled up to Mama. She tossed the measuring cup in her hands.

"Come over on this side," Mama said. She grabbed Maria's hand and twirled her to the other side of the table, where a blue-flowered mixing bowl filled with sugar rested.

"Two cups, sweetie," Mama said. Maria dug the cup deep into the bowl and came away with a mountain of sugar. "Two cups, baby," Mama said in that tone that indicated Maria's measuring skills needed improvement.

Maria looked at the grooves on the side of the cup and squinted her eyes to read the 2 CUPS painted on the side. Sugar sifted back into the bowl until the white powder was level with the line.

"Is this okay, Mama?" Maria asked. Her grandmother eyed the cup and released a smile that made her beam.

"Perfect, baby, just like you." Mama stretched over the table and kissed Maria on the top of her head, and watched as Maria poured the ingredients into the bowl. Mama mixed in the apples and cinnamon and syrup and jumbled them all together as Maria's stomach churned with anticipation.

Mama gathered the doughy strips and gently crisscrossed them over the roofless pie. Maria hopped in place as Mama transported the pie from the table to the oven.

"I'm so hungry, Mama." Maria moaned softly. She winced a little, knowing how her grandmother felt about whining. She kept an eye open for a smack to the back of her head, but her grandmother smiled and gave Maria a towel.

"By the time we see the ladybugs the pie will be ready."

"You mean ladybugs come for pie?"

Mama laughed and pressed her index finger to the tablecloth. "No, baby, these ladybugs. Once we clean this place up we can eat."

Maria moved pots and bowls to the sink with precise speed, careful not to drop anything but fast enough to hopefully expedite her dessert dining. She soaked her towel under the faucet and commenced to swabbing the table until all the specks of sugar and spices, apple bits and cinnamon sticks, and flour were erased. She leaned over toward her grandmother, who clanked dishes under the sink water and scrubbed every inch of plastic, copper, and steel until the remains of their Saturday afternoon ritual were wiped away.

Sure enough, all that was left on the table were the hundreds of printed ladybugs on the plastic tablecloth that covered the kitchen table. Suddenly Maria heard the soft ding of the oven timer.

Mama slipped on oven mitts and opened the stove as a flash of heat burst through the room. She plopped the pie on top of the range and proceeded to pull out a carton of ice cream, plates, and silverware.

Maria couldn't hide her smile as her grandmother sliced into the pie, placing a gigantic chunk on Maria's plate. She felt the warmth that covered her body. She knew even back then that the tingling that ran through her was not from the food she ate with her grandmother. Legs swung wildly under her chair as she munched and laughed with Mama. She occasionally rubbed the ladybugs between her fingers as she filled her mouth with pie and ice cream.

The ladybugs dissolved in a haze of steam and Maria was back in the shower with just her single friend, who had managed to climb almost to the silver shower rod. After a few more moments it vanished over the top of the curtain. It disappeared with her happy memories. Now it was just her under a scalding shower, red with pain, numb from losing nearly everything she ever cared for in her life. She knew it was time to get out of the shower and face her life.

After applying ample supplies of moisturizer to her skin and making sure her entire body had dried, she entered the world and walked to her bedroom.

"Q," Maria called out. She heard SpongeBob blaring on the TV and moved to her bedroom. Her fingers fondled a picture of Q that sat on the dresser. He was so handsome, just like his father. She wondered how much of Damon's personality Q had inherited. Would he cause his girlfriends as much pain as his daddy caused her? Would Q ever have to make a decision that would separate father from seed, woman from man? Would he have to see the insides of a jail, like his father would most likely see?

She threw on a baby tee and shorts and gazed at a picture of Damon in a startlingly vulnerable pose. It was her favorite. He was not posed for the camera, but just sitting on the couch looking away from the photographer. His head sank back in a fit of laughter. She couldn't remember what he was laughing about, but she knew it was one of the few times she ever remembered him being happy. How do you turn in your heart? How do you separate from the only thing that made you feel real for so long?

She knew after talking with Ms. Bates that surviving this mess meant that she would have to make a decision about who was more important in her life.

"I know you love him. I love my husband too," Ms. Bates had said as she walked to the car with Maria a few nights earlier. "But you are a mother first. You have to think about Q." She pulled in closer to Maria. "You are the only one who can make a difference in your son's life now. You have to make choices that cover his future."

Maria faced her shoes as tears spilled out. She was right, but Damon was all she had for so long. How could she survive without his love, without his touch, without him?

"They don't want you, and I think we both know that," Ms. Bates continued in the car. "But if there is no one left they have to blame someone. And you have to fight for your baby's future, even if that means destroying your present situation."

"That's easy for you to say," Maria muttered. "You got a good husband, who loves all y'all and does right. Damon didn't have that life. But he gave us what he could."

Ms. Bates let out a laugh and shook her head violently. "I know you are not that dumb."

"Excuse me." Maria swung her head around. Her hands scrunched into tiny hard fists.

"I know you don't think you are the first silly girl who did something stupid for her man. Half of all love songs are written 'cause some man done messed up their life." Maria stifled a giggle, but Ms. Bates continued. "And you ain't all innocent in this thing, either. You were more than willing to be the Bonnie to his Clyde. All I am saying is that now it's time to grow up and think about someone other than yourself."

Maria knew she was right. The only way she would be able to survive this situation was to give the police everything she knew about Damon and pray he wouldn't kill her. She also knew ratting out Damon would mean the end of any hopes of their relationship. They would be Q's parents, but never a unit. She wanted to slam his picture into the wall, but resisted the urge. Instead she gently placed it facedown back on the dresser.

"It's about Q now," Maria said to no one in particular. The only thing she could offer Damon right now was a life for their son. And she had to stay out of jail to do that. She pulled her hair into a ponytail and walked back into the hallway.

"Q, baby, you hungry?" She heard him giggling and wondered what nonsense cartoon he was watching. "Baby, you haven't eaten since lunch and I don't feel like cooking. I figured I'd order us a pizza."

"Make sure mine has pineapples on it."

Maria's mouth fell as she entered the family room and saw Damon staring at her. His arm was around Q as they sat watching television. The smirk on Damon's face shook her insides. She felt like she was about to lose her balance and gripped the wall for support.

"Daddy's back, Mama." Q smiled at Maria and then went back to his show.

"I see." Maria tried to parade a smile, but the muscles in her face quivered. Her eyes locked with Damon's. He didn't blink and just scanned her from head to toe like some futuristic judging machine. He pulled Q onto his lap and gripped him tight and then said, "Yep, Daddy's back and he ain't leaving ever again."

Chapter XIV

Cold breath blew into the night as Oscar tackled the last hill leading out of his neighborhood. He glanced at his watch between puffs of air. The dial flashed one and a half miles—just two and a half more to go. When he reached the hill's summit he keeled over and sucked in air like a vacuum. He looked back at his house, its green roof sticking out just higher than the other homes'. He didn't know if he could live in the city, having grown up there all his life. But when his wife took him to Inman Park several years ago, he discovered the difference between city living and inner-city living.

His old neighborhood was spotted with boarded-up homes and homeless men wandering the trash-filled streets. But just a few miles down the road gentrification had settled into the area, and houses were gobbled up by carpetbaggers with real estate mogul aspirations. Within ten years houses had been refurbished with gleaming windows and newly landscaped lawns. Fences reached up toward the aging trees that lined the streets. Shacks were gutted and crews of construction workers and contractors revived homes on their deathbeds.

Roads were repaved, tattered concrete ripped up, and soft black asphalt poured into the crevices. Chipped paint was scraped off walls, and expensive, glossy paints like Calvin

Klein, Ralph Lauren, and DKNY were smoothed over the age spots.

"This starter home is more than seventy years old," the slightly rumpled real estate agent said as they eased their way into the home's driveway. The agent ran her fingers through her tangled hair and surveyed her gum line for a moment in the mirror before swinging her door open and calling back, "You coming?" to Oscar and Adrienne.

"Seventy years old," Oscar moaned. He had his heart set on one of the suburban pop-up homes in Gwinnett County or Conley. A nice new house with all the amenities, including a dishwasher and a washer and dryer, fit his taste. Maybe they'd find one in a cul-de-sac. He had always envied his suburban classmates and their neighborhoods tucked away from the often-abrupt reality of poor black living. That had always been his dream.

"That means it has character." Adrienne placed her hand on Oscar's hand with a "Just keep your mouth shut and don't embarrass me" tone. They climbed out of the SUV.

"Oh my God," Adrienne said as she stepped through the front door and entered the circular foyer with a skylight pulling sunbeams into every corner. She entwined her fingers with Oscar's as they moved forward.

"This has a French modernist feel, very welcoming with all the light, no?" The woman looked at Oscar as if she dared him to refute her ramblings. "Do you see those moldings all around the room? You would pay eight thousand dollars for something like that to be put in one of those cookie-cutter houses."

Adrienne smiled, and Oscar rolled his eyes and walked into the living room. He had to admit to himself he was impressed with the space of the place. The birch-colored hardwood floors seemed to stretch for miles. And the double doors that fronted every room in the house were supercool.

"There is plenty of space for the kiddies to play in," the woman said. "How many did you say you have?"

"None yet," Adrienne said.

"We only want one or two," Oscar interjected. This was before the kids fell into their laps like an Atlanta rain, quick and unexpected.

"Oh my God," Adrienne squealed. "Look at this kitchen." With each scream, Oscar could see his bank account dwindling. He looked at his wife, so pretty when she smiled, running her hands along the stainless steel refrigerator. She giggled more with every inch she covered.

"Honey." The agent pressed her hand to her own chest as if the information she was about to deliver caused her indigestion. "The entire kitchen has been remodeled. The previous owner was an interior designer."

"Seriously?" Adrienne clapped her hands together.

"Yes, wait till you see the work upstairs." The agent grabbed Adrienne's arm, figuring out who the real CEO of the family was, and they scampered off toward the second level. Oscar shook his head and headed to the window. A smile broke out on his face when he looked out into the thicket of lawn that rambled for miles in the back. It escaped the white picket fence that encased the house and pushed back behind an army of maple and pine trees fighting for space at the edge of his sight line.

Oscar imagined touch football games with his future NFL-star son and the less adequate neighborhood kids. He could see the barbecues, and finally getting a chance to own a hammock. He would tie it to the small curved trees hiding in the corner of his backyard.

"Your property sits right behind one of eight parks in the neighborhood." The agent hunched over him like a vampire ready for her next victim—his pocketbook.

"Lots of rapes and robberies in parks." Oscar turned around and smiled. The woman's bugged-out eyes were his reward. He turned to catch his wife's eyes. Her lips pressed together as she stared at him. She tilted her head and mouthed "strike one" under her breath so only Oscar could hear. He knew he would be hearing a speech later.

"He's just kidding, Ms. Davis." Adrienne shook her head. "He's a cop. They have a bad sense of humor."

"Oh, it's okay." She clutched her pearls. "My husband has a unique sense of humor too."

Oscar and Adrienne exchanged flat-lipped glances and then Adrienne smiled and walked up to him. She cradled his hand in hers and whispered, "What do you think, baby?"

Oscar knew she meant "This is my house—you can either live here or check for vacancies at the local YMCA."

"It's real nice." Oscar smiled. Adrienne, confident her wishes were articulated, turned to Ms. Davis, who was dabbing her lips on a piece of tissue. "How much are the owners asking?"

"Oh, it's practically a robbery for this neighborhood." Ms. Davis elbowed Oscar and winked, and then turned back to Adrienne. "Only 335,000."

Oscar felt his throat go dry and his knees shivered under the weight of his body.

"But the resale value is astronomical, right, Ms. Davis?" Adrienne interjected before Oscar could scream.

"In five years this property will double in value."

"We will be living in a shelter by that time," Oscar said.

"Honey, it's an investment in our family's future." Then Adrienne gave him her "damn-it-all" kiss, the one where her soft lips pressed against his just long enough for him to forget what he'd been thinking ten seconds earlier. His hand rubbed the sweat off his face and she buried her head in his chest.

"Damn it all," Oscar whispered in her ear.

"We'll take it," Adrienne screamed again and the deal was done. That was their house for better or worse. And there was a lot of better. The kids being born, the lovemaking in almost every room in the house, even the pillow fights in the bedroom. The memories raced around in his head.

But where was that love now? He used to wake up early

every morning just to kiss, tease, and caress her body, till she finally turned to him and they made love. Now they both raced to start the idle business of their independent lives.

After spitting out children almost back to back, she wanted to make use of the law degree she obtained sans kids. She got a job at Legal Aid.

Oscar always wanted to go to law school too, but had known they both couldn't afford it at the same time. But he wanted to be a public servant. So on a whim he applied to the Atlanta Police Department. But what started as a job to help his people turned into a boiling hatred for the very people he was sworn to help.

He woke with cases on his mind. Notes of robberies, killings, and rapes filled his head. He obsessed over all the potential loss, all the people who seemed all too willing to not only choose the wrong path, but to continue to do it, even if it killed them.

And in his glorious anger he lost the one thing that kept the balance in his life, his family.

Now Damon was the only thing that took priority in his thoughts. The boy he had shot hoops with and seen movies with was not only a man, but a felon and attempted murderer. And it was Oscar's fault. Oscar had abandoned Damon the second he was accepted into school. His scholarship was his Get Out of the Ghetto Free card. Damon and everything else in his neighborhood was a part of the unmentionable past, only to be told in flashback footage when he was a congressman one day.

He would show how someone could grow up in the 'hood and become a pillar of the community, be faithful to his wife, not beat his kids, and be Black. But what of the people he walked away from? He didn't even want to move back into the city. If it hadn't been for Adrienne convincing him to buy the house, he would have taken a position in one of the suburbs until he finished law school himself. Then they would be off to Washington for him to start his political career.

But Damon would tell a different story about Oscar, one of smoking weed, sleeping with groupies, and skipping classes in school. That would not make the press release of his life. What about the severed friendship between Damon and Oscar themselves?

Was he in such a rush to leave his old life that he couldn't think of his best friend and the drama he was going through? Oscar shook his head and headed down the sloping sidewalk that led to the train station. He heard a beep in his pullover pocket.

"Hello?"

"It's late," Adrienne said in a monotone mothering voice.

"Just going for my run."

"Are you still mad?"

"I'm not mad, but I really don't want to talk right now."

"Oscar doesn't want to talk." Adrienne blew into the phone. "That will be on your headstone, just so you know."

"Adrienne." Oscar wanted to finish his run, take a shower, and go to bed—not argue.

"I'm leaving you alone, but sooner or later we need to have a talk about what is going on with us."

"I just have stuff on my mind."

"Nigga, we all have stuff on our minds. It doesn't stop you from being a father and a husband and a human being."

"Jesus, Adrienne, can you give me just one second by myself to sort things out?"

"You have walked around this house like a freakin' zombie for months, and now with this new case you're alienating us even more."

"Baby, this is not a cell phone conversation."

"It's not a phone conversation. It's not an e-mail conversation. It's not an in-person conversation. It's just the thing that is breaking up this fucking family."

She said it and quiet filled the space between the lines. She was right; there was something going on with him. Something he could not control was pulling him away from his wife, family, and most importantly, himself.

"What do you want me to do, Adrienne?"

"Think about what you'll miss," she said coolly and hung up. Oscar picked up his pace and ran until his heart thumped in his ear. His left foot landed on a rock and before he could balance himself he fumbled forward and landed on the grassy lawn in front of him. A pain shot up his leg and he cradled it like a baby.

The pain was so intense he couldn't think of a proper swear-word to blurt out. He massaged the ankle. It wasn't twisted, just throbbing and beaten, like his spirit. Oscar limped over to a lonely bench in front of a bus stop. He lifted his leg up onto the seat and stretched out. The pain had already subsided, but his heart still hurt. He looked around in both directions and only saw a sprinkling of parked cars on both sides of the street. Only the streetlights kept him company.

"God, what is going on with me?" Oscar screamed. He beat his fist against the bench until he heard the wood split and buckle under the force of his punches. His eyes caught sight of the dual halogen lights cruising toward him, up the hill. By the time he recognized what it was, the bus clicked on its turn signal and edged toward the corner he was lying near. Instinctually Oscar rose to his feet. The double doors swung open and Oscar faced an old man behind the wheel staring at him.

"You getting on?" the man said. Oscar looked back at his house, the life he was damn near ruining, and having nothing else to lose, he boarded the bus.

"How late does the bus run?"

"This is the last run, partner."

"Perfect," Oscar said as he flipped a couple of dollars into the machine and took a seat on the back of the bus. He watched as his neighborhood became a gaggle of houses, then lights, then only stars glaring in the distance."

Chapter XV

Damon delighted in watching the color escape from Maria's face. Her usual auburn tone fused into a chalky yellow hue. He could see her hands shaking. He picked up Q by the stomach and lifted him into the air.

"Stop, Daddy," Q giggled as he fell into his father's arms. Maria stood staring at him for a full five minutes before she finally said, "How'd you find us?" Her voice chirped like she was singing a song.

"Damon, can I talk to you for a second alone?" Maria asked. She leaned back against the wall and almost had a pleading look.

"Oh." Q beat his head on his father's chest. "Daddy, you're in trouble."

"Daddy is not in trouble." Maria pointed her tongue at her son. "I just want to talk to him without a Nosy Posey in our faces."

"Whatever," Q huffed. He got up and walked down the hall past his mother.

"I just remembered there is some pizza already in the freezer. Can you pull that out for me?" Maria asked.

Damon jumped up from the couch and walked up to Maria.

"You gotta go. This is my sister's house and she is going to go crazy if you're here and . . ." Her eyes wouldn't meet his.

"All I wanna know is why?" Damon said. He kept his voice low and monotone.

"Why what, Damon?" Maria threw her hands in the air. "Why I didn't want to go to jail? Why I didn't want to lose my baby, our baby? Why I never wanted to rob a fucking bank in the first place?"

"The plan was for us." Damon felt the blood steaming through his skin. His hands dripped with sweat and he wanted to ball them into fists.

"That plan was for your broke ass, so you wouldn't have to get a fucking job."

"I be hustling my ass off to put food on the goddamn table."

"You think playing Playstation till seven at night and going out and selling that little bit you sell for two hours was putting food on the table?"

Damon felt his arms shaking and trembling until he had to retaliate. But he aimed for the wall and punched a hole through it. His fist hit a wood beam and he drew back a bloody nub.

"Shit." Maria darted down the hall and ran into a bedroom. Damon traced her steps and closed the door behind them.

"Get away from me, Damon," Maria screamed. She held a baseball bat in her hands. A soft knock on the door interrupted their fight.

"Mama." Q's worried voice could be deciphered through the wood.

"We're just playing, baby." Maria held back tears. "I'll be right out to heat your pizza." She wiped the lines of tears that covered her face and turned to Damon. "Look, if you gone kill me come on wit' it, but I ain't going without a fight. I am going to be here for my baby."

Damon stood looking at Maria as his blood dripped on

the carpet. He saw the look of fear swelling in her face. He looked back at the door keeping his child away from the potential murder that could be the last thing Q remembered about his father. He checked himself. He pulled off his jersey and then his wife beater.

"What are you doing?"

"Mami, I don't want to fight no more." He offered a toothy smile as Maria eased the grip from her bat, but kept it cocked back over her shoulders, ready to swing.

"Seriously," Damon said as he unbuckled his belt and let his pants drop to the floor. "I came to find you 'cause I love you."

"Damon, please."

"And I miss you, Mami." His voice was a low growl. He slipped out of his boxers and stood buck naked before her. "I miss being with you."

"I can't, Damon," Maria whispered. "I can't be hurt no more."

"How can I hurt you like this?" He walked toward her, jumping on the bed. "How can I hurt you if I do this?" He kissed her forehead and placed his hands on her shoulders. Her arms fell to her sides, but her shoulders were still tense. He kissed her neck. He had forgotten how it smelled like a citrus grove. Her skin was softer than the cashmere sweater he had bought her for Christmas last year. Her lips tasted like Jolly Ranchers lip gloss. She was completely edible.

"Damn," Damon said. "I miss you, baby," He grabbed her waist and felt Maria let go and straddle him. He pushed her against the wall and pulled her shirt off. His lips explored her breasts as his hands felt the familiar spaces that were always home for him.

His manhood was fully charged and they landed on the bed. As soon as he pulled her shorts off, he was inside her. He loved the way she moaned with each stroke.

"Damon," Maria purred as they wrestled on top of the bed for what seemed like hours. Each movement seemed to mesh their bodies. Damon grabbed Maria's hands and stretched them out to either side. He pressed himself inside her until she screamed his name.

"Damon!" Sweat and tears mingled and dripped down his neck. He felt the end was near and increased his speed while she gripped his hands harder. Finally Maria could not hold it in anymore, crying out some nonsensical phrase before erupting into a violent seizure of shivers. Within seconds, Damon followed suit.

When they were done, Damon spooned Maria on the covers and he caressed her stomach with his hand until they both fell asleep.

The sun was threatening to invade the bedroom when Damon awoke. The covers were pulled over his naked body, and a towel was wrapped around his injured hand. Maria was balled up on the small chair that decorated a corner of the room. Her hair covered her face, so Damon couldn't see if she was awake or not.

"Maria," Damon whispered to her.

"I have to think about Q," she whispered. Damon barely heard what she said.

"What?"

"Q," she repeated. "I have to look out for our son."

"I love my son," Damon said. He balled up in bed so he could face her.

"I know you do," Maria said. "But sometimes love isn't enough to stop the pain, the consequences."

"I know I hurt you and promised you all kinds of shit." Damon felt a queasy feeling in his stomach, like he hadn't eaten in days. "But I'ma change. Things can be different if you let them be."

"I told you it isn't about you and me anymore."

"I love you, Mami. Maria, I can't lose you and Q. I would die." Tears pressed out of the corners of his eyes.

"I don't know if I will survive without you, either," Maria said. "But like I said, I can't be concerned if either one of us makes it. My main concern right now is my son's future."

"A future without his daddy, without his family together, is no future."

"I said that to myself for eight years, Damon." Maria's voice sounded hoarse and exhausted. "Every time I had to cover up a black eye. Or run another scam just to put food in our mouths. Every time you went out to take care of business and some girl kept calling my house with wrong numbers."

"I done told you that was all in your head, you know I don't be cheating."

"It doesn't matter anymore," Maria pressed on. "This life, or fantasy or whatever we've been living, is dead."

"Maria, I still have the money." Damon shot up and moved toward her. He was on his knees. "We can still get to Florida and start our lives over."

"I am not running from my reality anymore, baby," Maria said. "What's real is who is down the hall watching television. That is the only reason God has me here, and I can no longer make him a part of this bullshit."

"So we're bullshit, that what you're saying?"

"Maybe not before, but now . . ."

"Now what?"

"Say good-bye to your son, Damon."

"Fuck that."

"You can either spend some quality time with your son now or behind a glass wall."

"You fucking snitch."

"Leia tried to call the police the second she found out you were here. I got her to wait until you say good-bye to Q. But you should know the second you finish she is calling the police."

"I can't fucking believe this."

"Believe it." Maria stood. "Your son is waiting in the living room."

Damon watched Maria slink out. He glanced out the windows, but saw only the sun outside waiting for him. He gathered his clothes and walked stealthily down the hall to his son, who was sleeping on the couch.

Damon sat next to him and put Q's head in his lap.

"Hey, Daddy."

"Hey, Baby Boy."

"Can we play basketball at the park today? I have to show you my new shot."

"You have a new shot?"

"I can hit three-pointers."

Damon pulled his son up and landed Q on his lap. "You can?"

"Well, I hit one once," Q exclaimed. "But if you teach me, I know I can get better."

"I would love to, but your daddy has to go on a business trip for a minute."

"Another one?" Q moaned. "Dad, you were gone way too long."

"Yeah, I know it was a while, but I am hoping this one will be shorter."

"How much shorter?"

"Don't know, but I do know I will have to leave." Q slouched in his father's arms and grimaced. Damon wanted to start bawling, but held his composure.

"Look, I need you to keep an eye out for your mom and do good in school, all right?"

"Who is going to read me my bedtime stories?"

"You're a big boy. You should be reading them to Mama."

"It's not the same," Q whined.

"You gone have to be the little man I know you can be while Daddy is gone, okay? No whiny talk."

"But," Q whined.

"Q."

"Yes, Daddy."

"Give your daddy a big hug good-bye." Q held Damon so tightly he was afraid he would suffocate him. But Damon was even more afraid to let Q go. He contemplated running off with him. He looked into Q's big watery eyes and knew he had to leave.

Damon got up and said, "Be good, buddy."

"I will," Q cried.

Damon walked down the darkened hallway till he reached the front entrance. Leia and Maria guarded the door.

"Nigga, if I had my way I would have shot you in your sleep," Leia said.

"You are nobody," Damon mumbled to Leia, then turned to Maria. "I will never forgive you for betraying our family."

"That's the weird thing," Maria said. "I have forgiven you."

"So you really called the police on your man?"

"They're on their way."

"You probably got about five minutes to get out of here." Leia smiled.

"Take the car," Maria offered.

"Girl, is you crazy?" Leia looked at her sister.

"Get to where you can think and do the right thing."

"The right thing left my fingers a long time ago."

"You do what is right for you, but know I am doing what's right for your child," Maria said.

"I will never believe that."

Damon gave Maria one last glance and peaked out the door. Seeing the empty street, he hurried to Maria's car and cranked the ignition. He put the car in reverse and skidded to a stop in the street. He contemplated going back in and grabbing his girl and child. He debated turning himself in. Then he heard the distant sirens of his impending doom and sped off toward the sunrise.

Chapter XVI

The phone had been ringing off the hook since the party. After my hasty exit from the club, a certain someone told everyone—including the press—I might be dying. Naturally, it didn't take long for most of my clients to release me from their service.

"I just think you need to take some time to get better," Carlos told me on the phone last week. "We want your pretty self to stay around for a while."

Though he was sweet, he and everyone else switched to my competitors, leaving my infamous contacts about as valuable as a case of syphilis.

This time I didn't fight my bed's natural healing abilities. I lay under the down covers for days, only getting up to adjust the air when I got too hot or cold. I had trained myself to ignore the phone. But I was fumbling, trying to erase my contact numbers out of the caller ID, when it rang in my hands. Out of instinct I picked up.

"Jean Catherine, why are you awake?" The shrill voice rattled my nerves through the phone.

"Hey, Mom."

"Oh, these people can't drive in Atlanta. Anyway, dear, I'm on my way down to your house."

"Why?" Jesus, I did not need this crap. I could already feel my fingers twirling my hair into tiny unmanageable knots as my mom breathed into the phone. I was snuggled under my bed, trying desperately to forget the last few months of my life. And here this woman comes to throw it all in my face.

"Because you are sick and need to be taken care of." And, of course, my mother was exactly who I want to take care of me. This was the same woman who entered me in baby pageants to raise the money for her acting head shots.

"Well, that's why I invested in a husband, remember?" I tried to keep a friendly tone, but my mother usually brought out the venom in my voice.

"The last thing you need to do is bother your husband at work with all your little issues."

"Little issues?" Was this woman for real?

"He's a businessman, honey. He can't be disturbed with the woes of womanhood."

"The woes of womanhood?" It was bad enough that Oprah wasn't coming on for another three hours, but now I had my own personal Susan Lucci about to deliver more drama than I was willing to handle.

"Honey, I'm coming up your driveway. Meet me at the door."

The phone clicked and I jumped up to see if my worst nightmare was arriving on my front doorstep. Sure enough, the devil not only wears a blue dress, but she apparently drives a gray late-model Volvo. I scrambled for a comb and plowed through the naps just enough to give my hair some type of order. I made sure my terry cloth robe covered all the body parts susceptible to insult and headed for the door.

I had barely gotten the door open when my mother pushed it and me back as she charged inside.

"Look at my new head shots." She flipped a black-and-white glossy in my face. "I decided to use my maiden name, Deborah Bourgeois. Isn't it so pretty in embossed italics?"

I nodded politely, took the photo and placed it on the table beside the door.

"Why are ya here, Mama?" I asked. I felt my side pockets to see if I could locate my aspirin bottle. No such luck. I rambled through every drawer as I followed my mother down the hall.

"How you can live all the way out here in Alpharetta so far away from your mother I don't know," Deborah said, and then turned to inspect me. "Are you going to walk around in that thing all day?"

"I am sick, remember?" I could feel my voice rising. I took in as much air as I could and then blew it out in one long stream. "I thought you were coming over to comfort me."

"Please, all you need is a stiff drink and a little . . ." She jiggled her butt in small circles. I held the vomit inside.

"Where are your drinks?" Deborah sifted through the drawers and cabinets in my kitchen. She rummaged through the refrigerator and fingered the wine rack till she spotted something that made her mumble "humph." She pulled a bottle out of its cradle and walked over to the island in the middle of the kitchen.

"Where is your corkscrew?"

"Third drawer down." I pointed as Deborah pulled the corkscrew out and proceeded to grab a wineglass.

"Uh, we usually save that wine for special occasions."

"Me in a room is a special occasion." Deborah let out a cackle.

I wanted to swipe the wine bottle and crack it over her head, but I knew I would be too weak to hide the body. So I succumbed to the torture and grabbed a glass of my own. Hopefully I would pass out before the third drink.

"So what is your deal?"

"Excuse me?"

"Why are you sick?"

"You mean why was I pummeled on the street, losing my child?"

"Oh." Deborah cupped my face in her palms and shook her head. "I know you had a rough couple of days, but you have to learn to rise above it. If I let all the drama in my life get me down, I would be dead."

"Drama like what?"

"Do you think it was easy being the premiere black actress in the Deep South?"

Lord, the struggling actress bit. I had heard this saga a million times. I downed my second glass, hoping to numb her voice.

"I struggled as a young wife and mother to get through Spelman. Then I had to raise you and your brother while building an acting career in the South. Not New York or L.A., where they begged me to go."

She twirled around the island like a dancer, careful that the drink fell only into her mouth, not on the floor. "At one point in time I had to go through picket lines to rehearse my lines."

God, this was so ridiculous. Why would she seriously drive all the way over here to make me feel guilty? I tried to ignore her, letting her words sink into a familiar buzz in the back of my head, like smooth jazz or algebra.

"Then your father starting losing his mind, quitting his job to study acupuncture. It's just sad, a man using anything to make him feel special."

"Yeah, that is crazy." I rolled my eyes.

"So, are you trying to have another child?"

"Mom, it hasn't even been eight weeks since we lost the baby." My hand wanted to slam across her face, or even better, body-slam her into the refrigerator. But she wouldn't die. And even if she did, her spirit would float around here bugging me.

"Oh, honey, the best way to get over something is to replace it."

"It's not a dead goldfish. It was my child." My chest felt heavy, like a chain was pulling my shoulders down.

"It was awful. I prayed for you every night." Deborah

wrapped her arms around me and rested her head on my back. I jerked her off.

"You didn't even come to the hospital to visit me." I splashed more wine in the glass. I was up to three drinks and ready to fight.

"I was three weeks into a show in Tennessee. You know I never missed a show in my life."

"Just a few recitals, a graduation, and a couple of anniversary dinners." Sarcasm dripped off each word. "No big deal."

"Okay, okay, I have missed a few events. But I'm here now. And I want to help you."

"Help me how exactly?" I asked.

My mother pulled me to the dining room table and sat down next to me. "I want to move in with you and take care of you."

"Mom." I stared into her eyes. Taking care of me was something my stage mother had never aspired to do. "What is your angle?"

"No angle. I'm just here to make sure you can relax after all you've been through."

"And how will you help me do that?"

"I am your mother. I know how to take care of my own daughter."

"Usually mothers have some kind of *experience* taking care of their children."

"Girl, don't act like we didn't provide for you."

"I never said you didn't provide. But taking care of me is a different story altogether."

"Just imagine me washing your clothes, cooking your meals, and all you have to do is get better."

"Since when did you learn how to wash and cook?" I glanced at my watch, hoping it was time for David to come home and put an end to this madness. Of course, time with my mother always stood still, and the bottle of wine was gone and I was still nauseated.

"Oh no, I will interview and find a great housekeeper." Deborah pulled a piece of paper out of her purse. "But I will be there to do mom things."

"Like what?" I was so interested to see what "mom things" my mom thought she was going to do with a twenty-seven-year-old woman.

"Like comb that hair." Deborah pulled at a few strands of hair, while shaking her head. "Maybe redo your makeup so you don't look so much like a drag queen."

"Do you know I still have glass in my back? Do you think I give a . . ." I was about to lose it. But I was not about to do the typical Deborah-versus-J.C. heavyweight battle we had every time we spoke. And honestly, I was too exhausted to really fight. I had to heal, get my career back, and do a million other things better than arguing with an old woman. So I did the unthinkable. I compromised.

"Why don't you just come visit me on the weekend? I'm sure David would love to have you over for a couple of days."

"The thing is . . ." Deborah threw her head back and let out a little laugh. I knew I was in trouble.

"I got this new part at Alliance Theatre." Deborah bopped around in excitement. "It's a lead role. A lead role! Do you know how hard it is to get a lead role at my age?"

I could imagine grabbing my mother by the back of her blazer's collar and yanking her ass to the door and out of my house. How selfish could she be?

"So Griffin is just way too far to drive into town. But if I stay with you, then it's a quick hop on the Connector and I will be downtown.

"Mom, that isn't gonna work."

"Why not? It'll be fun. I can work on your nails and try to find your toenails underneath all that gunk."

"Seriously, I just don't think it's a good idea."

"Why?"

"Because I just am not in the mood." I really couldn't take

it anymore. My stomach crunched on top of itself. My head throbbed as I moved toward the couch.

"In the mood for what?"

"All this! The insults, the 'acting' career. All this shit."

"I am only looking out for my baby." My mother blinked back crocodile tears. "And my career helped feed us."

"No, Dad's job fed us. Your career was just an excuse to legally ignore your children. And now you come in my house not out of concern for me, for your daughter being almost killed, or out of worry that my migraines feel like they are hacking my head into two separate parts, but so you can be closer to another stupid play in which the director obviously doesn't care about good acting."

Deborah burst into tears and clutched her throat. "You are just so hurtful."

"I'm hurtful?" I screamed. "Just get out!" The words vibrated in my head. I could not believe I was evicting my own mother. But there was a thrill along with my racing heart. For years I usually rolled my eyes and ignored my mother whenever she discovered some harebrained scheme to add more pain to my life. But now, in my weakened state, I couldn't take any more. Enough was enough.

"I cannot believe you are kicking me out, your own mother." She swaggered toward the door.

"I just can't deal with your shit right now." I beat her to the door and swung it open for her to make her exit.

"Don't call me when you need me."

"When have I ever done that?"

My mother pouted and headed out the door yelling, "Well, don't start now." She got into her vehicle and skidded off, out the gated entrance and back to Griffin, while I scoured the house until I found my holy grail in the bathroom cabinet— a full bottle of Tylenol.

Chapter XVII

Christopher eased his Mercedes around the corner on Ashby Street, and debated whether to stop through the drive-thru at Krispy Kreme. He spotted four guys gathered on the edge of the street, near the intercom. Their pants fell down past their butts, displaying their boxers to the world. Their oversized T-shirts hung to just above the line of their pants. Yellow Timberlands and spotless white tennis shoes sat underneath overlapping jeans. The guys' hands flew in every direction as they talked.

Christopher felt his fingers easing toward the lock mechanism on his door. He resisted the urge. He refused to be scared of his people. But, with his aching stomach, he decided against the donuts and made a U-turn back out of the driveway and continued down the street.

The complex where his father resided sat close to the street. Small windows lined each floor, reflecting the sun's light like a greenhouse. A sparse collection of trees grew between walkways, adding a slightly residential feel to the overall urban area. People were everywhere, rambling down the street engaged in pockets of conversation. As the car drew to the curb, people turned to peek at who was inside Christopher's car.

"A couple of kids rushed to the driver's-side window. Christopher slid the window down a crack.

"Excuse me, sir." A cute girl with braids curling on her shoulders extended a box of M&M's toward Christopher. "Would you like to buy some candy for our basketball team?" Christopher raised an eyebrow at the thought of a six-year-old girl on anyone's basketball team, but he reached inside the change drawer, retrieved a five-dollar bill, and gave it to the little girl.

"Thank you," she said and turned away as another cute child replaced her position in the begging line.

"Sorry, she took my last dollar," Christopher lied as he rolled up the window. He flipped up his phone and dialed his dad's number.

"Hey, Dad. I am out here."

"I'm still getting dressed, come on up."

"Dad, why aren't you dressed yet?"

"Boy, stop acting like an old woman and get up here."

The phone clicked off and Christopher rolled his eyes. He grabbed the directions from the passenger seat and exited the car. He scanned the street signs until he found the address that matched the numbers on the paper. He walked past black iron doors and knocked on the door. A rumbling sound echoed behind the door. And then the door swung back and Alonzo peeked out from behind it. He swiveled his head in both directions and then whispered, "Come on." Christopher followed his dad up a flight of rickety stairs until they reached a small tattered door warped at the corners by age.

Alonzo pulled his keys from their resting place on his belt and fiddled with the lock on the door until it pushed open. Christopher followed his father into the small efficiency. With a little effort he could touch all four walls from the center of the room. A pallet made of thin blankets sat in one corner of the room, while a kitchen consisting of a miniature stove and refrigerator occupied the opposite side.

A window the size of a coffee table book was guarded behind cast-iron bars. A poster of Beyonce from Destiny's Child stared at Christopher from across the room. Her mouth puckered and she seemed to be whispering in her most seductive voice: "Get out before it's too late."

Alonzo opened the door to the bathroom and hurried inside. Christopher heard water splashing and then his father yelled, "I know it ain't much, but as soon as I get settled I'm looking to get a town house or something like that."

"It's fine, Dad." Christopher scanned the room for a place to sit, and settled on a rickety chair near the kitchen. The chair creaked as he sat down.

"My famous soup is in a Tupperware bowl in the refrigerator," Alonzo said. "I just have to take a crap and we can go."

"Uh, Dad, you can, uh . . . do that at my place, too, you know." Christopher cringed at the thought of smelling feces in such a cramped space.

"I am not about to go to someone else's house just to lay a big one." Alonzo slammed the bathroom door and Christopher headed for the window. He managed to lift the pane a couple of inches in the air. He moved to the kitchen and opened the refrigerator door. He gasped at the sight. A legion of roaches scurried around the near-empty space. They climbed over the plastic container like marathon runners surmounting a rough hill. Christopher resisted his urge to vomit and slammed the door shut.

"All right, son." Alonzo came around the corner, zipping up his pants. "You grab the soup?"

"I think someone else has beat us to it." Christopher opened the door again to display the bugs.

"Shit." Alonzo rubbed the back of his head. "I thought that Borax took care of those damn things."

"Yeah, well, roaches can be a bit tough to kill."

"Now, how the hell would you know that?" Alonzo fired back. "You live in that palace across town."

"I had roaches in my dorm room at college and in my apartment in New York, thank you very much." Christopher slammed the door. "Besides, I believe me and Mom lived in our share of roach motels when you left us."

"Are we going down that road?"

"It's the only road I've traveled with you."

Alonzo slammed his fist into the wall and Christopher jumped back. "Son, can we ever just have a civil conversation?" Alonzo slumped back into a corner. "Damn it, I just spent twelve years in jail, and all I thought about was the chance to see you."

"You see me, Dad." Christopher bit his tongue. He didn't intend for his words to be so harsh.

"I heard you got shot and I thought I missed my chance to ever get to know you."

"Dad . . ."

"And take care of you."

"I'm thirty-two, Dad. I don't need to be taken care of."

"Boy, I'm fifty-one, and I wish I had someone to call me other than my parole officer."

"Dad." Christopher looked in his father's face and suddenly saw the man he used to idolize as a kid. The man with strong arms that threw him in the air and always caught him before his feet hit the ground. That same arm had rested on his back as he practiced his free throw shots at the school playground.

"Just visualize the ball going in," his father said, rubbing his back for good luck. Christopher had been hitting bricks all day. He knew his arms veered to the left each time he released. He was nine and determined to make the elementary school basketball team, despite the fact he was only five feet tall. His growth spurt of fourteen inches would not occur until his junior year in high school. But he kept practicing every morning and every evening, four hours a day.

"Just imagine the ball going in the bucket this time," Alonzo said. His voice was soft and reassuring. It was devoid of any of the slurring that punctuated his drunken speech most days. Christopher closed his eyes for a moment and concentrated on watching the ball swish through the netted material without even touching the rim. The seconds felt like hours as he concentrated on the image until his head rang at the temples.

He built up the nerve to bounce the ball a couple of times and promised to keep his arms out straight. He drew his arms back and swung them forward like a catapult, releasing the ball and watching it soar through the air until it reached its destination inside the hoop.

"Yeah," his father screamed. "That was a shot that Michael Jordan would be proud of." Alonzo patted his son's back and Christopher beamed until his cheek muscles hurt. "That's my boy."

Christopher remembered how those words resonated in his ears. It was the first and last time his father would ever use them. He savored them when his father left, and when he learned of his incarceration. Every time he endured a father-son career day alone, he repeated those words in his head till he could almost hear his father mouthing them.

He looked at his father now, buckled with age, but still holding a piece of his heart in his hands. No matter how many years had passed, he still longed to hear the words again.

"Dad, how much do you pay a month for this place?"

"I rent by the week." Alonzo grimaced. "About 150 dollars per week."

"Why don't you hang out at my place and save some money to get a nicer spot?"

"Boy, you live in West Hell." Alonzo rose to his feet. "How am I supposed to get to work?"

"I have an old Nissan I store for the winter. You can use that to get to work."

"I don't know," Alonzo stammered as Christopher moved to him.

"Look, I thought I was going to have a . . . uh, roommate. But that didn't work out. You would be doing me a favor, keeping me company for a while till I get better."

"Your mother is going to lose it."

"Let me handle her."

"Son." Alonzo gripped Christopher's shoulder. "I appreciate the gesture. But let's be real. I haven't seen you in years, I got issues, you're settled in your life, and I am old and crabby."

"Dad." Christopher smiled. "I hate to break it to you, but you were like that when I was a kid."

"I was a bastard, wasn't I?"

"How do you want me to answer that?"

"With the truth." Alonzo's eyes were wide and pleading.

"There were some bad days. Many days, actually. But I always knew you loved me."

"Really?"

"Always," Christopher lied. Why should the old man live his last days in guilt? Christopher thought to himself.

"I have to ask a favor."

Christopher stifled a sigh. He knew it would come. He was going to beg for money, or ask him to invest in some crazy business scheme. "Go ahead."

"Will you give me a fair chance?" Alonzo's voice sounded pleading.

"Chance for what?"

"To be your father. Just give me a fair shot."

"Well, will you do me a favor?"

"I'll try my best."

"Just be my friend. That's what I need right now."

"I think I can manage that."

"Oh, and a few ground rules."

"You are giving me ground rules?"

"Property owners can do that."

"Shoot."

"No drinking, no drugs, no gambling." Christopher watched his father's face drop, but he kept eye contact. If they had a chance to rekindle any type of relationship they had to be clear about the boundaries.

"Okay, I have a rule for you too."

"A rule in my own house?" Christopher chuckled and then said, "Go ahead."

"I want you to be free to be yourself. I know about your life and I want you to feel comfortable in your own house."

"I will," Christopher said. "But I appreciate that."

"Aiight. Now that we got that settled, let me just grab my things and we can dip."

"How offended would you be if I asked you to leave everything here?"

"Shit, I only got three pairs of pants and a couple of shirts anyway."

"You're about my size. You can raid my closet till you buy some more stuff."

"Wow! Who would have thought having a snobby son would work to my advantage?"

"Life is full of surprises."

"Yeah, this moment is one of them." A slice of silence wedged between them as they awkwardly stared at one another. Christopher moved in for a hug but bent over and grabbed Alonzo's shoes on the floor.

"The gators can come too."

They both laughed as Christopher flipped the boots upside down and shook them hard, just to make sure he was only taking his father and the shoes home."

Chapter XVIII

The palms of her hands were so sweaty, Maria could have slicked her entire head of hair back. But she rubbed her hands against the grain of her shorts until all that remained was a sticky residue.

She peered out the window to make sure that Damon had left. Her car was gone, but there was no telling if he had just parked it around the corner.

"Don't be stupid," she whispered to herself. If Damon wanted to get her, he would have attacked her while he was in the house. There was ample opportunity. She couldn't believe she had let her guard down and had made love to him. She caressed her belly as she thought of Damon's body on top of hers. She mustered a small sigh and pulled herself away from the window and went back into her room.

Now was the time to make decisions about her life. Chances were that as long as she cooperated with authorities she would most likely get probation. But even if she didn't go to jail she was still in a prison. No job, no money, and a sister who clicked her tongue every time Maria made a move in her house. Her twenty-fifth birthday was pushing toward her like a runaway train and what did she have to show for it?

"The police said they would patrol the area and try to catch him. Hopefully they will retrieve your car." Leia walked up on her like a cat searching for a mouse. Her footsteps padded until she pounced on her prey. "God, I hope they nail his monkey ass."

"Leia, can you ease up a little? That is Q's daddy. And my husband."

"Ex-husband," Leia snapped. "May I also add ex-beater, too? How could you sleep with him again after all he put you through?"

"I love him." Maria stared at the floor, as if the truth forced her chin to lower toward the ground.

Leia squinted her eyelids into slits and mumbled, "Stupid bitch."

"Hey, Leia." Maria twisted around. "What the hell is your problem? Are you that upset I have a crappy husband or jealous because you don't have anyone?"

"Jealous of what?" Leia screamed. She maneuvered her body so that they stood face-to-face. "Cute boys with big dicks don't pay the bills. Besides, I have a house, a new car, and a job I go to every day. That's why your ass wasn't living out on the street. 'Cause I let you stay here."

"And I'm grateful."

"Then start acting like it."

"What?"

"You come here and not forty-eight hours later have the very man who broke you down screwing you in my house— my house!" Leia's hands flew everywhere as she talked.

Maria stepped back, afraid an arm might accidentally jab her and they'd be forced to fight on principle.

"What were you thinking?" Leia asked.

"I don't know. I guess I just missed him."

"See, that's what I'm talking about." Leia mounted her hands on her hips. "He beats you. He treats you like shit. How could you miss that?"

"It's hard to explain love."

"It isn't hard to explain stupidity."

"Jesus, Leia." Maria looked at her older sister. Her deep-set brown eyes seemed almost frozen over.

"Look, I am not going to let you ruin your son's future so you can be in love."

"Q is my son."

"Yes, he is." Leia poked her finger at Maria's face. "But you made him my responsibility when you walked through my door."

"I know how to raise my child."

"Do you?" Leia turned in disgust and walked down the hall. She paused a moment and then came back. "I hate to admit this, but that bastard was a better parent than you."

"What?" Maria said. "He wanted me to help him rob a bank."

"Yeah, he did," Leia continued. "But he at least wanted to do something about his son's future."

"First you hate him. Now you defend him."

"Trust, I am not defending him. But he did something to help his child. All you did for the last few years is lay up with that nigger, let him beat you down."

"He made me quit my job."

"You quit that job 'cause you wanted to be taken care of. Be lazy. Well, you can't afford to do that with a child. I would never let my son go through this."

"How could you? You won't even let a man get close enough to screw you, let alone have a child."

"Please." Leia's voice shook.

"You talk about me, but you won't let anyone get past your one hundred and one controlling rules. You can't understand love 'cause you never opened up enough to feel it."

"If love means being broke and unhappy I don't want it."

Maria moved to her sister. "You may be broke and unhappy in love sometimes. But not all the time. The love me and Damon have is for real."

"But is it worth your life?"

"I don't know."

"Is it worth your son's life?"

"Of course not. No!"

Leia placed her arms on Maria's shoulders.

"Understand, if you give in to him again, you may not be so lucky. They could take your son. And some stranger would raise Q. Is that what you want?"

"No." Tears welled up in Maria's eyes. "He's all I have."

"Then you need to start looking out for him," Leia said. "It's time to grow up and stop thinking about yourself."

Leia turned away and headed down the hall. "I made some breakfast, if you're hungry."

"I'll be there in a minute." Maria scoped the living room for Q and saw it was empty. She moved to his room, where she found him huddled in a ball on his bed. All his books were scattered on the bed. She eased inside the room and stared at her son. His forehead pressed down against his knees. Only the mass of curly locks was visible. God, even the back of his head was like Damon's.

How was he going to survive living without his father? Would his heart always ache with the loss? Would he hate her for it? She moved in close to the bed and sat down on the edge.

"Hey, buddy, how ya doing?"

Q gripped his legs tighter and began rocking back and forth in a slow and steady movement."

"Q." She placed a hand on his knee, and Q jerked it away. "Talk to me, honey. How you feeling?"

"Why did you make him leave?"

"Your father had to go."

"No, you told him he had to go." Q lifted his face. His cheeks were swollen and red from tears."

"Your father had to go away to take care of some business."

"You said the police were going to get him. You said they would take him away."

"Mommy was angry. I didn't mean it. The police aren't going to get him."

"I want to go with him."

"You can't, honey. He is going to be gone for a minute."

"I miss my daddy."

"I miss him too, but he'll be back one day." Maria moved behind her son and gently pulled him into her arms.

"Who is going to read to me?"

"I can if you'll let me. Or maybe you can read to me."

"It's not the same."

Maria wanted to deny his statement, but the truth remained. It was not the same. Everything she thought about her future was eradicated the day she had stopped in front of that bank. Maybe even before then. But whatever the situation, their lives had changed. And worse, she had no idea what would happen to them. She had no plan of action, no safety net. All that remained was a woman and her son dealing with the holes in their hearts.

"Look, buddy." She turned Q around until he was facing her. "We have to have faith and be strong. If you pray real hard I am sure one day you will see your dad again. In the meantime, we have to be strong for ourselves. Mommy has to take care of us both, and that means making some big decisions about our lives. It may be rough but we'll make it. You believe me?"

Q rested on her bosom and wouldn't look at her.

"Do you believe me, Q?"

"Yeah."

She could feel his head nodding against her chest. "You hungry?"

"Mmm, a little."

"Why don't you go ahead and get something to eat? I'll meet you there in a second."

Q slowly rolled off the bed and shuffled to the door.

He looked back and asked, "Mama, are you going to leave me too?"

Her face shattered at her son's look. His eyes looked broken, his spirit killed by her and Damon's dual irresponsibility. He looked utterly lost.

"No, baby. I am not going to leave you, ever," Maria said. "You believe me, right, baby?"

"Yeah, I guess." Q lifted his shoulders and walked off. Maria made sure she heard him in the kitchen before she quietly closed the door to his room and broke down. She keeled over in a fit of tears. Her chest seemed to crunch the breath out of her body. She lay on the floor for what seemed like hours until she could find no more comfort in self-pity. She rose and moved to the phone on the nightstand.

She called the only person she thought could help her.

"Adrienne Bates," the voice on the other end answered.

"Ms. Bates, it's Maria, Maria Adee."

"Hey, how are you?"

"Not so good," Maria managed. Her voice crackled on the phone line. "Uh, Damon was here."

"What? Did he hurt you or Q? Are you okay?"

"Yeah." Maria paused. "He spent the night and left this morning."

"I see."

"He has my car."

"Did you call the police?"

"My sister did. She told them everything I am telling you."

"Okay."

"I was calling 'cause, well, I have no one else to talk to. I have to help my baby but I don't know how. I don't want him to have a bad life, but all I bring him is trouble."

"You also bring him peace and love, Maria."

"Right now he is devastated 'cause he knows he will never see his father again. And it's all my fault."

"You made some mistakes, Maria, but I think we all have

at some point. What really matters is what you are going to do now."

"I just want to give my son a future, a chance at a real life."

"Then you have to tell me everything about what you and Damon had planned so I can make sure you'll be around for your son's future."

Maria nodded to the phone.

"Maria," Adrienne said. "Given what happened last night, it will be harder to convince a judge that you were a victim in this situation. I'm just being honest."

"I understand. Will I lose my son?"

"I will try my best to make sure that doesn't happen. But you need to get a stable job and a place of your own to prove that you can provide for him."

"I can do that."

"And you need to promise me that it is over between you two. No more contact. It will determine whether you keep your son or not. Do you understand?"

"Yeah," Maria sighed. "I do."

"Good, then let's have lunch tomorrow and we can go over your testimony."

"Okay."

"Maria, everything will be fine in the end."

"I know. I just never thought the end would come to this."

"No one ever does."

"Thank you, Ms. Bates."

"Adrienne."

"Thank you, Adrienne."

"You're welcome."

Maria hung up the phone and wiped her wet cheeks. She stood and took one last peep out the window. Then she pulled away. She was ready to leave the past behind. She opened the door and called out, "I hope somebody left me some pancakes."

Chapter XIX

His favorite place in the park was the bridge that overlooked the pond. Evergreens circled the water as their leaves fanned out into a blanket of green. Ducks under the bridge waded past Oscar, their black feathers tickling the water as they pushed forward.

The wooden planks underneath him creaked as he adjusted his weight from one leg to the other. The morning air nipped at his face, but the rest of his body was comfortably baking underneath the layers of cotton, rayon, and polyester. The smell of coffee brewing from a nearby restaurant caused his stomach to churn.

He looked at his watch: 6:30 a.m. He was officially dead. No doubt about it. The sun was already poised in an early salute to the sky. He thought about calling but realized there was no point. He had already broken the two biggest rules of their marriage: Never go to bed angry and never stay out all night without calling.

He noticed the caller ID box on his phone was suspiciously empty. *God, I bet she's pissed*. Oscar laughed to himself in that sad way that married guys make jokes they know aren't funny to their spouses. He stretched his arms to the sky and continued his trot along the pond as the water rippled and swooned behind him.

His eyes spotted the fishing hole where he, Damon, and his youth group used to pretend to catch trout. A sad little tree leaned over the mass of rocks that formed a makeshift bank. Only a small man with humongous eyeglasses was there, flipping his rod back and releasing the line. The lure bounced on the thick green water before plopping to the deep, leaving only Oscar and the man to exchange quick smiles and head nods.

Oscar's mind meandered back to the days he used to take Damon to the park for fishing excursions. It usually took ten minutes to mount and tackle the hill that ran from their houses to the west entrance of the park. But once they braved the peak, running down the hill was as fun as any roller coaster ever ridden. By the time they reached the foot of the hill, one of them had tripped to the ground, dropping fishing rods and spilling the can of worms they had squeamishly collected the night before.

Damon always fell down first in a fit of giggles. But once he had his fill, he jumped up, gathered his equipment, and called back to his friend, "Catch up, slowpoke." He always seemed to be in charge though he was six years younger. They needled each other with their elbows as they walked along the gravel path that led to the fishing pond. On Saturday mornings, only Mr. Ellis was up and about, already scoping out the best place to catch his fish.

"You boys better hurry up and find you a spot before we're mobbed." Damon and Oscar always scanned the deserted pond before exchanging muffled giggles.

Once they unloaded their equipment and found a cool spot under a tent of trees, the real day began. This was Damon's time to ask his big brother any question under the sun, away from the cockeyed stares of administration at the community center. Damon knew Oscar would answer him truthfully, no matter what.

"You get some yet?" Damon asked, pulling his line back and recasting it back into the murky waters.

"Get what?" Oscar half smiled.

"Some ass, nigga. What you think I'm talking 'bout?"

"Damon, I'm only sixteen." Oscar dropped his jaw and bucked his eyes in mock shock.

"You be bullshitin'," Damon countered. "You on the track and baseball team and you ain't had sex yet. My cousin Terry has a tiny little arm and he has three kids and he's sixteen."

"Well, your cousin sounds like a stand-up guy."

"Yeah, but he is ugly."

"That's kind of raw."

"Real ugly."

"Well, maybe he has game."

"I'm trying to see if you got game."

"Well, I got some skills, and I do have a girlfriend." Oscar felt a tug on the line and pulled the handle back, only to rip some weeds out of the water. He took them off the line, and double-checked the worm that flailed helplessly on the hook. He tossed his line back into the water.

"What she look like?"

"She's nice."

"Is she fine?"

"Yeah, I would say she is."

"How big is her ass?"

"Damon . . ."

"All my bitches gots to have big asses."

"Aiight, little man. That's enough on the bitch and ass talk." Oscar shook his head. This kid talked like a soldier on leave from an eighteen-month tour of duty.

"I'm just saying I have standards with the women I date."

"What women do you date?"

"I'ma player from way back."

"Back in elementary."

"You ain't funny, dog. I gets mine."

"You get your what?"

"I be tapping that ass."

"What'd I just say?" Oscar cast a parental stare at Damon, who rolled his eyes.

"I be tappin' that booty."

"You saying you have sex?"

"On the regular."

"With who, your hand?"

"With honeys at school."

"You use condoms?"

"Them things hurt."

"So you don't use condoms?"

"I ain't got nothing."

"What if the girl does?" Oscar watched as Damon's brow crunched up, and his lip poked out. "Aren't you worried about STDs or AIDS?"

"Man, AIDS is for faggots."

"Do you think Magic Johnson was gay?"

"Man, whatever. Look, I ain't been with nobody but my main girl and my side friend."

"Damon, what happens if one of them gets pregnant?"

"Damn, why you all in my business like this, man? I thought we was cool."

"We are cool." Oscar took the time to pat his friend's shoulder. "I just don't want you to miss out on your future, doing stupid stuff today."

"Aiight, I get your point, Daddy." Damon exhaled about a gallon of air into the atmosphere. Suddenly his body stiffened and his arms flexed against the fishing rod.

"I think I caught something."

"Reel it in!" Oscar yelled and ran behind Damon.

"It's heavy!" Damon tugged at the line and replanted his feet on the wooden boards. His hands fumbled with the crank and he desperately tried to gain leverage on the mighty beast that fought for its life in the sea.

"Let me help." Oscar, who was a full foot taller than Damon, grabbed the pole above and below Damon's hands and they began a group tug-of-war with the fish.

"This thing is heavy." Damon smiled, as Mr. Ellis, the boys' fishing guide at the park, came over to peer in the pond.

"There it is," Mr. Ellis yelled, pointing into the haze of weed, fish, and murk.

They struggled for several minutes, inching their way back from the platform, reeling in their catch. The line gave a high-pitched squeal, like a child, as the battle drew to an end. The rod bowed and looked like it would break, until finally the fish popped out of the water. It wiggled in the air, flapping its tail wildly. Oscar reached out and grabbed the line a foot above the fish and drew it toward them.

"That's it?" Damon questioned, his face drawn in a dark smirk. The fish could not have been bigger than the size of his hand. Oscar convulsed into a heap on the ground. All he could hear was his own laughter. He could barely hold the fish. Mr. Ellis grabbed it from his hands just as Oscar lost his grip.

"Well, I think this is a fine first fish." Mr. Ellis placed a hand on his chin, as if he were inspecting the fish for auction. "I mean, you been coming down here all summer and you finally caught something other than a shoe."

Oscar could barely breathe now. The pain stabbed his sides each time he tried. Damon play-kicked him in the back, and his face grew to a full-grown grimace. His arms crossed high over his chest.

"What you laughing at, boy?" Mr. Ellis locked on to Oscar. "It only took him a summer to catch something. I seem to recall it taking somebody, what, three years before you pulled a fish out of this little bitty pond?"

Damon snickered as Oscar stood to gather himself.

"I caught lots of fish."

"Correction." Mr. Ellis cut the line and grabbed the fish

with one hand. He pulled out the hook with his other hand and moved slowly toward a cooler lying next to his fishing rod. He plopped the fish inside. "I caught a lot of fish. You caught a lot of attitude sitting there with just your worms to keep you company."

"Whatever." Oscar lost some of the joy in his face as Damon now giggled on the side.

Oscar couldn't remember what happened after they walked back home that day, but he did remember feeling Damon was as close to a brother as anyone else. It was weird. Oscar had been the one who signed up to be a big brother, but Damon gave him the friendship he couldn't get anywhere else. On the track and baseball field he was a star. At home he was the breadwinner. At school he was the A student. But with Damon he was nobody but Oscar.

But leaving for college destroyed any connection they'd had. Stupidly, Oscar thought they would remain in contact throughout his years in school. But as Oscar got busier, so did Damon. Just not the way he planned it. Years later they were like two opposite sides of a coin. Molded in the same neighborhood, but shaped by different grooves that had formed in their lives.

Had Oscar stayed in town, would Damon's outcome had been different? Would his own life have been different? Should he have sacrificed a full ride to a top college to help his brother? He never would have met Adrienne, gotten married, or had his beautiful children. No, of course not. He had made the right decision. But he still ached for the loss of the one person who had actually been his best friend.

The platform across the pond was no longer filled with his memories. There was no Mr. Ellis, or laughter, or anyone now but a young man sitting on the platform, his legs pointing toward the water. Oscar blinked a few times at the man who looked vaguely familiar. As his eyes squinted and he focused on the head half covered by a hood and shadows, Oscar could swear he'd seen the man before.

As the man leaned back, his arms stretched back to support his weight. Oscar's mouth dropped. It was Damon. He wasn't looking at anyone or anything, but just staring blankly into the pond. Oscar wondered if he was reliving the same memories of their youth, wondering what had happened.

Instinctively, Oscar padded his side for his gun. But he knew it wasn't there. And for the first time he really didn't feel he needed it. If there was any chance of reaching out to Damon like he did before, this was the time and place. Maybe there still was a connection between the two. Maybe he could talk sense into him before some other cop with a grudge or just doing his job blew Damon away. Oscar would not be able to forgive himself.

But if Damon refused to cooperate he would bring him down. There was no doubt in his mind. This ordeal had gone on long enough. Too many people were hurt, and were still hurting, for this to continue. Damon had to stand up to his past.

Oscar smirked a little bit at his own self-righteousness. He was playing judge over one man while he had yet to face the demons in his own life.

"One thing at a time, baby," Oscar said to himself as he drifted off the platform and headed over to meet Damon.

Chapter XX

The ground in the back of the park was just soft enough to serve Damon's purpose. He threw the bag of money to the side and dropped to his knees. After one more quick glance to look for witnesses he began turning over the earth with his hands. He scooped pile after pile of wet dirt until the hole in front of him was deep enough to fall into. Not as deep as a grave, but enough to disappear from the world. Once he was satisfied with the depth and width of the hole he grabbed the bag and took one last look at its contents. As he gazed at the crisp green bills that looked more like play money under the shadow of night, he tossed the bag in the cavity and quickly replaced the empty space with dirt.

He stomped on the dirt and scraped the money pit with his shoe to scatter the dirt around enough to look random. His breath was the only thing visible under the moon's blue haze of light. He moved quickly back into the lamplit path that decorated the park at night. Damon pulled out his bundle of cash and recounted the wad. It was still five thousand dollars, enough to brave a train to L.A. Then he could reevaluate his options. He had known he couldn't go to Miami as planned when he saw Maria's face. He knew she would tell the police everything to save herself.

He really couldn't blame her at this point. She had to worry about Q. As much as he hated her for causing this whole mess (Why couldn't she have just waited outside till he finished the job?) he knew she would do anything to protect their child. The only way he would ever see his son again was to convince her he'd change and move her wherever he ended up. And this time he had to be legit. With the cash he stashed they would be able to do just that. But he also needed to get a regular job to play it off.

L.A. would be good for him. It was big enough to hide in, but not as crowded as New York. He hated the idea of living with all those people on one tiny island. He needed space, maybe a house and an SUV. Get Q into the right schools, maybe a chance for a legitimate future. He noticed how much Q liked to read. He devoured the reading books they worked on and always peeked through the pages of the music magazines Damon left on the living room table.

In the morning while police were groggy from their night shift and no one wanted to open their eyes let alone recognize a felon, he would board the Amtrak toward his new life. But with the police no doubt locked in on his last destination, he had to go somewhere no one would suspect. He also had to hide the money where no one would think to look. He hadn't been to a park in years—especially this park.

Damon hugged himself for warmth as he scoured the area for a nice place to hide out and catch a few moments of sleep. He settled on a hill that opened to a view of the entire park. He could see anyone who was coming his way. But with the maples lined up above him and the occasional birch rooted at the foot of the hill, no one could see him mingle within the darkness. He lay back on the grass and nestled into a limp ball.

His eyes flickered as his mind settled into deep thought. Thoughts raced from his son to Maria to the robbery, the thing that got him in this situation in the first place. Why did he even think he could rob a bank? Was it the blunted meeting of the minds with his boys? Or the numerous rejections for jobs he knew he would hate working anyway? Or did he secretly hope he would be shot in the process and not have to live one more day in misery? His mind scanned the faces of all the people he hurt. Q, Maria, his mother, the man he shot. God, he shot a man. Watched his eyes roll back in his head as he dropped to the ground like a dumbbell. Blood oozed everywhere. But he ran, ran, ran, and pulled a woman out of her car to save himself—a pregnant woman! Her belly was as big as Maria's when she was carrying Q. The look on her face, her eyes poked out like she would die right there. He left her on the street. God, what kind of man leaves a pregnant woman out on the street to die?

"Serves the bitch right for being in my way." His mind tried to convince his heart. But he knew better. He winced from the combination of the memory and the cold. Pictures of the past flickered past him at light speed until, like a movie that ran out of film, there was just white light.

"This is not your end," a voice echoed in his head.

"What?" Damon questioned. He could not see anything but he knew there was something there.

"I will turn everything around for good in the end," the voice said. Damon wanted to stretch his arms and touch the light, but he couldn't see anything beyond its brilliant radiance.

"Brotha man," the voice said in a slightly groggy voice. The stench of alcohol seeping through human flesh permeated his nostrils.

"Brotha man," the voice repeated, and Damon was sure it wasn't coming from the light. He gained control of his eye muscles again and clicked them open to find a man leaning over him. His eyes glowed a haunting yellow as his jagged teeth fought for space in his mouth. Instinctively, Damon pushed the man forward and watched him tumble down the hill.

"Who the fuck are you?" Damon asked.

The man at the foothill rose and swaggered to his feet.

"Brotha' man." The man stumbled toward him again. "Brotha' man, I don't mean to disturb you but I was wondering if you had a dollar you could spare."

Rage boiled in the pit of Damon's stomach as he felt his hands shaking to get at the man.

"Nigga, I'm sleeping in the park just like you." His tone was more like a question. Damon was gripping his jeans so he wouldn't lunge at the man. "Get the fuck out of here," Damon yelled at the man, then bit his tongue at his stupid actions. Parks were known to have police patrolling at night to keep gangs and fags from tagging walls and sucking dicks while they were closed. He scanned his surroundings and though he heard and saw no movement, decided to push toward quieter, more isolated ground.

His mind skipped back to the voice in his white noise dream. Yes, later the voice turned out to be a bum's, but at first it sounded like something completely different. Something he hadn't heard in a long time.

As he walked down the long paved walkway, he watched the moon retracting in the sky and the sun blooming on the horizon. How long had he been dreaming? Must have been at least a few hours, he thought, as his eyes caught sight of a dusted path that strayed off the cement pavement. He followed it down, feeling somehow familiar with its bumps and turns to the bottom. Sure enough, his eyes opened up to an unused fishing pond, barren of fish and fishermen. He could see clear across the pond to the other platform that sat on tall wooden beams above the water. It looked like it had been deserted for years. He moved to the edge of the platform and sat down. His fingers rubbed over grooves made by scuffling shoes, storms, and time. Suddenly, he felt something familiar and jumped to his feet. He leaned over and saw his name etched in the beam.

"Jesus, the fishing spot," Damon mumbled to himself as

the history of the platform hurried back to him. Oscar and Damon used to come here for two years. Their bond was inseparable until Oscar had deserted him for school and left him alone to deal with his shitty life.

Damon let his feet dangle and leaned back on his arms for support. He closed his eyes and tried to dream again of the light, the voice, but only darkness enveloped him until the sun's heat became unbearable on his skin. He inched his torso up till it was perpendicular to his legs, and checked his surroundings. He only spotted a few mice scurrying across the edge of the pond, and a man who seemed to be leaving the platform across the water. Still groggy, he couldn't make out the face, but the tattered jogging pants led him to believe it was another bum.

Still, Damon looked at his watch and knew it was time to head to the train. He had to catch MARTA to get there, and Lord knew how often it ran in the mornings. He began to mount back up the hill when he heard the sound of breaking sticks up top. He slowed his pace, and peered up to try to make out any humans walking down. Sure enough, a figure surfaced through the foliage. But as his vision cleared, his eyes widened in amazement. A lump rose to the middle of Damon's throat as the sight of Oscar walking down the path hit his brain.

"Fancy meeting you here." Oscar looked at him with that damn self-righteous smirk Oscar used to give when they were kids and he would win an argument. Prick.

"Damn, they must really pay cops hella overtime to be kicking the bushes this early."

"To find you, I would work twenty-four hours straight."

"You found me all right." Damon's palms pushed out moisture like a faucet. The small of his back suddenly became clammy and his legs shook.

"So how we gone do this?"

"You tell me, supercop." Damon looked around and above

him. There was no escape except back down the path or through Oscar. "I'm just the criminal."

"Then let's finish this quietly and maybe I can help." Oscar took another step.

"I don't need your help."

"Maybe," Oscar said. "But I can guarantee I will be nicer than the next cop who comes in contact with the guy described as 'the baby killer.'"

"That was an accident, I . . ." But there was no denying the truth. He pulled that woman out of the car and threw her on the ground like unwanted trash. He trampled everything in his path. Now he just had to decide if he was going to trample over Oscar too.

"Damn it, Damon, just let it go. It's over. You have caused enough damage."

"Well, so have you!" Damon shouted.

"What the hell are you talking about?"

"You just up and left me here in this fucking city and didn't even care." Damon would not cry, he promised himself.

"Damon, I had to go to school for the same reason you did what you did, 'cause you felt you needed to."

"Man, I needed you."

"At the time I needed me more."

"So it was just fuck me."

"I couldn't be your daddy, Damon."

The words struck harder than any blow originating from a fist. Damon didn't know if it hurt so much because it was true or because it was coming from the one person he wanted to hear the opposite from.

"You are a smart young kid, Damon. There could still be a life waiting for you if you just stop blaming everyone and—"

"Fuck you," Damon yelled and ran toward Oscar. He leaped onto his midsection and pushed him onto the ground. They tumbled down the hill like old times; only fists replaced laughter.

Chapter XXI

After the third stranger had put a finger in my vagina, I decided enough was enough.

"The damage to your uterus does not seem to be the cause of your pain and blackouts," Dr. Wong said to me after an exam so thorough I could swear she was an alien seeking information for her mother ship.

"Have you thought of the possibility"—*Oh, Doctor, don't say it*—"that it could be psychological?" There the words were now, just sitting in the room uncovered and free. Whenever a woman hears those words, a deadening chill shivers through her body. Because if she is suffering mentally, every action she takes will be blamed on her "condition."

Did you hear she was thirty-seven cents off balancing her check book? It's because she's crazy, you know. You know she's stressing at work 'cause she's bananas, didn't you hear? When a man breaks down he can seek help, recover, and jump back into his life. A woman who loses it has lost. God, I didn't want to be another sad woman relegated to eating crackers and watching Lifetime television all day.

"Could there be any other physical cause we haven't checked?" I pleaded. Hell, I hated physical exams, but the idea of being pitied was too much to bear.

"Well, I'm the third doctor you've seen and it says from your chart that we all agree." Dr. Wong shifted from the small sink behind my chair and sat next to me.

"Look. You have been through a traumatic experience and sometimes we don't heal as quickly as we'd like." Her hand rested on mine. "I know some excellent doctors that provide excellent care."

What else was I supposed to do? After the incident, it seemed everything I touched corroded. My career, my relationships; I couldn't go on denying that I needed someone to help me sift through my life. But it was just so humiliating. I had been begging my mother for years to seek psychological help, and it looked like I was going to beat her to the punch. The doctor scribbled on a piece of paper and then passed the note to me.

"Here are my favorite two doctors. They are both female and very understanding, but make no mistake—they are the best in the business."

I reluctantly grabbed the paper, thanked the doctor, and headed out the door.

By the time I reached my home, I had decided on the best hiding place to lose the little note. I never looked in the top drawer of my dresser for anything. It used to house my jewelry, but since David bought me that beautiful mahogany jewelry box, I only kept junk in there. I would hide the note in the drawer and forget all about it.

I was about to drop it into the abyss of my bedroom. But my hand wouldn't let go. I looked at the two names etched in almost indecipherable script on the piece of paper. Dr. Anita Melan and Dr. Lynn Talbot. I sat on my bed and contemplated calling the numbers.

I picked up the phone and clicked through the caller ID as one last distraction. Passing through the usual calls from David and my mother, I noticed a ridiculous amount of calls listed as *Private Number*. God, solicitors were so tricky now.

But as I recalled the last few days, my mind couldn't pick out any unwanted calls. But then, David was on the phone working for a long time.

You're procrastinating, J.C. Damn right. I just couldn't bring myself to dial a shrink. It was either that or live with the numbing headaches and stumbling abdominal pains. My fingers punched in a few numbers and then I hung the phone back up. *Come on, stop being a punk.* I clicked on the TV and decided to call after a couple of hours of *Sex and the City*. If Carrie and the gang couldn't make me feel better, then I would have to call the doctor. Then we'd have reached emergency status. I was poking around the nightstand looking for a DVD when a photo on television caught my attention. The eyes were unmistakable. It was him: the man/child who had delivered me to the brink of destruction. I sat in fear of my life, though he was only on television. I stumbled for the remote to hear the newscaster:

"The man responsible for the armed robbery of Southern National Bank in downtown Atlanta has been identified as Damon Harvey, a twenty-six-year-old man from Atlanta. He was captured in Piedmont Park by an off-duty officer who discovered the suspect hiding by an unused fishing pond. Harvey reportedly stole over two hundred thousand dollars, nearly killing one man and brutally attacking a woman. Harvey's arraignment is scheduled for next week, as the district attorney wants to process this case as soon as possible. Though Harvey has been captured, there is no information on whether the money has been recovered or not. For *Channel Seven News*, I am Leslie Morales."

My mouth dropped, and I lay across the bed in shock. I couldn't believe I was so terrified, but I could barely move. I wanted to turn the TV off, but I just sat petrified looking at the man's face. When the clip finally went off I fell back on the bed and burst into tears. My body jerked and I could barely breathe. I had to get over this. I had to do something.

I moved back to my phone and picked up the note that lay next to it. I dialed the first number and let it ring until voice mail picked up. I quickly hung up and punched in the second set of numbers. I heard a voice on the other line.

"Dr. Talbot's office, how may I assist you?"

"Yes. My name is J.C., uh, Jean Catherine West. I'm a referral of Dr. Wong's. I'd like to set up an appointment."

"Of course, do you have a date in mind?"

"As soon as possible would be great."

"Let's see." The woman paused and I could hear her clicking on a keyboard. "I have one cancelation on Friday. We could schedule you for that time, one thirty p.m. Is that okay?"

"That's perfect, thank you."

"Thank you and have a great day."

Surviving the day was hard enough. Having a great day would be more akin to a miracle. I clicked off the phone and decided to call David. I was sure he would be relieved that I had not completely lost my mind. I got his voice mail. Suddenly my husband was all I could think about. This poor man had lost a child, lost the romance with his wife, and even suffered a financial setback with the demise of my business. Yet through it all he had been there for me. God, I had been so selfish. I decided it was time to give something back to my husband.

It was late afternoon by the time I reached David's office, but his secretary assured me that David would be working late today, and so it would be the perfect time to see him. Before I got out of the car I surveyed my surroundings. This was only the second time I had been back downtown since the incident. I got out of the car and proceeded to check myself. I had my favorite Jimmy Choo stilettos, the ones that hiked me up six inches, with open toes. My sheer black dress clung to every inch of my body; I loved how it draped just below my bustline, to give the illusion of fullness. I draped my favorite cashmere shawl over my shoulders and pulled out the wicker picnic basket and wine bottle. I turned the knob on the office door but it was locked. I used my keys to get inside and walked past the empty secretary's desk and moved toward his office.

Since David worked by himself, it was common for him to be gone all the time seeing clients, but at least the secretary should be here. Had she left without telling him? Or worse, was the business in a slump? God, David was a workaholic; he wouldn't be able to handle that. I tried his office door, which turned without hesitation. I entered the dimly lit room and felt my heart stop for the second time in one day.

David was holding a head in his palms, his pants scraping against his knees, and a woman's hands rose up his shirt. His head was cocked back and he moaned softly, almost trance-like. The woman moaned louder as if they were competing in a battle. After the shock wore off, my favorite emotion sprang to life—anger.

"Are you serious?" I called out to the pair. David fell out of his trance and looked across the room at me. When his eyes recognized me, his dark face bloomed into a deep purple.

"J.C.," he yelled and pushed the woman off him.

"What the hell are you doing?" the woman said, and then tracked his eyes and turned around. When I recognized her the flesh on my skin began to burn. Damned if it wasn't that bitch Nicole on my husband.

"Anyone but her," I yelled at David. "Hell, your secretary is cute. I would deal with her before this heffa." Pressed with an urge to react, I threw the wicker basket at him. It fell short and landed on the desk.

"Now, J.C." Nicole stood up and tried to adjust her shirt back onto her surgically altered breasts. "I know this is hard to take, but David and I are in love."

"The hell we are." David separated himself from her and moved toward me. "Baby, I was just so frustrated. We hadn't had sex in months and with all that was going on . . ." He looked as if he wanted to continue, but my stare kept him from proceeding.

"David." Nicole moved in closer. "You need to decide who you love. I thought you said you wanted to have a family with me."

The words punched my chest like boxing gloves, swift and precise. I slung my arm and threw the wine bottle, hoping to hit the portrait above her, but it clocked her in the head. Nicole stiffened and fell back like a cartoon character. I almost envisioned stars circling her head.

"J.C." David ran toward me, but got caught up in his unbuckled trousers. He struggled to pull them up as I headed for the door. He caught me in the foyer.

"Hey, are you going to let me explain?" he asked. "To apologize?"

"What's the point?"

"J.C." He grabbed my arm and I punched him in the face. He buckled forward. I resisted the urge to help him. He massaged his jaw and continued. "I'm sorry. I don't have any excuses. But can we please just try to work it out?"

"Work it out," I screamed. "There's a whore bleeding and unconscious on the carpet I picked out for you. You were getting head below a portrait of us at our wedding."

"You always said I never live dangerously," he attempted to joke, and I wanted to laugh. That was just the type of ill-timed sarcasm I loved about him. But I held my best angry face in place. He continued: "Okay, okay, bad joke. Can we just go home and talk about it?"

I sat there pondering if I should return to my husband and work things out. For all intents and purposes he was a good man, loving, and up until this point, honest. Though up until this point I had been hiding everything under the rug, hoping it would eventually disappear, my problems weren't going anywhere, and I had to face them.

"David, I am going to stay at the Ritz-Carlton for a while. I have some issues I have to deal with before I can talk about us." He nodded and hugged me.

"I love you," he said. "Please don't forget that."

"I know you do," I said. "But I have to love myself first." I hopped back in my car and drove down the street. From the rearview mirror I could see David crying in the distance.

Chapter XXII

Shots of pain sliced through Christopher's arms and back. The sheer volume of hurt he felt in the morning was almost enough to knock him back into bed. But today he had to get up. He had an interview. He pillaged his night table for two horse-sized pills and chugged them sans water. Literally rolling out of bed, he slumped into the bathroom and turned on the shower. His eyes caught himself in the mirror staring at the stitches that climbed his chest to his shoulder blades.

As the steam enveloped the room he pulled out the clippers and tried to find his face underneath the new growth. After he tapered the edges of his goatee, he ran his hand across his face to check for stray stubble. Smooth as silk. He disrobed and entered the shower just as the bathroom door burst open.

"Chris, Chris," his father yelled through the steam. "You gotta come see this on TV. They caught your boy."

"Dad, I'm in the—" The realization of "your boy" socked his brain and he swiped his robe off a hook and moved to his bedroom TV and clicked it on. Out of instinct he switched to CNN and immediately wanted to kick himself. Dressed in a quiet gray suit that Christopher had bought was Vince offering his best serious-journalist pose in front of the county jail. It was amazing how good people looked after you broke up with them. His teeth looked extra white and his chiseled jaw-line was shaved and polished. Christopher settled back on his bed and tried to focus on the newscast:

"Harvey has been given the nickname 'Midday Masher' for his blazoned daylight robbery of a downtown bank a few weeks ago. He reportedly injured a woman and nearly shot a man . . ."

"There was an awkward pause and Christopher rose in his bed a little. Vince looked at his paper as if he had lost some notes, and then gave his smile and continued. "Sorry—shot a man in the back, critically wounding him. A quickie arraign-ment has been scheduled and Harvey will be placed in the county jail until his trial. He is not expected to receive bail. It is not yet known who will be Harvey's defense attorney."

"There are a lot of unanswered questions. One thing is for sure—police have searched the city for the money and have come up empty. Apparently, Harvey is tight-lipped on the whereabouts of the more than two hundred thousand dollars in hundred-dollar bills he stole. For CNN News, I'm Vince Leagues."

Alonzo chuckled at his son and slapped his knee. "I'll say one thing. You sure know how to pick 'em. I'm almost at-tracted to that boy."

"We're not together anymore."

"Really?" Alonzo's eyebrows arched high on his forehead. "What'd you do?"

"Now, why the hell do you think I did something?"

"I'm just saying, big-time reporter on TV takes a liking to you and then he's gone. Just asking."

"Well, don't ask. I am not really comfortable talking about this stuff with you."

"You mean the gay stuff. Look, Son, I was in jail, don't nothing surprise me no more. In fact—"

"Hold." Christopher released a defensive chuckle. "Uh, I

am really not ready to hear any Oz-like tales, especially from my father. So can we change the subject?"

"That's cool." Alonzo rose from the bed. "Anyway, I just wanted you to see that they caught that little bastard."

"Yeah." Christopher stared at the muted television. "I mean, it has been so weird. I didn't expect to still be upset about what happened. But every time they mention his name I get queasy. I thought getting shot was just the luck of the draw, you know, like boarding a plane that crashes or getting in a car wreck. But this feels so personal. I just can't shake it."

"You were shot, Chris," Alonzo said. "It will take time to heal your insides and your outsides."

"Yeah." Christopher's voice conked out. He was still in pain, but hated to admit it had more to do with Vince than with the bullet fragments they had removed from his body.

"Besides you already making a new start with your new job and . . ."

Christopher looked at the clock as Alonzo yammered on.

"Oh, crap." Christopher sprang out of the bed and returned to the bathroom. "I'll talk to you later, Dad. I have to get dressed for this interview or there will be no job." After a quick scrub-down, he rushed to his suit closet and picked out his favorite Kenneth Cole suit, which looked as if it had been hand-stitched in Italy. It had a grayish black quality that Christopher loved. He slid to the tie section and perused his options. Usually he favored a nice thick red tie with no patterns, just soft silk. But this time he wanted something different. He picked a yellow Jones New York with muted blue squares lined up like soldiers down the middle.

"Perfect," he murmured to himself as he placed the blazer over his shoulders and posed in the full-length mirror. He noticed something on his eye. He moved in closer, then pulled back in horror.

"No," he moaned in an overexaggerated tone. He brushed his eyelashes aside with his fingers to discover a gray hair embedded between the black ones. He grabbed the tweezers from the medicine cabinet and extracted the hair with a surgeon's precision.

"You are officially old," he said to himself as he clicked off the lights to his room and hurried down the stairs to his car. "No job, no man, no joy, no life."

"Hey, man, can you pick me up some bacon on your way back?" Alonzo yelled from the kitchen.

"Excuse me?" Christopher wanted to ignore him, but the request stunted his movement.

"Bacon, man. Bacon." Alonzo turned the corner and rubbed his hands in small circles on a dishrag. "You've heard of that, right? Well, I like bacon with the BLT sandwiches I take for lunch, and I forgot to go to the store the other day. So can you pick up some bacon?"

"Uh, sure." Christopher suddenly became acutely aware of his father's presence in his house. Burnt cigarette smoke had already invaded the house, despite his insistence that his father only smoke outside. The pungent aroma of socks and sweat settled near the front door, as Alonzo's array of work boots and shoes lined the wall by the door.

Part of him cringed at the pure gross realignment of his house. The other part fluttered with excitement at the sight of seeing his father on a regular basis. Something he longed for all his life.

"Good luck, Son." Alfonzo smiled in that way that only his father could. His encouragement was not so much evident in the words, but in the way he uttered the word "son." It was as if no one else but his son deserved luck. Christopher smiled and ran out the door."

"Wow, a B.A. from Morehouse, an M.B.A. from NYU. Quite impressive," the woman said, peering over the rims of her oversized glasses, as if looking above the prescriptive lenses helped her sight.

"I must say, your resume as a whole is quite amazing for you to only be thirty-two." She giggled to herself. "I know I am not supposed to mention age, but most guys your age are just settling into their careers. You're well established."

"Thank you," Christopher said, though he glanced up at the woman with more than a little trepidation. The way she paused after saying the words "well established" didn't feel right at all.

"Blanc Finance is a much smaller institution than the bank you last worked for," she said.

Christopher reacquainted himself with her nameplate and decided to head her off before this went too far. "Ms. Reeder, I know there may not be a lot of positions that require all my experience. However, I'm willing to take a lateral position in the hopes of learning something new."

"The only person with as much expertise as you would be the comptroller or maybe the CEO." She weighed the page in her hand as she continued. "And the only lateral position I could even think was worth your time would be my position." Ms. Reeder cackled like an insane person who was sharing a private nonsensical joke with herself. But Christopher got it.

"With all due respect," he said, "why did you ask me in if you didn't have any positions available?"

"Well, if I may be candid," Ms. Reeder said, moving in close to him, "Eric Miles, your old boss, is a friend of mine. He asked if I would at least give you an interview. He knew it would be tough for you to get back on your feet."

Christopher rose and snatched his resume from the woman's hands. "I need to give this to real employee seekers." He headed for the door and turned around to add, "And that prick Eric used to work for me."

Christopher wanted to slam her door but resisted the urge.

When he reached the street, he hollered like an old dog and slammed his briefcase against a mailbox.

He peered down the one-way street and could see Peachtree traffic already lined up for the lunch-hour rush. He traced the path from his location to the bank where he had spent years developing his career, honing his craft. Now, because of some idiot and a crime he had nothing to do with, his career was over. He glanced at the picture of Damon Harvey, encased in the *Atlanta Journal-Constitution* newspaper box. He kicked it so hard he dented the fenced wire that protected the box's hard plastic. A shooting pain rose up his foot and Christopher hopped along until he landed on a nearby bench.

Was this what all the work was for? All the years of struggling to be a success, only to lose it all in one quick flash, was that life? He looked up to the sky, not knowing who to address or what to say or where to go.

"I don't know who to ask or what to ask for, but I need your help." Christopher had never been a religious person, but he knew sheer will could only get him so far. "A little help would be wonderful."

A drop of rain plopped on his head from the gray sky, and Christopher busted out laughing. Soon the trickle rushed into a midday storm and Christopher spread his hands and took in the shower. After several moments he finally got up and headed for his car, but bumped into a woman rushing out of a door in front of him.

"Whoa." The huge box she was carrying crashed into Christopher, and the woman muttered something and took off down the street.

"Come back, Melissa," a young woman called after her.

"I just can't take this bullshit anymore." The woman with the box lifted a hand out of exhaustion and continued on her path. The other woman sat on the stoop of the steps, her face hidden in her knees.

"You all right?" Christopher asked.

"No." The woman wiped tears from her face. "We just lost our third youth director in eight months."

"Director?"

"I'm sorry, this is Heaven's House. It's a nonprofit organization that helps boys get back into school, learn math skills, and think about college."

"Oh," Christopher said. "Why did she leave?"

"Why didn't she leave? Bureaucracy, crazy church people, crazy kids, no money, you name your issue."

"Sorry," Christopher said.

"No, I'm sorry. I don't even know you."

He extended his hand. "Christopher Roberts."

"Pastor Dana Patterson." The woman grabbed Christopher's hand and shook it lightly. "It's just we're already behind the eight ball with everything else that needs to be done. And it would take a miracle to fill this position."

Christopher looked up to the sky and laughed.

"What's funny?" she asked.

"Nothing. Do you mind if we have a cup of coffee? I'd like to hear more about Heaven's House."

Chapter XXIII

Maria kneaded the linoleum floor as she paced up and down the small hallway that led to County Courthouse room twelve, where the fate of her family would be decided once and for all. The brown loafers she had borrowed from her sister scraped against the light sheet of dirt that had accumulated on the floor after years of sanitary neglect. Her hands kept pressing down the wrinkles that bunched up near the peak of her dress. After she was satisfied the bends in the fabric could not be subdued anymore, she tackled her hair. Her fingers pulled off the clip that held her ponytail together. She ran her fingers through it at least a dozen times, making sure every follicle was in place, then arrested her hair again with the small black clip.

"Honey," Adrienne said, looking up from her notes. "You are really going to have to sit down. I can't think with all that shuffling."

"Sorry." Maria sat next to her and attempted to relax. After a few seconds, she commenced wringing her hands until they looked chapped and worn. She dipped in her purse and pulled out her lotion bottle. She squeezed a glob in the palm of her hand, and rubbed little circles into the creases of the skin. She suddenly smelled a tart aroma from her breath and rummaged back in her purse, searching for a piece of gum. She pulled out a paperback book and a ratty brush before a hand fell on her arm.

"Maria, please." Adrienne put her books to the side and turned toward her client. "You are really going to have to calm down.

"Maria tried to form a smile, but it resembled more of a maniacal grimace. "Do you think they'll put me in prison?"

"Honestly, I don't know. I mean, you were going to drive the getaway car."

"But I drove off. I didn't go through with it."

"I know, but you helped plan it. You could still be brought up on attempted robbery charges."

"Oh my God," Maria whined.

"Look, it's most likely the D.A. will want to make some sort of a deal with you for information on Damon. But I gotta tell you, this particular judge is a bit conservative on family values. She may want to make an example out of you."

Maria pushed back against the hard bench. "Are you serious?"

"Don't lose it yet." Adrienne smiled. "You have a couple of pluses on your side. You have a sister with her own home who is willing to take you in until you establish residence. And Q is an excellent student."

"What does that have to do with anything?"

"A judge will be less likely to move a well-adjusted child from his environment." A smile cracked Maria's face. "How have you been coming with that job hunt?"

"I looked everywhere. The only place that called me back was McDonald's."

"I don't care if you put on a big purple Grimace suit and throw hot fries at the people in line. We have to establish that you are at least trying to create a good work history."

"But how am I going to raise my baby on McDonald's money?" Maria clicked her tongue against the bridge of her mouth, letting out a soft sucking sound.

"It's not about where you work at this point." Adrienne turned to Maria. "It's that you do work. Do you feel me?"

"Yeah." Maria coiled back at Adrienne's scolding tone. She would normally cuss someone out for using that voice with her. But Adrienne was right; she needed a job. And Adrienne had been the only person in the last few weeks who bothered to even listen to what she had to say. She returned to rubbing her hands when Adrienne tapped her knees and rose to her feet.

"Come on, sweetie. It's time to talk to the judge."

Maria gulped back the dry knot in her throat and followed her lawyer into the room. To her surprise, it was a small, windowless room with three conference tables positioned into a U formation. A small woman with square glasses sat behind the center table reading a stack of papers. A tall man with a bush of brown hair sat on the left, and Adrienne motioned for Maria to sit on the opposite side.

"I have a full day today, so let's get started," the woman said without looking up from her papers. "Ms. Adee, you are charged with attempted robbery, reckless endangerment of a child, and two counts of child abuse." Maria's face sank as the charges were being read. She looked at Adrienne, who was reading her notes again. Adrienne seemed calm and unaffected by all the charges against Maria.

"Your Honor," said the man across the table, sliding a piece of paper to the judge. "We are willing to drop the attempted robbery charges in exchange for testimony against Damon Harvey."

"Does this sound right with the defense attorney?" The judge threw a glance toward Adrienne.

"Yes, Your Honor." Adrienne passed some papers to the judge as well. "We have agreed to all terms set by the D.A."

"Lovely." The judge stacked the forms she collected and put a set of them to the side. "I may get a lunch after all." She gave a long sigh and looked at Maria.

"Okay, Ms. Adee, that just leaves the child abuse charges. Do you understand the charges brought forth?"

Maria leaned to Adrienne and saw her nod and said, "Yes."

"Okay, Defense. Do your job."

"Your Honor." Adrienne leaned into the table, placed all her paperwork on the desk, and looked directly at the judge. "Ms. Adee has never been arrested and her child is an A-plus student reading at a high school level. Given the fact that he will soon lose his father, we ask that the court recognize that having his mother will benefit him and help him continue on his path toward becoming a positive member of society."

"That is unless Ms. Adee helps her son rob a bank, hmm?"

The words jabbed into Maria like dull scissors. She wanted to retaliate, jump up, and slam that snobby judge against a wall. But what would happen to Q?

Adrienne held her ground. "Your Honor, Ms. Adee was abused physically and mentally to the point where she agreed to Mr. Harvey's wishes just to stay alive."

Maria heard the words. Yes, Damon beat on her a lot, but had she ever really thought of him as abusive? It seemed Adrienne's version of her life resembled a Lifetime movie, when Maria always pictured it as a tragic love story.

Adrienne continued: "She has bruises all over her body, and managed to escape his grasp. Lord knows what Mr. Harvey would do if he caught up with her again."

The judge wrestled with some more papers. These were the reading-est people Maria had ever met.

"Explain this to me—if Ms. Adee was so threatened, why did she let her husband spend the night one day before she was captured?"

Adrienne fell back in her chair. She tapped a pencil on the table. "Mr. Harvey was holding their son captive when she woke up. She had to placate the man for her family's own safety."

"Hmm." The judge blew more air, like a full balloon with

its lips slightly parted. "Here's what I am going to do. You prove to me that you can keep a job"—Adrienne winked at Maria as the judge continued—"save some money, and establish a residency, and we'll consider dropping these charges."

Maria smiled and grabbed Adrienne's hand.

"Until such demands can be met by Ms. Adee, the child must be placed in foster care."

"What?" Maria flew out of her chair. "You gone take my baby? That isn't fair. I'm all he has left."

"Life isn't fair, Ms. Adee. Ask your husband's victims, you know, the one with the dead baby and the man who almost died."

"I didn't do that," Maria cried. "I left! I didn't do that!"

"No, but you were an accessory and you're lucky I don't charge you for that."

"Your Honor, can the child at least stay with the sister?" She has a stable job and her own house. Surely she can keep the child in Ms. Adee's absence."

"Look, you can file a petition to have the child remanded to the aunt." The judge rose. "But until then, the child is not going to suffer any more of this girl's foolishness."

"Please," Maria shouted. She felt her legs shaking under her dress. Bile had risen from her stomach and threatened to eject itself. She cradled her stomach. "Please don't take him away."

"We're done here." The judge walked off.

The district attorney moved over to Adrienne and said, "We're going to need her testimony and her signature before the end of the day. And she may have to testify."

"We'll take care of it." Adrienne put her arm around Maria and rubbed her back. The man left the room and Adrienne closed in on Maria.

"If you want your child back, you're going to have to be strong."

Maria nodded and tried desperately to wipe the globs of mascara and tears that burned her eyes. "I know."

"I will get your son back for you."

"I know. I just . . . when are they going to get him?"

"Probably by the end of the day."

There was no consoling Maria now, as her legs gave and she fell to the hard, carpeted floor. Adrienne huddled beside her, rocking Maria in her arms.

Maria was tired of crying. She had shed so much water her body felt dehydrated. She looked at her son's face as the doorbell rang. She explained as best she could that he was going away only for a little while so Mommy could get a job. His screams and kicks reminded her of when he was first born, fighting for his space under a gaggle of hospital blankets.

"Mommy, please don't send me away," he cried. "I'll be good. I promise."

Maria stood silent as her child hollered.

"I want my daddy," Q demanded when he realized Maria was powerless to move.

At that moment she thought of Damon. She wanted his touch, his arms, to hear his lulling voice saying, "It's gone be all right."

Her mind wandered to the if questions. Had she waited for the garbage truck to move and returned to pick up Damon, would things have been different? Had they driven off together, would she be saying good-bye to her only son?

What if she had stayed? Would they be tanning under a blazing Miami sun, sipping fruity drinks like she imagined? Would she finally get a small house with bay windows that peered into a majestic living room? Would Damon have been able to start his custom auto parts store? Would Q really get into private school like she had dreamed for him?

She continued to ponder as a woman in a dark gray pantsuit knocked, came into the house, and exchanged some unmemorable words with her. She watched as the woman scooped up her wailing child and walked to an unmarked police car parked in her sister's driveway. Leia held the doorway for comfort and pressed her face into the wood so Q wouldn't see her crying. Maria wanted to grab him back, but the fight inside her had washed away like a receding tide.

"Bye, baby," she moaned. "We'll see you in a few days." Q no longer looked up. He just stared at his lap as he was placed in the backseat of the car. It took exactly forty-seven seconds for the car to reverse out of the driveway and head down the street. With no energy pulsing in her body, Maria slid down the wall and landed in a heap on the floor. Her mind raced to a few days ago when Damon had sped off in her car.

In a matter of days the only two things in the world she loved had driven away from her. She could truly only depend on herself now.

Chapter XXIV

A clump of officers gathered around the area where they had found Oscar and Damon. They poked through shrubs and leaves, split ferns, and uncovered half-buried debris in search of evidence that could be used against the man who lay face-down on the ground. His arms and legs were hog-tied by steel handcuffs. One officer talked on a cell phone while his combat boot dug into Damon's back. Oscar sat leaned against a tree, dabbing a wet towel on his busted lip.

"He socked you pretty good there, Parks." Sergeant Walters stood over Oscar, his aviator sunglasses deflecting the hot sun's rays. "You want to tell me how you just happened to be in the same park he was in at the crack of dawn?"

"I was dealing with stuff and just came here to get some air." Oscar used his tongue to push his lip out as he talked. "I guess he was doing the same thing."

"Rumor has it that you two are friends," Walters said.

"We were friends," Oscar interjected. "A long time ago. When we were kids."

"I was just wondering 'cause you seem real close with this guy. I mean, you interviewed his wife. Your wife is defending her case, I believe."

"Had nothing to do with me." Oscar rose slowly to his feet.

A defined pain settled into his back. He doubled over for a moment.

"I hope not, 'cause APD don't have no dirty cops." Walters smiled and Oscar frowned.

"Right." Oscar let the word sit in the air for a moment. "Well, I can tell you we aren't friends anymore. Haven't been for years."

Walters stood silent for a moment as if analyzing Oscar's statement, then turned quick like a knob and walked off. "Good job, Parks," he rattled off without looking back.

Oscar winced as he moved toward the crowd surrounding Damon.

"Where did you hide it, you little dick?" a tall, thin officer with spiked red hair yelled at Damon. "We're gonna find it sooner or later."

"Don't know what you're talking about." Damon smiled and the man set his foot back, like a timer ready to go off, on Damon's face.

"Whoa, hey." Oscar moved in between the men. "Can I talk to him for a second?"

"What, so you two can plan a new hiding place?" the officer asked.

"Watch yaself, partna." Oscar's eyes closed to small lines.

"Everyone thinks you're in on it."

"If I had access to that kind of money, then I wouldn't give a shit about rules and would beat your ass right here." The man took a baby step back, and Oscar noticed. "Please say you want to try me today. I need more exercise."

"We're watching you," the man rebuffed.

"Could you watch me over there, so I can talk to the suspect?"

The man stood still for a full moment, his eyes darting from Oscar to Damon and then back again. He watched Oscar's eyes, which held firm, not blinking. The officer slowly retreated to the flock of police now talking in fragmented cliques throughout the grassy valley.

"So, you gonna tell me where the money is?"

"Fuck you." Damon spat globs of blood as he spoke.

"You know I'm still your friend." Oscar kneeled down and leaned over Damon. "I could help you."

"Help me like you helped me a few minutes ago?"

"This is my job." Oscar smiled. "I'm a cop."

"Exactly." Damon turned his head away. "So why would I trust you?"

"Because we used to be tight."

"Used to be, nigga, till you sold me like a slave for an Uncle Tom–ass school."

"Oh, I get it." Oscar laughed. "I'm supposed to keep it real like you. Sell out my family, my future, for a couple of bucks."

"I was trying to keep my family together."

"You tore your family apart." Oscar strained to keep his voice at a manageable decibel. "Your girlfriend is facing jail time. They may take your kid away." Damon remained silent, but Oscar could see his eyes quiver at that last statement.

"I am all you have right now," Oscar said.

"Then I'm already lost," Damon said.

"If you tell me where the money is, we can return it and maybe they'll have a lighter sentence and you may have a chance to see your son grow up."

"Man, why don't you get it?" Damon arched his back so he faced Oscar. "I needed you back then. Back then when we were kids I would have done anything you said."

"I left for school, Damon," Oscar said. "You could have too."

"Man, you was the only nigga I knew checkin' for some damn college. And what'd you do? Up and left me alone."

"You can't blame me for moving on with my life."

"Why couldn't you have moved me along with you?"

Oscar paused for a second. He hadn't really thought of that. When he graduated from high school, he was in such a hurry to leave the ghetto, he never thought of the bonds broken by his departure. Had he bothered to look back he would have seen that Damon needed him more than he realized.

"I can't change the past, Damon," Oscar said.

"Neither can I, son," Damon said. "What's done is done."

"So that's it? You're still gonna be hardheaded."

"There is nothing to talk about." Damon swung his head around again.

"Fine," Oscar muttered. "Have a nice fucking life in jail." He walked off, reeling from Damon's words. Had he deserted the very people he had planned to help when he became an officer? When had he become an enemy to his people? A job protecting his people had become a battle for his soul. The pride he felt driving past his neighborhood was replaced with contempt and hatred for what his people had become. Worse, Oscar was afraid he had nothing left to contribute to them or himself.

His mind thumped from the thoughts that bounced from every corner. He didn't hear Adrienne calling him in the distance.

"Oscar," she screamed, navigating her way down the jagged hill. "Oscar!"

When she reached him she grabbed hold of him so tightly he felt his last grain of energy squeeze out from her grip.

"Oh my God, your lip." Adrienne touched it with her soft fingertips. "Are you okay?"

"Yeah. He rattled me a bit, but I'll survive."

"I didn't hear from you all night, and then your precinct called and said you were here. They wouldn't even tell me if you were alive or dead."

"Not dead." Oscar laughed. "You can't cash in the policy yet."

Adrienne punched him in the chest. "Don't be flip."

"Ow!" Oscar yelled. "You gonna get a piece of me, too?"

"I'm just happy you're alive."

"Yeah." Oscar moved back and turned toward the hill. His back faced Adrienne.

"What's wrong with you?"

"What do you mean?"

"I mean, you won't talk, you work ridiculous hours, leaving me alone with our four kids, and now you're out all night and end up almost getting killed fighting criminals."

"Do you think I am the same person you married?"

"Huh?"

"Am I the same person you married?"

"The guy I married was fifteen pounds lighter and a lot more considerate."

"I'm serious, Adrienne."

"Oscar." Adrienne approached him and rubbed his back. "We're all a little different now than we were ten years ago. I mean, remember when we went clubbing on the weekends before the kids? Dancing till five a.m. and then eating breakfast at Waffle House?"

"Yeah," Oscar said. "You could tear up some French toast."

"Now all I can stomach in the morning is juice and a multigrain bar. And we usually both fall asleep by eleven p.m."

"Do you think my ideas have changed, though?" His look was pleading as he stared at his wife, as if her answers provided the keys to his life.

"Lots of things I believed at age twenty-three changed again when I went to law school. They changed again when I had the kids, became a property owner, blah, blah, blah. That's life. Change."

"I just don't know what I'm here for anymore."

"What?" Adrienne chuckled. "You have been fighting for justice since you were like two. Everyone knew you would be a cop, like we know you'll go to law school and then be a politician. It's your dream."

"It's hard to decipher my dreams these days." Oscar rubbed

the back of his head. "I used to have everything planned. Now I feel like I am not making any type of difference."

"We all go through that."

Oscar grabbed Adrienne and led her away from the crowd. "Sometimes I hate us, you know what I mean?"

"Us being . . ."

"Us." Oscar lifted the back of his hand up and tapped and rubbed his skin.

"Oscar," Adrienne sighed. "There are times when I want to tie you and the kids up in the basement of the house, light a match, and start all over."

"Damn, Adrienne." Oscar frowned. "Please tell me there was a point in that statement and not just premeditation."

"Oscar." Adrienne invaded his personal space. "I love you all so much sometimes I get physically sick when I worry about you. But I am human. I can't stand y'all sometimes. Sometimes I would sell my car to get my personal freedom. But in the end I know there is no place I would rather lay my head than on your arm at night."

"It always falls asleep under your big head." Oscar smiled.

"Whatever," Adrienne said. "Look, maybe you should take some time off and figure some things out. Maybe consider going back to school now that I have a job."

"I have to see this thing through first," Oscar said.

"You still care about him, don't you?"

"He was all I had for a while growing up."

"Then stop judging him and help him."

"Why did he have to be such a fuckup?"

"He was not your responsibility," Adrienne argued. "I mean, you were only a few years apart in age."

"But we promised to be brothers—to take care of each other."

"Then be there for him."

"But how?" Oscar said. "It's over. He's going to jail for sure."

"Does life end in jail?"

"I doubt he would talk to the one person who put him in jail in the first place."

"I don't know," Adrienne said. "But I do know if you just let him rot, you'll be the one who dies."

"Hmm." Oscar peeked past Adrienne and glanced at Damon, who was now being led away. His face was covered in facial hair, but he still looked like the boy Oscar had shot hoops with, talked about girls with, laughed with. Didn't Oscar owe Damon his friendship, even if Damon didn't want to accept it?

"Adrienne, why don't you go to the car? I'll meet you up there in a second."

"All right." Adrienne nodded. "Just hurry up. I had to leave the kids with the next-door neighbor, and I think she steals money from our change drawer when we aren't there."

Oscar stole a kiss from Adrienne and walked back to Damon. "Damon," Oscar called as Damon rolled his eyes. "No matter what, I will watch over Q for you."

He half expected Damon to lunge at him again, but Damon just stood there, eyes full of dirt and tears. At that moment Damon looked like the scared boy talking smack at the youth center so many years ago, trying hard to impress but, deep down, his knees were caving together from fear.

Oscar and Damon stared at each other, both afraid to move, both afraid to stand dormant. Damon moved toward Oscar as the officers yanked him back.

"Hey, take it easy," Oscar yelled.

"Don't let him grow up like me, man," Damon said. His words fell like Oscar's heart. Then the two officers each grabbed one of Damon's shoulders and walked him around Oscar, through the clearing to a waiting sedan. The door was already open. The seat seemed all too familiar, too planned to be spontaneous, Oscar thought. Perhaps the squad car door had been left open, waiting for years for Damon to arrive and be taken away.

Chapter XXV

Damon sat in the courtroom, his eyes fixed on the empty podium that jutted out from the north wall. His head moved back and forth from the judge's empty chair to the seat in the center of the adjacent wall. The long hand of the clock stood petrified at 11 while the short hand had already landed on 9. He scanned the room for a familiar face, but recognized no one. He pulled at the starch-drenched shirt collar that scratched his neck. He wiggled the tie, which had sunk into the space above his Adam's apple.

His lawyer leaned over his table, whispering to the lawyers at the other table. Their familiar giggles caused his stomach to quake. He steadied his hands on his lap to keep them from shaking. But he couldn't hide the sweat. It creeped down his back. It dripped under his arms, finally caught by the cottony cushion of his T-shirt. Damon glanced back at the clock. The long hand inched its way toward 12, and eventually his lawyer sat up straight in his chair.

"All rise." A bailiff rushed through a side door, a clipboard pressed in his hand. "The Honorable Jeffrey Rosenbaum presiding."

A tall man stretching out of his robe sauntered up the steps. His small-rimmed glasses rested on the brim of his hook nose. Once he sat down, he glared at the crowd and zeroed in on Damon. The look was momentary, but it settled deep under Damon's skin, causing his hairs to wrestle on his arms.

"Be seated," Rosenbaum said. He planted himself in his seat, tossed papers around, and nodded to the bailiff.

"The case of Damon Harvey versus the State of Georgia, Your Honor," the bailiff read off his clipboard.

"Ready, set, go, counsel," Rosenbaum muttered, his head bent forward to his desk.

"Your Honor, the state is charging Mr. Harvey with armed robbery and third-degree manslaughter," the D.A. said, standing at his desk.

"Mr. Harvey, how do you plead?" Rosenbaum asked. There was that expression again. His eyes pierced through Damon.

Damon's jaw dropped and his tongue seemed to widen across the circumference of his mouth. He wanted to plead his case. He was just trying to feed his family. His options were as stifling as the shackles binding his wrists and ankles.

"No contest, Your Honor," Damon managed to spit out, his voice crackly and worn.

"Yeah, okay," Rosenbaum said. "Got that out of the way. You understand that by pleading no contest you have waived your rights to a jury trial?"

Damon looked for reassurance to his lawyer, who winked at him. Damon said, "Yes, Your Honor."

"Fine. We will set your sentencing date for three weeks out." Rosenbaum slammed the gavel and it was done. Officers moved in like hawks and grabbed Damon's arms. They pulled him away from the table and guided him out the back hall and down a small corridor to a field of press. Lights stole the color from his face as cameras flashed.

"Mr. Harvey, are you sorry for your crimes?" a voice shouted at him.

"Are you afraid you'll get the electric chair?" Damon felt his face crunch up at the thought. His lawyer never mentioned anything about dying. What if the judge was crazy and thought pushing that woman, making her lose her kid, was the same as murder? He bowed his head forward, trying to avoid giving photographers a direct shot of his face.

"Are you concerned that your child is now in foster care?"

A fearful rage whirled inside Damon. He dashed toward the voice and yelled into the crowd, "Who the fuck said that? Who told you that?"

"We did a feature story on it on *Channel Eight News*," a female voice countered. "He was taken into protective custody until your girlfriend can show she's fit to raise him."

Fit? Damon's head was murky with thoughts. He wanted to break free and find his son, but knew even if he did manage to barrel down the guards and escape, he wouldn't get far. He knew what he had to do. When he got out of the media circus he sidled up to his attorney.

"I need to talk to my girl," he stated plainly and calmly.

"I don't know if that would be such a good idea," his lawyer said. His curly locks pushed slightly over his face. It came to Damon that this guy was about his same age, maybe a year or two older. Suddenly, standing next to his counterpart, the dark corners of the life he lived seemed obtuse and out of place. Here was a man just like him but who, because of a different background, different stimulus, and different goals, led a totally opposite life. The lawyer probably never had to ask anyone where his son had been taken, or whether he would ever see him again.

"I'm not gonna ask twice." Damon stopped the brigade of officers, lawyers, and courtroom staff.

"She is working with the prosecution right now. It could be a conflict of interest to strike up conversations now."

"I need to know where my son is." Damon turned so he was eye to eye with his lawyer. They were almost the same height, so Damon could see his sea-foam-colored orbs widen as Damon moved into his personal space.

"Let me make some calls," the man said. "Maybe I can figure out what happened to him. I am sure he's in good hands."

"You ain't understanding me, yo." Damon watched the hot spittle leave his mouth and land on his attorney's nose. "I want to talk to my girl right now. And I ain't leaving until I do."

"All right, partner. Let's get you back to holding and we can all discuss this in private," an officer said, leaning into Damon's ear.

"Get the fuck off me." Damon thrust his head back, slamming into the officer's face. He felt blood gushing on his head.

There was a snap of silence, as if the eye of a storm had passed over the courtroom. Then they pounced on him. Damon watched as they pushed his lawyer back and then fists pounded his face and neck. When he finally fell to the ground, the kicks registered. They jabbed his groin, thighs, and stomach. He didn't even try to fight. He resigned himself to his subconscious, which quickly led him away from that place.

Damon's reflection in the holding room window was like spying on a different person. His acute features were blurred by a mixture of dried blood and swollen skin. A deep gash rode up the side of his face, from his eye right through the brow. A soft white bandage covered his nose, but Damon felt as if it was keeping his nose in place on his face. He dabbed fresh ice packs over his jaw, which felt dislocated. But he sat quietly waiting. Throughout the whole ordeal he refused to move. Despite the beating and pain, he didn't budge until his lawyer agreed to get Maria to come in to see him.

Now he sat in the waiting room, trying to think of ways to diffuse his anger, but he could not. His hands tapped against the metal base of the chair. His legs crossed and he wriggled his feet in small circles, until he finally saw her through the glass. She entered and spoke to the guard. Damon was praying she would be leading their son by the hand, but she was alone. The guard directed her to a seat behind the glass. She sat down and picked up the small receiver positioned to the right of the window.

He moved up to her seat and sat down. He picked up the receiver.

"Oh my God." Maria placed her hand on the window. "What happened to your face?"

"Don't worry about it," he mumbled under his breath.

"Don't worry," Maria moaned. "Jesus, Damon, you look a mess. Are you all right in here? I mean, I know it's jail, but I . . . are they feeding you?"

"Where the fuck is my son?"

Maria's eyes bucked and she pushed back a little in her chair. "They took him away." She turned her head away as she spoke, her tone decreasing several decibels.

"How the fuck could you let that happen?" Damon screamed. His finger tapped the glass. "You his mom, you supposed to be there."

"I'm supposed to be there?" Maria moved in close to the window. "What about you?"

"You're the reason I'm in jail."

"No, you're the reason you're in jail." Maria's face reddened, and she let out a giggle. "You know, I wasted so many years, took so many beatings trying to love you, when you don't even love yourself. You just keep hurting yourself and everyone around you."

"You hurt me," Damon screamed. "You was supposed to be my down chick, my ride-or-die chick."

"I did die, Damon. I died each time you pulled me into one of your schemes, each time I had to apply some extra makeup to cover marks on my arms and face. Now I'm dying again knowing I sacrificed my son in order to love you."

"Where is Q?" Damon demanded. He slapped the window,

wishing it was her flesh. He pulled back his red palm and balled it into a fist.

"They took him away." Maria flicked back tears. "Took him away."

"If anything happens to my son—"

"It already happened to him, Damon," she cried. "You left him, and then they ripped him away from me and it's taking all my strength to get him back."

"Why would you let them take him?"

"We all can't start fights and beat people when things don't go our way," Maria said. "Look at you. Look how far it's taken you."

"Fuck you!"

"Not anymore," Maria said. "My only focus is getting my son back and getting him as far away from you as possible."

"You ain't taking my son anywhere."

"You don't scare me anymore, Damon," Maria said. "All my fear left when they carried my son off. You know what I do now? I work ten hours a day at McDonald's trying to save what little I can to get an apartment in my name and build a home for our son. Something I should have done years ago."

"When I get out I'll take care of us."

"No." Maria was hysterical now. "I don't want your money, your help, your anything. All I need for you to do is forget us!"

"I am not gonna forget my only son."

"You don't have much of a choice." Maria rose to her feet. "This is my last visit and you best believe I will not be bringing Q here so he can try to be a jailbird just like his daddy."

"I'm gonna kill you when I get out of here." His throat was on fire. He could barely breathe. He wanted to get at Maria so badly that his fingers ached. But for all he tried, she still wouldn't obey him. For the first time he felt helpless in front of her.

"It doesn't matter," Maria said. "It doesn't matter anymore. We're done."

Her words hit him harder than any blow she could have mustered from her body. As she stood up, he realized his last connection with anything he loved was leaving him alone again. He banged halfheartedly on the window, knowing she would not turn around. He sat negotiating the tears that ran down his cheeks with the back of his hand.

His mind flashed to Q, his square jaw, just like Daddy, set back in a rounded smile. He thought of him growing old without his father. He bent over on the table and sobbed until the guard placed a hand on his shoulder to lead him back to his cell.

Chapter XXVI

"Your Honor, we would like to call Ms. Jean Catherine West," the lanky man said, extending his open hand in my direction.

I sat crumpling a tattered piece of paper in my hands. I gathered myself and rose, halfway hoping I would faint before I reached the small podium. At least I didn't have to endure questions, like I thought. This was sentence hearing. All I had to do was make a statement about how that knucklehead destroyed my life and I'd be out.

I had avoided his stares all morning. I felt his dark eyes scanning me as I sat in the front row, just a few feet away from him. I couldn't read his face from the corner of my eyes, but he didn't resemble the madman who threw me down. Maybe it was the muted gray suit that lent him credibility and a pinch of remorse. It wasn't so much in his facial expression, which held about as much emotion as an abstract painting. It was more the way his hands interlocked quietly on the table. He wasn't slouched over in his chair, either. There was a sort of repenting curl in his spine, as if he was surrendering within himself after a tough battle.

I shrugged my sympathy off and reached the podium in just enough time to lose my voice. I cleared it several times before the judge calmly said, "Take your time, Ms. West."

It wasn't that I was truly scared of speaking in public. I had a knack of being "on" in social settings. But the letter in my hand was so personal, and even though it was meant for Mr. Harvey's ears, I felt a rush of embarrassment swirl inside. I couldn't believe I was going to spill my insides to a total stranger, in front of fifty other strangers, no less. Granted, Mr. Harvey and I had become very intimate very fast before he sped off and left me to die on the street. Nonetheless, I felt awkward. How in the world did I even end up in this predicament?

"Have you ever thought of confronting the man who hurt you?" Dr. Lynn Talbot had asked as she systematically pulled loose hairs off her face and combed them back into the massive sea of brown locks that rested behind her shoulders.

"Who, me?" I asked, praying she meant some other patient. Alas, I was paying $170 per hour for this one-on-one session, and it looked like I was going to finally get my money's worth. "Um, no." My eyes hit the floor. "I just figured it happened, let it go, ya know?"

"Dr. Lynn let out a soft "hmm," which I calculated meant, along with her near-incessant scribbling in her notepad, that I had given the wrong answer.

"What do you think would happen if you expressed your true feelings to Mr. Harvey?" Dr. Lynn threw out the question in between thin-lipped smiles and after glancing at the clock hanging above the chair I usually occupied during our weekly visits.

"Huh," I replied, not exactly sure why or where the statement came from. "I, uh, I don't know."

"I was just wondering because I read in the paper his sentencing was coming up. I didn't know if anyone had contacted you."

"Yeah. I got a lot of messages I haven't gone through yet," I lied. In reality, the D.A. in the case asked me to come down to make a statement. It would help when they sentenced him. I ignored the message partly because I had my own drama right now but mostly because I wouldn't know what to say. Yeah, it was awful, yeah, I lost my kid, but life moves on, right? But here we were, again addressing the same issues.

"What do you think you would say to him if you had a chance?"

"Honestly, I have moved on from that part of my life." A half truth. I really did have to move on from a lot of stuff. Maneuvering through seven suitcases in a one-room hotel suite was tough enough to deal with. Not to mention the husband ringing my cell phone off the hook.

I wasn't really pressed to deal with a man who was going to jail anyway. But Dr. Lynn kept probing.

"Have you thought about writing some of your thoughts down?" Dr. Lynn reeled me in. Once she clamped her teeth down on a subject, you couldn't beat her off it.

"I'm fine with that, really," I said curtly. "I just don't see a need to see him ever again."

"Do you not think he affected your life in some way?" Dr. Lynn's British accent tilted the words as she spoke. They sounded so romantic, even though she was getting on my nerves.

"Yeah, I guess in a way," I said. "But that was so long ago and what happened just happened."

"Yes, but it has changed you, no?"

"In a way."

"Think about what you were doing before." Dr. Lynn moved her hands in small circles as she continued. "Now think about that moment when your life changed." She stumped me. As much as I wanted to pretend that meeting that man didn't change my life, he was a part of me now. And I had to do something about it.

In a gesture to appease Dr. Lynn and explore my thoughts, I had started writing about the incident. Now here I was, coughing into a microphone in a room packed with people. And all I wanted was to erase this memory from my brain completely.

"Whenever you are comfortable, Ms. West." The judge smiled at me reassuringly.

I stole one last look at Mr. Harvey. Our eyes met and he nodded his head. His eyes were red and though his goatee and hair were trimmed, he looked mangled, like he had wrestled with his bed a few moments before he entered the courtroom. I fiddled with the deep creases embedded on the paper one last time, and finally began.

"Mr. Harvey. I don't know if you remember me, but I was the woman who you robbed that Monday afternoon downtown. You may not remember my face, but I remember yours. Every time I close my eyes, every time I dream, every time I wake up, I see your face. When I walk down the street and pass a black man, for a split second I see you and clutch my purse. I feel awful for doing that. I never did that before. But I am afraid it is you."

I swallowed hard to coat the tickle caught in the middle of my throat. I pressed my hand on my neck as if to will the fire inside to calm down.

"I thought I had a perfect life. A husband who loved me, a job I loved, and a baby on the way. Now because of you, I lost my job, I left my husband because I can't even imagine touching another human being anymore, and then there is Sonja.

"Sonja is . . . was my baby girl. She was six months along when you showed up. We had already painted her room and were looking at preschools. Do you have any idea what it is like to hear the sound of a machine sucking your baby out of you? To be half high on painkillers and watching your husband's face as his child is taken away? Do you even care that I probably can't have children anymore due to the damage from the fall you caused and the miscarriage? I wake up and wonder how one person, who I didn't even know, can change my entire life before I have my third cup of coffee." I could hear muffled sniffles from the back of the room and wished I could cry. But I had no tears left.

"I understand you have a son, Mr. Harvey. Imagine if someone had done to you what you did to me. Imagine not getting to hear your child laugh, or cry, or hug you. . . ." An ache rolled through my belly and I placed my hand on the origin of my pain. For a brief moment it felt like Sonja was back.

Suddenly I realized what I had lost. Not just my child, my daughter, but my connection with life. I just couldn't face another day knowing I was all alone. The life I was responsible for had been taken away. What did that say about me? What, God didn't think I was fit enough to be a mom? Was I too selfish? What? I looked at Mr. Harvey, searching his face for answers. He held his head low, hands covering his face.

"I am not an advocate for the death penalty and I know you would not receive it anyway, but I want you to realize that you did murder someone. And you did ruin my life and no doubt countless others. You were a storm we never expected to hit us, but now that you have, all I can do is pray. Pray that you take the time given to you in prison to change your life. You owe it to us to reform. You owe it to your soul to be something other than a cancer on society. You owe it to the child you may actually get to raise when you get out. Let him know that he doesn't have to make the mistakes you made, hurt people like you. Let him know that he can come into someone's life and change it for good."

I folded up the paper and added, "That is all I ask of you, Mr. Harvey." I turned around and walked out of the courtroom. My energy evaporated and I walked to an empty bench and sank back into the wooden frame.

"Excuse me," a male voice said over me. I looked up and saw a handsome man standing in front of me.

"I'm sorry to interrupt you." He smiled.

I rolled my eyes, as I had seen sly reporters grin before.

"I ain't doing no interviews, sweetie." I brushed him away with my hand. He didn't budge, but sat down next to me.

"I'm not a reporter," he said. "My name is Christopher Roberts. I was shot the same day you were . . . robbed."

"You're the guy he shot?"

"Yes, I . . ."

"I don't know why, but I leaned over and hugged him. He tensed under my arms for a second, and then I felt his arms squeeze around my back.

We finally pulled free and smiled at each other. "Sorry," I said.

"No problem," he said. "I just wanted to say how brave you were up there reading your statement. I wanted to but I just chickened out."

"I wanted to chicken out but then I thought, 'Why should this prick get off without hearing what I have to say?'"

"True," Christopher said. "Well, I just wanted to thank you for articulating so many of my feelings. I know we went through our own thing but . . ." He smiled again and continued. "Well, do you think maybe you'd like to do lunch and maybe talk about it sometime? I mean, I know we don't know each other, but it's just kind of hard talking about it to people who haven't been there, ya know?"

"Yeah," I said, relieved someone could actually share in my madness. "And that would be real cool." I dug in my purse and drew out a pen and an old business card.

"I wrote my new number on the back." I beamed back. "Call me soon, okay? And good luck to you." We shared a quick hug again and I rose to my feet and started for the door. I turned to see Christopher waving and smiling in my direction. It was good to know there was at least one person out there who got what I was saying on that podium. And if you can reach one person, you're doing something.

Chapter XXVII

"I need a drink." Armando laughed as he threw his luggage in the back of Christopher's car, and then climbed though the passenger door.

"What's up?" Christopher and Armando exchanged a brief hug and then parted to their sides of the car. "You can't be ready to drink already," Christopher said. "You just got off the plane."

"That's the best time to drink, while your ears are still popping." The two laughed as Christopher's car darted out into moving traffic.

"Well, it's already eleven p.m. We might as well grab something to eat and then head out. I assume you want to hit the clubs?"

"Fo' sho," Armando said. "I am going through colored-man withdrawal at Berkeley."

"There are colored folks in California."

"You know I need a soldier." Armando cracked a smile.

"Lord." Christopher laughed.

"Don't act like you don't want one."

"I've evolved." Christopher laughed again. "I'm looking for a meaningful relationship."

"You are just a retired whore, too old to stay up till four a.m. like you used to, so now you're looking for a relationship." Armando curled his index and middle fingers on both hands as he said "relationship."

"I'm serious. You see what I was trying to do with Vince."

"And you see how that worked out," Armando said. "I hate to say it but I'm starting to think homo-monogamous relationships are an urban legend."

"That's just the stereotypical shit people expect you to say, so we can justify being hos."

"I'm sorry, but I've been running with the rainbow camp for ten years and only had two relationships that lasted over a year. Two, man. I've had foot fungus longer than that."

"That reminds me," Christopher interjected. "Make sure you keep your socks on when you sleep in the guest room."

"Whatever. I'm just saying I need convincing that this relationship thing is feasible in our society."

"Well, there are lots of gay guys in relationships."

"White guys."

"Not true. I know three couples that have been together for years."

"Are they monogamous?"

"They live together."

"Are they monogamous?"

"They are on each other's insurance."

"They do all that but still can't stop poking other boys."

"I'm sure there are plenty of black and Latino guys in monogamous relationships."

"Well, I'm tired of needing a special decoder ring to find them. That's why I am embracing my inner 'ho."

"Is this some disgusting new theory you developed during heated yoga class?"

"No." Armando patted his spiked hair, looking into the overhead mirror. "I just realize that I'm too old to pretend I can change the way things are. So I have moved back to Slutsville."

"Moved back." Christopher laughed. "When did you leave?"

"Hey, I was celibate for three years," Armando countered. "And you just changed zip codes a few months ago."

"I left the second I turned thirty and couldn't eat a whole pizza in one sitting anymore. I knew things had changed forever."

"But they haven't really changed." Armando turned to Christopher so he could fully argue his case. "Ten years ago when we were young, thin punks on the scene and everyone wanted us, we thought we would be in relationships 'cause we were too cute to be alone. Well, it's ten years later and the only things that have improved are our credit ratings."

"Some things have changed," Christopher said. "We're older and wiser and don't have to accept the same ol' bullshit when we first went out. We can demand more."

"Come on now, playa." Armando chuckled. "In the end, after the degrees, political associations, houses, and cars, guys still always get around to the same sad question."

"T or B," Christopher sighed.

"Yep." Armando laughed. "And I'm a little too old to show these niggas that I'm an intelligent catch for the long run. You know why? 'Cause there is no long run. We don't even accept being gay—let alone being saddled with some man—for twenty years. It ain't gone happen."

"Well, I ain't losing hope."

"I don't need hope. I have alcohol and a prescription for Xanax."

"Can we change the subject, please?"

"Sure," Armando said. "What's it like living with your pops again?"

"Weird," Christopher said. "It's like I waited for years to get some quality time with him, and now that he is at my place, we see each other maybe a couple times a week."

"Really?" Armando said. "Why don't you schedule some time with him?"

"'Cause it's weird enough as it is getting used to him there.

I don't want to start making demands on him while he's getting his life together."

"Well, tomorrow you two should go out for lunch," Armando said.

"But you just got into town. I'm not abandoning you."

"Tomorrow I'll be recovering from a foreshadowed hangover."

"Well, maybe I should at least make some effort."

"Why have your father in your house and treat him like some roommate? Get to know him."

"I guess you're right," Christopher said. "Damn. Now I could use a drink too."

"Now you're talking."

Christopher slipped the key into the lock and swung the wooden double doors open. He rolled Armando's luggage bag and threw his car keys on the table in the foyer.

"Now, you mean to tell me you got this big-ass house and only you and your daddy live here?"

"We closed the underground railroad last week." Christopher smiled. "You missed out."

"They wouldn't have let my Mexican ass through anyway." Armando walked in a small circle and turned back to Christopher. "Man, I wish I had known your place was this big. I would have insisted we go to the club and pull some tricks back."

"Please, after two glasses of wine we were both nodding off at the dinner table."

"Getting old sucks."

"We're not old, we're in our early thirties."

"If you have to justify that you're not old, you're old, buddy."

"Whatever," Christopher said. "I'm proud of being old and

having a great new job and a nice house. And you should be proud too. You're a professor at Berkeley, for God's sake."

"You know, it's so funny, but when I come in some Saturdays at night, some of the security guards still think I came to clean the floors."

"Yeah, I used to get stopped by security at the bank when I first started. Till I got fed up and gave the director an eight-by-ten of me to stick on the wall. I said, 'Next person who stops me will be picking up his check at the unemployment office.'"

"Hell naw." Armando busted out laughing.

"Hell yeah," Christopher said. "Oh, we should try to keep it down, my dad is probably asleep."

"Sounds like a party in the other room," Armando said, as Barry White blared from the back of the house.

"Yeah, sometimes he watches movies and videos real late and falls asleep in front of the television," Christopher said. "I have to make him go to his room to sleep."

"Wow, how weird. You asked for a father and got a son too."

"Cute," Christopher said. "Let me go check on him and then I'll show you to your room." The two moved down the hall and opened the thick door that led into the den. The place was dark, with only the light from the fireplace warming the edges of the room. Christopher moved around the L-shaped couch and gasped at the sight in front of him. He tried to close his eyes, but the image fused to his skull like a car wreck during rush-hour traffic.

"Damn, baby girl," Alonzo crooned as he gyrated his hips onto a young girl. Her braids fell over a pillow like those of a model in a rap video. Her legs, locked together at the ankles, wrapped around his back. Her nails clenched his shoulder blades.

"Oh my God. Sorry." Christopher ran backward and

tripped over an end table. His torso shot back as his legs flew toward the sky. He landed on his butt. Alonzo ran over to him.

"Son, are you all right?"

"Put some clothes on, man," Christopher yelled. His father, standing in the buff, grabbed a pillow and placed it over his midregion.

"Hey, that is Ralph Lauren . . . which you can now keep."

"I thought you were hanging out with your boy." Alonzo gathered a blanket and placed it over himself. He moved to the woman, who casually lay uncovered on the rug.

"Cover up, girl," Alonzo pleaded with the woman who giggled defiantly, gathered another blanket, and slid it over her curves.

"Uh." Armando laughed. "Chris, can you show me to my room now?"

"Sure." Christopher stood and moved toward the door.

"Sorry, Son." Alonzo followed him.

"No, no." Christopher shook his head. "All naked people stay in this room. I'm closing the door." He slammed the door shut and hurried down the hall.

"Is she going to be coming to my room, or does she just cover the den?"

"I don't want to talk about it."

By morning the memory of his naked father sexing a woman had almost diminished in his head. But the pictures resurfaced as he stepped into the kitchen and spotted his father, thankfully covered in a robe, dancing in front of the stove. He flipped pancakes with a spatula and hummed as he moved from the left burner to the right.

"Hey, Dad." Christopher half smiled as he moved directly to the refrigerator and pulled out the container of orange juice.

"I'm making pancakes for everyone."

"Cool." Christopher grabbed a glass from the cupboard and poured juice inside it.

"Hey, man, listen," Alonzo said. "'Bout last night, I just wanted to say—"

"No, no, Dad. It's cool." Christopher chugged some juice. "This is your house too. I want you to feel comfortable doing what you normally do."

"Well, I never would have invited Camille over if I had known y'all were coming back so early." Alonzo laughed. "Y'all were supposed to be out partying."

"Yeah, well, we discovered we're not that young." Christopher cleared his throat. "Speaking of young . . ."

"She's twenty-seven."

"Twenty-seven." Christopher felt like someone had siphoned the air out of his chest. "Come on, Dad."

"Look. I know I am an old man and she is old enough to be my daughter."

"Granddaughter," Christopher blurted out.

"Watch yourself." Alonzo gave a stone-faced stare that reminded Christopher of the lectures he had received for talking back in class.

"I'm just saying that is a pretty big age gap."

"She makes me happy."

"Christopher pursed his lips in response, just as Armando walked into the room.

"Something smells good." Armando smiled at Christopher and then headed toward Alonzo. "What up, pimp?"

"You got it, playa," Alonzo responded, slapping hands with Armando. "There are pancakes here for everyone."

"Good morning," a soft voice shot from the doorway. Camille sauntered in wearing a silk robe, her hair tied in a ponytail. Her soft dark legs tensed as she moved toward Alonzo and planted a kiss on his cheek. "Hey, baby."

"You make a brotha' switch teams again." Armando

grinned, staring at Camille's backside, until Christopher nudged him in the arm.

"Can you turn off the whore button for like a second?" Christopher asked.

"It's on autopilot. What can I say?"

"All y'all come over here and get you some breakfast, 'cause I'm tired of cooking." Alonzo transported the pan from the stove to the kitchen table and disseminated food to the threesome who gathered around the table.

"Christopher, Armando, this is Camille." Alonzo smiled. "Camille, this is my son, Christopher, and his best friend, Armando." They all exchanged handshakes and grins and everyone began eating in silence.

Armando leaned over to Christopher and whispered, "Should we be concerned that your father is the only one getting some ass at this table?"

"I don't want to talk about it." Christopher shook his head. "I don't want to talk about it."

Chapter XXVIII

The cup of soda slammed down on the counter so hard, the lid split, sending a swig of Coke flying over the side.

"Sorry." Maria smiled and wiped off the spilled contents with the rag she kept tucked under her belt. She replaced the soda and handed it to a woman, who snarled as she snatched her Value Meal and walked out of the restaurant. Maria rolled her eyes and rushed through the last five people in her line. She turned the key on her register and then called to her manager.

"Pam," Maria yelled to the back. "Pam, I gotta go." Pam meandered to the front, a handful of fries in her chubby hands.

"Did you clean the bathrooms?" Pam's voice was curt as she stuffed the whole batch of fries in her mouth.

"Yep," Maria said as she released her hair from its ponytail. "Everything is done."

"Did you clean your station?"

"Did it an hour ago." Maria smiled.

"That was an hour ago. I need it done before you leave."

"Pam, no one even goes near that area." Maria's smile fell as she battled to keep her temper in check.

"Station five is your job." Pam dipped her finger in Maria's direction, and then readjusted her body so that her arms crossed over her ample chest.

"I know it's my station and I cleaned it." Maria caught her rising tone and forced herself to smile again. "Look, I have to go see my child. And I can't be late."

"I don't give a damn. You don't leave until your station is clean. You can't have no dirty station. The customers see stuff like that, and they are number one." "A man leaned against the counter as the two conversed. He raised a questioning finger when Pam glanced at him.

"This line is closed," Pam blurted and moved back to Maria.

"I'll clean her station." A young man next to the fry station, whose name Maria couldn't remember, smiled at her as he walked toward Pam. "I'm here till nine so I can do it."

"That is her job, Andre," Pam yelled.

Andre moved over to Pam and started massaging her shoulders.

"Come on, Pam." He winked at Maria. "I got it. Plus, I'll even do your station so you can sit and relax the rest of the night." His fingers worked her shoulders, and Maria watched as Pam almost melted under his care.

Pam stared at Maria. "Tomorrow, you better make sure you do your station."

"Thank you," Maria almost screamed and pressed out of the door. She was in the parking lot unlocking her sister's car when Andre ran up to her.

"Hey, Maria, wait up."

Maria was already in the car, cranking it on. She rolled the window down. "I seriously have to go, Andre."

"You owe me."

"I really do appreciate what you did." Maria smiled. "But I have some place to be."

"I know. I just wanted to give you this." He passed her a folded napkin. She opened it and found a series of numbers and a smiley face.

"Uh . . ." Speechless, Maria looked into Andre's chestnut-brown eyes. His dark skin almost shimmered under the light-posts overhead. "Thank you, but I don't date anymore."

"Well, keep it as a souvenir," Andre said. "It will be worth a lot of money when I blow up."

"Blow up?"

"I'm a rapper," Andre said. "Call me sometime and I'll spit a few rhymes at you, 'cause my heart is true, like a different kinda blue, 'cause I can't be with you, start something new, maybe find some new taboos."

Maria giggled, and then said, "Needs a little work." She rolled up her window and sped off. She crumpled up the napkin but decided to put it in the glove compartment.

"Before you go in there, we have to talk for a second," Adrienne said to Maria in the waiting room of Fulton County's Foster Care Office.

"About?" Maria had gotten used to disappointment this year, so she was careful not to get her hopes up.

"Your sister."

"Are they finally going to let Q stay with her until I get my own place?"

"Afraid not." Adrienne shook her head. "Your sister has a marijuana charge."

"That was not for selling. It was for possession and that was like five years ago."

"I know it sounds lame, but the courts interpret that as her being a bad fit for your child."

"Shit." Maria slapped her hand against the wall. She pulled back her palm, red from the throbbing pain.

"Don't lose hope yet." Adrienne smiled but Maria turned away.

"Hope left my house years ago," Maria bawled. "We're talking about snuffing out my prayers."

"I do have some good news."

"Please, anything."

"I know of an apartment that is available."

"I can't afford an apartment right now. You know that."

"I know the owners and they are real understanding of your situation."

"Really? You told them about me?" Maria perked up a bit.

"They is me." Adrienne smiled.

Maria gave a puzzled stare. "How?"

"Oscar has decided to go back to school, so we're in need of all the spare cash we can muster. So he converted the garage into a studio apartment. You'd have your own address and parking."

"And your husband is cool with this?" Maria smirked. "I didn't get the feeling he was too cool with me or Damon."

"He wasn't," Adrienne admitted. "But he really has been going through some changes, trying to figure out who he is and what he is here for, and it was actually his idea."

"Seriously?"

"He even plans to visit Damon in prison."

"Oh."

"Sorry. Sore subject."

"No, it's just weird to talk about him."

"Do you miss him?"

"Huh?" Maria froze. She was not prepared for the emotions that welled inside her from the question.

"Girl, it's me. You can be honest."

"I miss the idea of him. You know, holding me, kissing me, making me feel safe and secure. But the reality is he rarely made me feel safe, happy, or secure."

"I got ya."

"Whatever." Maria forced herself not to obsess over Damon. "This apartment idea sounds real cool. Thanks."

"I'll be happy when you get Q back." Adrienne sighed while she fixed her hair in the large mirror flanking the west wall of the room.

"Speaking of . . ."

"Yeah, let's go see your boy." Adrienne prompted Maria to do a little dance and they both giggled. They moved through the visiting room door and walked inside.

Q was already sitting inside. He was busy scribbling in a coloring book with a blue crayon. Maria covered her mouth with her hands, then, bracing herself, moved forward. She got a few paces when the light shifted and she saw the black mark that circled Q's eye.

"Oh my God." Maria ran to him. "Baby, what happened?" She gripped him in her arms, and Q patted her back as she cried.

"It's okay, Mama," Q said, weaseling out of her embrace and continuing with his drawing.

"Who did this to your eye?"

"Floyd." Q continued his sketches, until Maria politely slipped the crayon from his fingers. "He was saying that Daddy was going to jail forever and that he'd forget about me. So I hit him and then he hit me. And then I got this." He pointed to his eye.

"Adrienne," Maria yelled. "Is this supposed to be better for him? Getting into fights, black eyes? What's next?"

"I'll talk to the coordinator here and see what happened," Adrienne said. "But that's not really important right now." She nodded her head toward Q.

Maria forced her mind to digress. "So other than that, is everything okay?" she clipped her tone so it sounded flat and monotone.

"It's all right." Q finally turned to her. He looked a little thinner, but no worse for the wear. "We get to watch Spongebob before we go to bed, and I get my own room."

"Really?"

"Yeah, the one kid I was supposed to stay with got adopted."

"Wow."

"Mama?" Q asked. "Are you going to give me away for adoption?"

"No, sweetie. Of course not."

"If I promise to be good can I come back home?" His eyes were tearing, and Maria knew she would always remember this very second as the moment when she physically felt her heart break. The churning in her stomach was so severe, she knew she would vomit. Her head throbbed in sync with her rising heart rate. She wanted to snatch him and walk right out of this place, this mess, this life she had unwittingly dragged him into. But she had to ride it out. She held him in her arms and chose her words carefully.

"Q, the reason you are here is because me and your father made a lot of mistakes. And we are trying to make them right."

"Is that why Daddy is in jail?"

"Yes, and that is why you and I have to be apart for a while. I have to prove to the state that I am a good mom who can take of you properly."

"I think you're a good mom."

Maria refused to allow her heart to break twice in one day, so she moved past the comment.

"Thank you, sweetie," she said. "Look, we will be together real soon, but until then you have to promise me a few things."

"Sure."

"One, no more fights. You have to be good in here." Q nodded and she continued. "Two, you have to understand that me and your daddy will always love you no matter what. Do you believe that?"

"Yes."

"Finally, I need you to give me a great big smile before I leave so I can remember it while I'm gone."

Q grinned and showed a toothless smile. He had lost his two front teeth, and she hadn't even been there to tuck them under his pillow at night. That was the last straw. She wanted her son back now. And she was going to do everything in her power to get him.

"You be a little man in here, and I promise I will come get you soon." They hugged for so long, Maria halfway convinced herself she had successfully meshed him into her skin. But she knew better. She pulled away just as a young man in a tie came out of a back door.

"I'm sorry, but we have to get Q back," he said. Maria rose to her feet and blew her son a kiss. Then she walked back to Adrienne, who was waiting with open arms.

"He's coming home soon, Maria," Adrienne said. "You have to believe that."

"I believe I have totally ruined my son's life," Maria said. "Maybe some nice parents should adopt him and give him a better one."

"Maria, listen to me." Adrienne and Maria walked toward the exit. "There are some children I've dealt with who, to be honest, need a different set of parents. They need a different life because their parents would do nothing but bring them pain and suffering. I have seen it time and time again. You and Damon have made some huge mistakes, and Q is suffering. But I know in my heart that Q needs you in his life, more now than ever. And if you give up now, then I am afraid for his future. This is not the time for self-pity. It's time to be Q's mother, the person I know you are."

Maria wanted to blow Adrienne off, smoke a joint, and forget her life, but she knew her friend was right. The only person Q had right now was her. She had to fight to save him. If it meant starting over, or flipping burgers, or being insulted by fat managers, so be it. The least she could do for her son was give him a chance. She swallowed the pity and pain that bubbled in her throat and walked out of the building, determined to fight for her child.

Chapter XXIX

Oscar slid his gun and badge onto his captain's desk. He dropped his final evaluation and exit interview forms next to them. He pumped fists with his captain and left his office, stopping off at his desk to pick up his box of possessions. A couple of framed pictures of the wife and kids, a few medals and certificates of service, and a good-bye card with the word *quitter* emblazoned on top. Ten years of service stuffed in a cardboard box.

"We're gonna miss you, Parks." Freddie, the pimply-faced officer who shared his desk, patted Oscar's back and shook his hand. "But you left with a bang, getting the collar on that piece of shit who robbed the bank."

"Yeah." Oscar smiled and withdrew his hand. "That's the problem. I thought he was a piece a shit. But he is just another guy caught up on the wrong road."

"Are you kidding me?" Freddie squinted an eye in Oscar's direction. "That dude almost killed two people and Lord knows who else he would have killed if you hadn't have stopped him."

"I wonder what he would have done if I were there a little earlier," Oscar said.

"I don't get it." Freddie shrugged his shoulders, and Oscar

just grinned and grabbed his box. He had no need to explain his new mind shift or his new purpose. He just walked out the door.

He walked outside and spotted his SUV shaking four parking spaces away. The kids jumped from the front seat to the back as the radio blasted so loudly he could hear every word. Usher's *Confessions Part II* thumped across the parking lot. Oscar ran behind a parked car and approached his SUV from the back. He could hear them giggling from outside the vehicle. He flipped the SUV trunk up so fast the kids were still singing the chorus and dancing around. He threw the box in the car and let the weight shift their attention to behind them.

Tiffany snapped her fingers and sang into her McDonald's shake. Tre bobbed his head to the rhythm section, while Joy did a sad interpretation of the Harlem shake in the backseat. Terrence sat quietly engrossed in a Harry Potter book. When they caught a glimpse of their father they all screamed in unison.

"Shaddup." Oscar beamed. "I caught you. Your mother is gonna love it when I tell her how y'all were showing out in public."

Tiffany, already the litigator for the children, spoke up. "Daddy, you don't have to tell Mommy. We were just practicing our songs for choir."

"Do you sing Usher in the choir?"

"We were just practicing with him." Tiffany held the word "practice" on her lips, as if her case had already been proven.

"Um-hmm." Oscar closed the trunk and walked over to the driver's seat. He opened the door and scooted Tiffany to the passenger seat. "Whatever. I know not to buy y'all any type of sugar before dinner."

"Hey, Daddy, why did you retire from the police?" Tre asked from the backseat.

"Because I want to go back to school and be a lawyer like your mommy," Oscar said.

"Why do you want to copy Mommy?" Tre interjected.

"He's not copying, silly," Tiffany yelled. "Mommy just went to school first, right, Daddy?"

"Yep," Oscar said. "But I may be copying your mom a little." He winked at Joy as he navigated out of the parking space and out to the street.

"You don't like being a police officer no more?" Tre asked. He had moved up between the front seats and leaned on his father's arm, which rested on the middle cushion.

"I loved being a police officer. But I am trying to help people in a different way."

"Can I still be a policeman when I grow up?"

"Buddy, you can be anything you want to be."

"I want to be a dancer and a singer," Joy yelled from the back.

"I am going to be a lawyer like Mommy and Daddy," Tiffany proclaimed, as if God himself had whispered it in her ear.

"What about you, sport?" Oscar looked back at Terrance, who turned another page in his book. "You already know what you want to be when you grow up?"

"I either want to be Wolverine or Colossus from the X-Men."

Tiffany burst out laughing. "You can't be a superhero. That's not a real job."

"My regular job will be as an archaeologist. I will just be a superhero at night."

Tiffany rolled her eyes and ignored him. Oscar suspected she clammed up so quickly because she didn't know what an archaeologist was.

"Son, I truly believe that if you do whatever you can to help other people you are a superhero."

"That makes you a superhero, Daddy." Tre laughed.

"I could be, huh?"

"Not the way you smack at the table," Tiffany whispered out the window.

"You gone be my first supervillain if you keep it up."

"Get her, Daddy," Tre chimed in, while Terrence tried to hit Tiffany with his book.

"Hey, X-man, let me handle this one." Oscar shot an arm in Tiffany's direction, tickling her side as she jumped in her seat.

"Stop, Daddy," she screamed as her siblings fell out. "Stop being so immature." She tried not to laugh, but succumbed to the torture. They laughed all the way home. When they reached the house, Adrienne ran out to greet them. She waved them down as they pulled in to the driveway.

"Hey, Mommy," everyone screamed as they climbed out of the car and moved toward the door. Adrienne grabbed Tiffany and whispered something in her ear. Tiffany smiled at her mother, and then followed the other children inside.

"Do you want to hear some good news?" Adrienne asked Oscar.

"Of course I do." He moved up to her and planted a soft kiss on her waiting lips.

She whipped out an envelope from behind her back. "Emory."

"Emory what?"

"You got into Emory."

"Impossible. I never applied to Emory."

"Yeah, I know." She smiled. "But your controlling wife filled out your application 'cause I know that's the school you really want to go to."

"I thought we agreed on Georgia State 'cause of the cost and 'cause we are already paying off the ninety thousand from your education."

"I know that, but you wanted to go there before I did, and look what else I have." She pulled another piece of paper out of the envelope. "You got scholarship money."

"Seriously?"

"It doesn't pay everything, but it will put a dent in the tuition."

Oscar looked at the paper and saw the amount listed at the bottom. His face lit up like a bald bulb in a dark room.

"Yeah, it will!" He grabbed Adrienne and hugged her tightly. "Wow. I am really going to Emory."

"Yes, sir, you are."

"We have to celebrate."

"I'm way ahead of you." She smirked. "I couldn't find a babysitter so we have to improvise. Tiffany is in charge of the kids. They have pizza already ready, it just needs to warm in the microwave. They have movies that will keep them occupied for hours."

"Wow, you got it all planned." He smiled. "But you know how hard it is trying to get wild in the house. They always mess things up."

"We won't be in the house." She turned, her hand gliding toward the driveway and the garage in the back.

"Ooh, you are good."

"That's why they pay me the big bucks."

"Guess so."

"So you go make sure the kids are okay and then meet me in the studio in ten minutes."

"Cool." He kissed her lips one last time, and strained to break the embrace. He ran inside and slammed the door. He darted into the family room, where the children were eerily settled and quiet.

"Everything good in here?"

"We're fine, Daddy." Tiffany beamed from behind the couch. "Mommy put me in charge."

"And you're doing a great job."

"So you know we'll be right in the back and if you need anything—"

"Daddy, we are fine."

"Lock all the doors and don't answer the phone."

"Daddy!" Tiffany yelled. "Go!" She pushed her hands out in a sweeping motion, shooing him away.

"All right," he said, leaping out the back door and walking the fifty feet to the garage-turned-studio. He was proud of the renovations he'd made to the place. The garage door was replaced by a series of windowpanes surrounded by deeply ridged wood. He'd had an entire bathroom and minikitchen installed. Though it had been empty the last time he went inside, he could see the windows held tan drapes that blocked the last remnants of light from the falling sun. When he entered the small wooden door he was amazed at the inside.

Soft earth-toned furniture filled the space he'd left empty. A plush couch centered the room, while a dark mahogany coffee table held up a centerpiece of flickering candles. Candles also stood guard on a small mantel anchoring a wall. He was thoroughly impressed with the room.

"I'm upstairs," Adrienne called out from above him. He climbed the creaking steps that led to the bedroom and bathroom. At first glance the place looked deserted, save for a small bed placed in the corner. Pillows of all shapes and sizes floated atop the all-white comforter. He moved closer and spotted a silhouette behind the opaque shower curtain. He slowly opened it to find his wife barely hidden under a sheet of bubbles.

"Hi." Adrienne smiled, and Oscar felt himself awaken.

"Hey." His fingers clung to the top of the shower curtain.

"You look dirty." She winked, slurring the word dirty like it was unseemly. His clothes flew off and landed in a pile next to the tub. He eased his way into it behind her. She leaned back on his chest. He had forgotten how soft her skin felt on his fingertips. He moved from her shoulders to her arms and then clung to her tightly.

"You don't know how much I love you."

"I can guess." She pushed back on his body and he jumped down below.

"No." He kissed her neck. "You don't understand. I missed you so much. I really missed being with you, touching you, talking with you."

"I know you were going through stuff."

"But I shouldn't have checked out on our marriage. My changes are our changes."

"You're here now."

"Yes, I am."

"And you're definitely paying attention."

"All of me is at attention."

"Then listen to me." She squirmed around to kiss him. "That's enough talk." Their lips fused together as Oscar lifted Adrienne up and carried her to the bed.

When they finished, one of his arms locked around her waist. Her head lay on his other arm. Their legs interlocked like vines.

"I'm going to visit Damon in prison," Oscar said.

"You mentioned that before. That's great, honey."

"I want to help him, at least as much as I can."

"Well, you're letting his child and girlfriend stay in our apartment. I would say that's pretty good so far."

"Yeah, I know, but I wish I could just reach him, ya know. I mean, he was not always crazy." His lips nuzzled the collarbone protruding from the base of Adrienne's neck.

"I'm sure he wasn't."

"I think I owe it to him to give him a second chance," Oscar said.

"I agree, just don't get your hopes too high," Adrienne cautioned. "I know you mean well, but he has to find his own way, like I found mine and you found yours. And it may not be the place you would like him to go."

"Are you saying just butt out of his business?"

"No, sweetie." She turned to him. "I'm saying if you want him to be a man you also have to allow him to make the manly decisions in his life."

"Got ya."

"You know, like I pretend to let you make decisions for us." Adrienne smiled and crashed her head on his shoulder blade.

"Pretend?"

"Yep."

"Well, I'm going to pretend I don't hear you screaming."

"What are you—" Before she could get her bearings, Oscar was on top of her, tickling her sides and feet.

"Stop, stop!" she pleaded. But it was no use—he couldn't hear her.

Chapter XXX

"You know me?" the man asked, without diverting his gaze away from the book planted on his lap.

"Huh," Damon mumbled, masking the flash of embarrassment that turned his face a deep purple.

"You just look like I'm your long-lost daddy or something," he said. "And if that's the case, and it quite possibly could be, all I have to leave you are two pairs of shoes, some good hair, and a history of heart disease."

Damon chuckled at the little man who barely filled out his denim shirt. His legs crossed at the knee, as he lounged against the steel picnic table.

"Nah, man." Damon walked the few paces that distanced him from the man. "You was just so into that book I wanted to find out what it was."

"It's the only book that matters." He held up the tattered black cover, gold letters spelling out HOLY BIBLE in the center.

"Oh," Damon said. "I thought that was a novel or something."

"It's got all the drama you need, trust me." The man re-crossed his legs and settled back on the bench.

"Um, never read it," Damon said.

"I never did either till I got here," the man said. "It's the only book that made me feel like I could have a happy ending."

"I don't get it."

"Maybe you will one day, young buck." The man closed the book and extended his hand. Damon walked over to shake it and grabbed hold. "Xavier Giddings."

"Damon Harvey." He smiled at the old man, staring at the salt-and-pepper bush of hair, either an Afro or a work of abstract art. He hadn't determined yet. Damon's face froze over when he thought of himself aging in prison. His bones thinning out, his skin sagging as his son, his life, the world passing him by.

"So, what you here for?" Xavier asked.

Damon stumbled to find the answer. He wanted to blurt out, "'Cause my stupid girlfriend don't know how to take orders." But that didn't sound right. "Systematic racism" also wouldn't roll off his tongue with the same assurance as it had years earlier.

"I robbed a bank." The truth of the statement rang in the air. "I shot a man and hurt a woman real bad." He was suddenly hit with the horror of his life. A rumble in his stomach pitted against his sides.

"Wow, how long they give you for that?"

"Seven years," Damon mumbled. "Probation after three."

"Wow. You are blessed."

"Blessed?" Damon tilted his head in confusion. Was this old man trying to convince him spending time in this hellhole was a blessing? The stench of unwashed men in the shower made him want to vomit. At night the cells seemed to shrink in front of his very eyes. Not to mention the food, which never had any definable characteristics of meats or vegetables. Where exactly was the blessing?

"Yep," Xavier continued. "I got seventy-five years to go in here."

Damon's eyes widened and fell. He tried to calculate how

old he would be if he had to stay in prison that long. He knew he would be dead.

"Yeah, got here when I was twenty-three." Xavier set his Bible to the side and dug deep in his pockets. He retrieved two pieces of peppermint candy held tight in plastic wrappers. He moved his hand to Damon, keeping his palm down. Damon opened his hand, and Xavier dropped a piece of candy into his hand. Xaxier didn't bother asking whether Damon wanted a piece, and Damon didn't bother declining. He just began untwisting its plastic ends as the man continued.

"Yeah, I was into a lot of dirt. Gambling, mostly, but every now and again I would do some petty robbery just to pull up my change, you dig?" Xavier continued, not waiting for Damon to answer. "Well, I used to be on that heroin and needed fixes almost every day. So I decided to go find me someone to rob to get me some cash. Well, I found this little white boy walking out of his apartment building downtown. He went through an alley to get to the other street and I decided I was gone get him. I jumped up behind him and pulled out a knife. I told him to give me his wallet or I would stab him. You know, this joker jumps on me, starts whipping me real good. And I was so high I could barely feel anything. All I know is he was cussing and yelling something awful. And I knew the police would be round in a minute if I didn't shut him up."

Xavier paused to pull a handkerchief out from his shirt pocket. He dabbed at his eyes, and then continued.

"So I slit his throat."

Damon could feel a tingling sensation growing near his Adam's apple. He desperately wanted to check to see if his neck was still intact. But he knew how insane of a gesture that would be. Instead, he sniffed hard and pulled at the corners of his nose, hoping to alleviate the itch below.

"Well, I ran off with his wallet, which only had sixty dollars in it anyway, and as it turns out that young man was a reporter for what was then the *Atlanta Constitution*. Well, when word got out about him being murdered across the street from the paper, they went on a manhunt looking for me. I was so high I didn't even realize I was wearing the same shirt, with his blood splashed all on it. The jury reached a decision in seventeen minutes. I mean, I went and took a dump, came back, and got a life sentence."

"Damn" was all Damon could muster out of his mouth.

"I would have got the chair if the machine wasn't broken at the time."

"For real?"

"That's my testimony," he said. "The Bible speaks about giving testimony. I only hope it helped you, son."

"I think you're a little late, man, 'cause I'm already here." Damon threw his hands in the air and displayed his surroundings in true spokesmodel fashion. He forced a hollow laugh until Xavier finally stared in Damon's eyes.

"It's never too late, son, never too late." The conviction in his eyes forced Damon to take his statement seriously. He rose to his feet, ready to flee the spiritual cave he had mistakenly wandered into.

"Well, I . . ." Damon started, but Xavier had pulled a small wooden box from his side.

"Ya' play checkers?"

"Not in a while," Damon confessed.

"You'll pick it up again," Xavier said as he opened the box and poured the red and black checker pieces onto the table. He turned the box over to reveal a full checkerboard.

Xavier segregated the checkers by color and placed them on their separate sides. And, within a few matches, Damon did pick it up again.

Damon was ashamed to admit it but, after a few weeks, his moments with Xavier became the high points of his days. After meals and daily chores, there wasn't much to do inside a giant gray square. And though he occasionally hit the weights out of boredom, he never spent too much time outside. He preferred talking and playing checkers with Xavier. Their discussions between moves transcended from casual niceties to in-depth conversations about life. For the first time he felt comfortable talking to an older man. Xavier never scolded him. After Damon always arrived late for their games, one day Xavier waited till he had sat down and got comfortable and then politely packed his things up and stood to leave.

"I thought we were playing checkers," Damon whined.

"We had a scheduled time of one p.m." Xavier pointed to the wall clock. "It's one twenty p.m. Game time is over."

Damon was never late again. He got special joy one day when he arrived on time for a checkers session and found Xavier's spot empty.

He waited for several minutes imagining how he would tease his friend for being so late. But, after thirty minutes, he began to look around. He walked over to Xavier's cell and found it silent and undisturbed. In fact, the bed was still wrangled from the night before. He peeked inside and discovered the checkerboard mounted on a stack of books. A rush of anger flashed through him. He felt his body shake. How could this old man stand him up like that after weeks of playing?

"Fuck him," he said to himself. He walked down the catwalk as his eyes fixed on a group of guards leaning against a rail. He usually avoided all contact with guards, mostly because of his hatred for anyone with a uniform. He knew his feelings would be apparent through his sneer, his mangled mouth and sucked-in teeth. But he braved his doubts and stepped to one of the guards.

"Excuse me." Damon slipped a smile over his scowl and kept his voice in a higher range then normal.

"What?" the guard asked, his smile melting into his on-duty frown.

"Have you seen prisoner Giddings? Xavier Giddings?"

"What was his number?" The guard almost interrupted him.

"I don't know his number."

"Why the hell would I remember any of you miserable cocksuckers' names?" He had turned all the way around and his group had formed a semicircle around Damon.

"I'm sorry. I don't know his number."

"Then get out of my face," the officer said.

Damon knew if the man touched him, he would lunge at him and they would most likely go over the side of the rail. It would be worth it, he thought if he landed on the guard's head.

"Oh, you mean the old guy," another officer standing to Damon's right said. They all nodded and agreed that they knew who Damon was talking about. "Yeah, he's in the intensive care unit. He had a heart attack early this morning."

Damon thought his own heart would stop. He had to pat his chest to make sure he was still breathing. He ran past the guards and headed down the long path to the infirmary.

When he arrived, he saw a nurse standing over a sea of empty beds, their white sheets immaculate and perfectly stretched over the mattresses. He moved to the nurse and asked, "Is Mr. Giddings here?"

Her face immediately sank and she tilted her head and lightly patted her clipboard.

"I'm sorry, sweetie, but Mr. Giddings passed this afternoon. His heart couldn't take the bypass they performed on him."

Damon clutched the corners of a vacated bed so he wouldn't fall.

"Yeah, he was in his sixties and had led kind of a hard life when he was younger. I guess it caught up with him."

If ever there was a moment of clear defeat in his life it

would be this one. He turned, shell-shocked by both the news and his own reaction.

"Oh," she yelled as he slumped out of the room. "Are you Damon?"

"Yeah."

The nurse walked over to a desk and opened the top drawer. She rumpled some papers and then pulled out the leather Bible Xavier had clung to like a sword.

"He said he wanted you to have this." She thrust her hands forward and gave him the book.

He took it, whispered, "Thank you" to the nurse, and dashed out of the reception area.

He ran until he found a quiet space near a common area where no one congregated. His hands felt like they were on fire. The book almost seemed to scorch his skin. He slammed it onto the concrete.

"Why can't I have anybody in my life?" he yelled at the book. He fell to his knees and buckled forward in heaves of tears. He could barely breathe. The list of deserters in his life rolled through his mind like an army of AWOL troops—his father, Oscar, Maria, and now Xavier. He couldn't take the pain anymore. He couldn't fight anymore. Damon grabbed the Bible and cradled it near his tear-soaked chest until the guards found him and took him to his cell.

Chapter XXXI

I fumbled the pencil in my hand, trying desperately not to lose my nerves and walk out of this classroom. But my new editor at *Atlanta Style* magazine would probably strangle me if I chickened out on my first freelance article. Honestly, I don't know how my therapist coerced me into writing again.

"You need a hobby, something constructive to take your mind off all your issues," Dr. Lynn said.

"That's what TIVO is for." I laughed as the doctor pursed her lips.

"How about a sport, like golfing?"

"Boring."

"Do you like to swim?"

"Do you know how long it would take to dry my hair?" I paraded my ponytail in front of her as she rolled her eyes.

"Have you thought of doing any PR again?"

"I am the laughingstock of the entertainment community." I hugged the pillow innocently lying next to me. "I can't even get a reality TV star on my team at this point."

"What about writing something different, like entertainment or news articles?"

I was ready to belt out a "no," but the thought lingered in my head awhile. I had always fantasized about being a struggling freelance journalist like author Jill Nelson, kicking whitey and men's asses all over town. But New York was too dirty for me, and I was not sporting dreadlocks and living in a shack in Harlem to prove some Bohemian lifestyle. I loved my Mercedes, trees, and my kitchen's separation from my bathroom, thank you very much. My doctor's face perked, as she must have noticed me contemplating her idea.

"Surely you must have contacts in that business, since writing is so interconnected."

And as sickeningly accurate as she always was, I happened to have an old soror who worked for *Atlanta Style*, a start-up progressive—read *poor*—newsweekly in town. After a week of procrastination I called my friend and explained my situation.

"Girl, we always need good writers," she squealed. "Hold on. Let me pull up the editor's story list right now." I heard the clicking of fingers on keys and in a flash she was back.

"I have a great story for you," she started. "Do you know Carlos Vega?"

"We're familiar." I smirked through the phone.

"Well, he's starting an after-school reading program for young black and Latino boys. It's the first leg of his nonprofit organization. He even won some type of service award. We would love a story about him and the program."

"Wow, it's just that easy," I uttered in shock. "I always thought journalists were these handpicked intellectual dynamos who never watched television and scoured the streets for articles."

"Girl, if you can type we can use you." She laughed.

I laughed too, wrote down the school's address, and now, a week later, was soothing my shaking legs under a small wooden desk. I studied the clump of awards that lined the wall next to me. To ease my nerves, I rose to my feet and paced around the room. My hands fondled the knickknacks that made a home on a teacher's desk. A picture frame rested near the chair. I picked it up and stared at the pretty woman who sat holding her beautiful son in her arms. Their bright smiles were identical.

"Sorry I'm late." A baritone voice soothed the room.

I looked over and stared at Carlos. He had to be one of the most beautiful men I had ever seen.

"Oh, no problem." I quickly placed the photo down. I felt a little guilty for fondling it. I walked toward the man, who offered his hand.

"Long time." Carlos smiled and leaned in toward me. His sea of white teeth flashed between two perfectly sculpted lips.

I smiled back, praying there was no lipstick smudging my teeth.

I entered his arms and he squeezed me with the sensual electricity of an old lover. "How are you?" he asked.

"I'm doing okay."

"I was worried about you."

"Me too." I beamed. "But I think I'm on the road to recovery."

"That's good to hear." Carlos giggled and then released his hold on me. "Sorry."

Damn, I cried to myself. I was hoping we would carry on the entire interview in a bear hug. "No problem," I said. I pulled at my clothes and attempted to regain my sense of perspective. "Well, you have been pretty busy. What is with the nonprofit organization?"

"Yeah." Carlos blushed and managed to look even sexier. This was not going to end well. "It's called Write for Life and it's a reading and writing program to help at-risk minority boys with their English skills. But it's also a chance to help them see another career path beyond pimping, music, or sports."

"Wow. That is weird coming from a musician."

"Yeah, well, I always wanted to be a musician, but I never wanted to be a star. It just happened. I went to school and got a master's in composition from Roosevelt University."

"Stop playing." It is amazing how you peg a person. Here I thought Carlos was some pretty-boy crooner, and here he was deeper than the Indian Ocean. Suddenly I was very conscious about how shallow I was. I had no charity; the only organization I gave to regularly was American Express. And that was because they let me buy dresses and shoes.

"Yeah, even if I was not a star I would have a job somewhere in music. And that is all I'm trying to do. Offer these kids options in life."

"Wow. I'm speechless."

"Please don't be. I love hearing you talk." The corners of his mouth curled up and I busted out laughing. Were we flirting with each other or was this just more PR smoke between two old pros?

"Well, I'm glad I clicked on the tape recorder, 'cause I didn't write down anything."

"Tell you what. If you allow me to take you out to dinner, I'll give you an exclusive on my organization and all my altruistic endeavors."

"Wow, a girl can never pass up anything exclusive."

"I am definitely an exclusive kind of guy."

"Well, I better go." I knew I had to run before I completely dissolved in this man's arms. "I have to hurry home, do more research, and be ready with more questions."

He grabbed my hand again, this time with both hands, and moved his lips to my ears. "Let me give you one more scoop— I'm single."

My mouth dropped as he kissed my cheek so lightly I could barely feel his soft thick lips. But I could. Damn it.

"Can't wait to see you again." He walked toward the door and turned around. "Don't keep us waiting."

He walked out the door, and I scrambled to the desk before I collapsed. I fumbled to turn off my tape recorder. I didn't want any evidence when I let out the loudest scream I could muster.

* * *

I kept the smile on my face all the way until I pulled into the driveway of my rented condo in Dunwoody. But the sight of my husband's BMW parked in front of my house forced the muscles in my face to recoil and curl. I hopped out of my car and made a beeline toward the door. I had made it just a few feet when his car door swung open.

"I'm sorry for coming over like this, but you won't return my phone calls."

"There is nothing to say." I kept walking until he stepped in my path.

"Come on, J.C. We really do need to talk."

"About what?"

"About you, me, us, our marriage." David put his hands out like he was going to touch me, then quickly retreated.

"I told you that right now I can't think about that."

"Well, I think about it all the time." His voice trembled. "I think about us all the time."

"Did I cross your mind when Nicole was giving you head?"

"I said I was sorry," David pleaded. "I betrayed you and hurt you, I know that. But we're married. Hell, I have loved you since college. Doesn't that count for anything?"

"Apparently it didn't."

"Look, we have been through a rough year with the accident and the baby, and I made a huge mistake in my handling of it. But you just closed me off, and I kind of needed someone to help me forget about it all."

"That's the point—you did forget about it all!" I forced myself not to yell. "You forgot about me."

"Can't we just start over? Go back to where we used to be?"

I looked into his eyes, and saw the genuine sorrow and regret behind his pupils. Tears lined the corners of his eyes and quietly flowed down his cheeks like a leaky faucet.

"The problem is that no matter how badly I want to go back

to before that moment when I lost everything, I can't. We are stuck where we are and have to deal with it. I didn't just lose my baby, I lost myself and everything I thought I was. And I don't know how to get myself back. Or even if I want to get me back."

"So you want a divorce?"

"I want some time to think."

"We have been separated for months," he said. "I sit alone in that house and pray every night you'll come back. I miss your laugh and your smile. And your touch, and . . . you. I miss you."

He grabbed me and held me close to him. I could feel his heart pounding as he held me in his arms. He didn't want to let go. For a second I didn't want to let go. But I refused to let loneliness force me to make decisions I wasn't ready to make.

"I miss you too," I said. "But more importantly, I miss me. And until I find her again, I really don't want to see you again." I kissed his cheek and then moved around him to enter my house. When I got inside I peeked through the front curtains to see David sitting in his car balling like a baby. I wanted to run to him, but my legs stiffened like a marble statue. He stayed in the driveway till the sun fell behind his car. Finally he crept out of the driveway and drove down the road.

Chapter XXXII

The kids funneled through the doors like water at high tide. Christopher could barely set the spare chairs down around the circular tables before the boys ran, laughing, yelling, and teasing, up to him.

"Hey, Mr. Roberts," they hollered, some hugging him tightly, others slapping his hand, some just waving. They clamored around the tables. The buzz of noise shook the building. Christopher counted thirty children from his youth organization already there. But he prayed there would be more.

"I could use some help with the banner." He pointed to the huge piece of plastic rolled up in a corner. Two boys immediately ran over and pulled it out. Some others grabbed chairs and hopped on them. They hung the banner so the words read sharp and clear: ANNUAL SELF-RESPECT CONFERENCE!

Christopher stood back to admire the sign. Another group of children walked inside and a short woman with a cane waddled inside.

"Mr. Roberts." She moved toward him. "I'm Razell from Bethel Boys Home."

"Hey. How are you?" Christopher replied.

"Pleasure to meet you." She shook his hand. "I'm so happy

you are holding this conference. These boys need to see men like you up there teaching them how to be men."

"Well, thank you." Christopher blushed a bit. "But all I did was present the idea. The kids did all the work, even inviting your group here."

"I'm just glad someone is doing something to help these boys."

Christopher smiled and led her to a padded seat in the back. Through the picture frame window he could see another group of kids heading toward the door. But his eyes focused on the man in the back of the pack who directed them.

He was tall with locks that flowed past his muscular shoulders. He wore a formfitting T-shirt and jeans wrapped around athletic legs. The kids ran through the door.

"Hey, what did I tell you about running?" the man barked. The boys abruptly stopped like a scattered line of infantrymen. "Walk to your seats."

The boys obeyed, slowing their pace to a casual stroll.

"Sorry," the man said as he approached Christopher. "You know how kids get so excited."

"They're the same way here." Christopher looked back on his boys, who were already mingling with the other groups of children. It took only seconds before the three segregated groups meshed into a blob of teenage testosterone.

"You have to be Mr. Ellis." Christopher gripped the man's soft but brawny hand.

"Tim." The man held Christopher's hand. "You can call me Tim."

"Cool, Tim," Christopher said. "I'm Christopher."

"Yeah, we talked on the phone. Thanks again for inviting the kids to this. A self-respect conference, what a cool idea."

"We just thought it was necessary to address what respecting ourselves was all about."

"Well, you already have my respect," Tim said as he winked. "I'm gonna go check on the kids to make sure they haven't set the place on fire." They exchanged low snickers and moved to opposite sides of the room.

"Aaron," Christopher called to a lanky boy with a hood hanging over his head. "Since you are the facilitator for this conference, why don't you start it off for us?" Christopher pointed to his own head and made a jerking motion in the air. Aaron lifted the hood off his head and stood up.

As Aaron led the meeting, Christopher slipped back into his office and pulled his cell phone from the drawer. He frantically dialed Armando's number.

"What up, nigga?" Armando yelled through the phone.

"Is it respectful to lust after another youth director during Self-Respect Week?"

"Are clothes on or off?"

"What the hell? This is a kids conference . . . On."

"Did you French-kiss him in front of the kids?"

"Why do I call you?"

Armando chuckled. "Because I'm smart, or at least my degrees fool others into thinking that. And you would have to be a fool to believe being attracted to a good-looking guy, even at a self-respect conference, is disrespectful."

"I just was sort of staring at him in some kind of trance and he held our handshake."

"Strike one."

"And he winked at me."

"Strike two."

"Excuse me," a voice beckoned from the door. Tim was leaning against the frame.

"Hey."

"I forgot some statistics on teens and gun violence and wanted to pull them off the Web real quick."

"Is that him?" Armando yelled through the phone. "Erroneous diversion to get you alone. Strike three—he's gay."

"Gotta go," Christopher whispered through the phone.

"Details, man," Armando yelled. "You owe me details."

"Here." Christopher turned his laptop around so it was facing Tim. "You can use this."

"Thanks." Tim smiled and sat in front of Christopher's desk. "So, how long have you been the director here?"

"Only about six months," Christopher said. "I used to be in banking."

"Banking." Tim's lips shaped a sly grin. "What did you do?"

"I was a VP."

"Are you for real?" Tim laughed.

"Yeah." Christopher felt that nervous tinge he got whenever he talked about his jobs to guys. They either felt compelled to one-up him or belittle his accomplishments. He braced himself for both.

"Well, God must have put you here."

"Why do you say that?"

"Usually the more money we get the more we stay away from social service jobs."

"Well, I can't say I was compelled to work here," Christopher admitted. "I lost my job and then this just kind of fell into my lap."

"Isn't this program run by Dell Street Missionary Baptist Church?"

"Yeah," Christopher confirmed.

"God."

"Maybe you're right." Christopher had played with the idea of divine intervention when he first received the job. He certainly had no training or background in social services or urban policies. He was just desperate for a change. But listening to Tim he felt the dual blade of gratitude and guilt that he had accepted the job but not really learned more about the church that paid his checks.

"Printer."

"Huh?" Christopher fell back into the conversation.

"Where's your printer?"

"Oh, it's behind you in the corner." Christopher moved to

the back of the office and pulled the papers from the feeder. He turned around to walk back and slammed right into Tim. For a split second their bodies stuck. Tim placed a hand on Christopher's waist to steady his balance. Christopher braced his tennis shoe against Tim's Timberland. It felt like some weird slow dance. They both backed up slowly.

"Sorry about that," Christopher said, blushing.

"You never need to apologize for touching me." The smirk on Tim's face was so sexy, Christopher prayed for an interruption. He was relieved when Aaron barreled through the door.

"Mr. Roberts," he yelled. "We need you in here."

"You're pretty lucky." Tim moved toward the door.

"Why?"

"That probably would have ended in a compromising position."

"Aren't all positions compromising in some way or another?"

"Well, I have a pretty safe one." Tim turned back and grabbed the phone out of Christopher's shirt pocket. He punched on the number keys until he smiled with satisfaction.

"Here," he said. "My number is programmed into your phone."

"Thanks."

"Make sure you call me."

"I will."

"So, now I think having dealt with that issue, we can go back to our jobs."

"Oh yeah, our jobs." They both laughed and Christopher entered the room, ready to take on the world.

"Mr. Roberts," Aaron said. "We were talking about violence and how guns kill. And we wanted to know about when you were shot."

Christopher stood frozen. He rarely thought of that moment. He didn't recall telling his students about it, either. But here he was in the middle of it.

"What do you want to know?" He eased his way to the center of the room.

"Do it hurt?" one voice from the crowd asked.

"Yes, very much."

"Were you in the hospital?"

"For a couple of weeks."

"So what was you thinking when you got hit?"

"I thought . . . I'm going to die . . . alone. And I felt scared. All I could feel was warm blood all around me, and I was getting dizzy. There wasn't so much pain as there was this numbing feeling across my body. I watched the man who shot me run away. He was probably just a few years older than all of you. The officer on duty said some words to me. But I couldn't hear them. I only thought of being left out on the street alone to die. Who was going to take care of my mother? Would I ever talk to my father? Where would I go if I died? All my coworkers were around me, holding my hands, praying over me. But I felt like it was just me on the sidewalk."

"I don't know why I survived," Christopher continued. "I just know I am pretty lucky. But the fact of the matter is I could just as easily have died out there. And if you feel like you need to have a gun, understand that you could end up in the same place I did. But you may not have the chance to speak about it." A sudden rush of emotion caused Christopher to start hyperventilating.

"Excuse me," Christopher said and bolted toward the door. He leaned over the windowsill and braced his arms on his knees, taking in thick gulps of air.

"Wow. That was a pretty deep story." Tim leaned on the plate-glass window beside him. "Was that the first time you told anyone that?"

"Yeah, pretty much."

"Well, if it's any consolation, those kids are in utter terror of getting shot." They both laughed.

"Good."

"Well, this is no fair."

"What?"

"I was already impressed by you for so many other reasons and now you were shot, too. I just have a lot of catching up to do."

"Well, I didn't plan to get shot."

"But you still survived it."

"I had to."

"Why?"

"I didn't feel like I was done here yet."

"Well, I look forward to seeing what else you have to do." They smiled. "Are you feeling better?" Tim asked.

"Yeah," Christopher said. "I'm all right."

Suddenly Christopher's phone vibrated in his shirt pocket. He pulled it out and looked at the LCD screen. *Unknown Caller.* He clicked the TALK button.

"Christopher," a female voice said on the phone. "Is this Christopher?" Each vowel shook as the woman spoke.

"Who is this?"

"It's Camille, your father's friend."

"Oh, hey, Camille. Look, I'm a little—"

"It's your dad," she yelled. "I think he is having a heart attack."

"Where are you?" Christopher tried to remain calm.

"We're at my house."

"Can you move him?"

"Yeah, he's just sweating a lot and says his heart hurts."

"Where's the nearest hospital?"

"Piedmont, I think."

"Okay, if you can get him into your car, drive him over there. If not, call an ambulance. I'll meet you there in a few minutes. Call me if anything changes." He clicked the phone shut. "I need my keys."

"What is it?"

"My dad may be having a heart attack." Christopher searched his pockets till he found them in his back pocket.

"I can wrap this up in here."

"Would you?"

"Yeah, man, no worries." Tim patted his back. "Just go."

"Thank you," Christopher said and ran to his car. He sped down the freeway, praying his father would be all right.

Chapter XXXIII

"Just put it at the end of the desk," Maria directed Andre, who lugged the computer monitor down the tiny hall corridor into the cramped bedroom in the back. He set the monitor on the tattered desk in the corner of the room.

"Perfect," Maria mumbled to herself. She stood back and looked at the room that would be her son's. It was finally the way she imagined it should be. The small twin bed was adorned in a SpongeBob comforter. Posters of Ciara and Michael Vick were framed and faced each other on opposing walls of the room. Specks of light through the venetian blinds warmed the butterscotch-colored walls.

"It looks great, baby." Andre kissed Maria's cheek. "He'll love it."

"I hope so." She rubbed her hand on the birch dresser that flanked the bed. "Oh, forgot something." She ran into the studio area that served as her bedroom and living room. She dug through boxes hidden behind the couch till she uncovered the one labeled PHOTOS. She broke the taped seal and shuffled through the batch of memories. Her hands stopped on the picture she had vowed would stay in the box.

She caressed the photo of the three of them. Damon sat in the center of a bench. Q sat on his lap. Maria leaned back on

Damon's shoulder. It was summer at Six Flags Amusement Park. She hated the photo because her hair had been in its Halle Berry stage. The back was cropped so low it looked like a fade. Colored bangs fell just over her forehead. It had looked cute the first day she got it styled. But the merciless humidity and a barrage of wet rides had left it poofy, like a badly beaten Afro. By the end of the day she was wearing Damon's Braves baseball hat.

Damon had held her hand that whole day, something he hardly ever did. He would kiss her neck while they waited in line. He patted her butt while they watched some local band playing on the main stage. And she could hardly remember a time when Q was so happy.

"Daddy, let's go through the haunted house," Q pleaded, tugging at his father's arm. Damon just smiled, kissed her lips, and then said, "I'll be right back." Damon and Q ran off into the mouth of a ghoul, which served as the entrance to the haunted house. For a moment she feared some demon would devour them and she would never see them again. But after a few moments they rolled out of the exit laughing, Q riding on his father's back.

"Mama, it was so scary," Q said.

"Yeah," Damon said. "I was trying to front, but a brotha was a little scared." That was when a photographer asked to take their picture. She just knew Damon would curse the man out, since he was prone to random eruptions of anger. But he smiled and asked, "Where do you want us to be?" The man pointed to a bench in front of a batch of oaks, shading the trio from the sun.

The man passed them a ticket to collect their photo at the end of the day. After a litany of scary-named rides like Thunder River and Free Fall, Maria had all but forgotten the photo as they walked the long road to the parking lot.

"We forgot our portrait." Damon halted right in the middle of the road. Q was already asleep in his arms. Maria, bogged down with stuffed animals and bags, dismissed the idea of going back with her hand.

"You stay here, baby." Damon kissed her forehead. "I'll go grab it." He walked off with Q still in tow and returned ten minutes later with the photo in his hand.

"Tell me this wasn't worth waiting for."

Indeed, looking at the threesome, with a rare moment of unified joy displayed on their faces, it was worth the wait.

"You all right, baby?" Andre asked, peering around the corner of the hall.

"Yeah," Maria shouted back, arriving back to reality. "I'm just looking for a frame for this picture." She wrestled through another box and found a small silver frame. She slid the photo through the back opening and walked toward the bedroom. She placed the frame on the dresser. "Now, that is perfect."

"Great picture." Andre wrapped his arms around her. "Q will love it."

"I hope so," Maria said. "Just because I ain't dealing with Damon doesn't mean Q has to forget him."

"He seems like a great kid."

"Thanks, he is."

"So when will I get a chance to meet him?"

Maria let out a slow sigh. "Andre, you know I like you. But I have been working for almost a year to get my baby back. And that is my number-one goal."

"I know that." Andre eased back to face her. "I just want a chance to be in both your lives."

"I know." Maria hesitated and then continued. "But right now I need to make him my priority. And I don't want another man making me lose sight of what's important."

"So now I'm just another man."

"You know what I mean."

"We have been dating for eight months," Andre said. "Haven't I proven that I'm not him?" He pointed to Damon's likeness in the photo. "I never beat you, have never yelled at you. All I have tried to do is be your man."

"I know that and I appreciate it," Maria said. "But I have been away from Q for almost year. Do you have any idea what it's like to wake up and want to hold your child, knowing you can't because of mistakes you made? I can't let that happen again. I won't."

"Now I'm a mistake."

"I need time alone with Q before I introduce another man into his life."

"Wait," he said. "Are you breaking up with me?"

"I just need some time with my son, alone."

Andre sat on the bed and looked to the floor. "That is gonna be a problem, Maria. 'Cause . . . I think I love you."

Maria turned to face Andre, who now looked in her eyes. "I think I love you too, but it doesn't matter."

"Doesn't matter?"

"Look, don't ask me to choose between a man and my child."

"I know who comes first in your life." Andre grabbed her legs and pulled her close. "I'm just asking you to make room for me in there somewhere." He placed his hand on her chest.

"If you love me you will give me the time I need."

"Man, I knew you were going to be a tough case when I met you." Andre laughed. He rose to his feet. "Okay, I have to finish up my album anyway. I didn't want to mention it before, but Sony is coming to the studio this week to hear me spit."

"Seriously?"

"Yeah."

"Andre, that's great." She hugged him.

"I'm gonna go handle my business and make my cheese. But I am not giving up on you. Don't shut me out, Maria."

"I'll try," she said.

"That's all I ask." He kissed her lips softly and slowly, and then left. Maria lay on the bed as she heard the door shut behind him."

Oscar and Adrienne insisted on barbecuing despite the fact that clouds blocked the sun, giving the sky a grayish quality.

"We are gonna celebrate whether the sun decides to show or not," Adrienne said, setting the bag of plastic plates down on the picnic table. Her children canvassed the backyard doing a variety of chores. Oscar flipped burgers over the grill's flame. Maria paced away her nervous energy until she heard the muted crackle of tires on the gravel driveway. The same beige sedan that had taken her child away had returned her son. The social worker opened the driver's seat and waved at Maria, then circled around to the passenger side. She opened the door and a lanky boy stepped out.

It was her son but he looked different. Q had lost all his baby fat, and seemed to have sprouted a few inches. His short hair had grown and was braided across his skull. His striped shirt swallowed his thin frame. His jeans sagged off his rear and came to an abrupt halt at his white tennis shoes.

A gruesome breeze whipped through the backyard. The last remnants of winter swirled in the air. But Maria burned inside. Sweat dripped down her sides and met the cold air. She shivered as she walked toward the car.

"Hey, baby." Maria held her hands out. She watched as Q hesitated a moment. It felt as if time froze. He stood there almost contemplating his next move. He finally shifted his weight and headed toward her. When his head rested on her breastplate, he trembled in a fit of tears. "I missed you so much, Mom." Speechless, she held him in her arms as he released the pain that had been caught inside him for the past twelve months. When he pulled back her T-shirt was drenched.

Adrienne stepped over to the social worker and put her hand on the woman's arm. "I'll handle all the paperwork."

"Hey, Q." Tiffany walked up to Q and waved. "My name is Tiffany and that's my little sister, Joy, and the twins are Tre and Terrance." The children all waved as their names were called. "That's my mom and dad."

"Hey." Q smiled and wiped his eyes, acutely aware now that he had been crying in public.

"Your apartment is over there, right behind our house. It used to be a garage."

"Thank you, Tiffany." Adrienne smiled and then beckoned her daughter to her side.

"Would you like to see your room?" Maria asked.

"I get my own room?"

"Yep," Maria nodded, grabbed his hand, and guided him to the apartment. "We'll be right back."

Once inside, Q probed through each room. He stopped at the television in the front with the PlayStation 2 stuffed under the console. "Wow, all we had at the home was an old Nintendo system."

Home—Maria cringed at the sound of the word. Her son had been stuck in a group home for a year, away from everyone he loved. It was amazing he didn't want to kill her, she thought.

"Wait till you see your room." Maria pointed to the hall and he moved down the dark corridor to the small enclave that served as his bedroom. He sat on the bed and felt the comforter. He giggled at the Ciara poster and focused his attention on the computer.

"Oh my God, Mom," he screamed. "You got me a computer?"

"You'll need it to catch up on all your homework."

"You got all this working at McDonald's?"

"You can get everything you need working an honest job, baby." Maria sat on the bed. "It may take a little longer, but it feels so much better." She watched as he moved to the picture on the dresser. He stood mesmerized for a moment.

"I remember this picture," Q said. "Six Flags, right?"

"Yep. You were only seven then."

"Man. I was so tiny."

"We thought you'd never grow."

"We had a good time, huh?"

"It was one of my favorite moments together."

"Hmm." Q looked at the photo again, and then turned to his mom. "Thank you, Mom."

Maria shot up. "Thank me, for what?"

"For keeping your word, for getting me back."

"I had no choice," Maria said. "I would be lost without you."

"I love you, Mom."

"Oh God." Maria ran to him. "You don't know how good it feels to hear you say that." She embraced him again and truly feared she would never let him go.

"Mom?" Q asked.

"Yes, sweetie?"

"I'm a little hungry."

"Well, what do you think all that food was outside? Let's go eat."

"Cool," he said and started for the hall.

"Hey, Q," she said, as her turned and smiled at her. "Welcome home."

Chapter XXXIV

Oscar felt a nipping sensation near his heart as he walked to the bulletin board. It was an almost-paralyzing tingling sensation. If it was a heart attack, he hoped it would drop him before he could read his score. Torts class was his worst subject, and he hated it. He felt much more comfortable in the human rights and international law classes, where his experiences seemed applicable. But torts were just foreign. He needed to be in the 90th percentile to pass the course. As he neared the board he saw his name and scanned the line and saw a 76. His body burned with fear. Would he get kicked out of the school? Would he lose his scholarships? Now a few inches away he retraced his name and guided his finger down the line till he reached a 97. He followed his name to that number at least eight times until he was confident that was his score.

"Thank you, Jesus." His legs gave way and he fell to his knees.

"I think you may be looking for the Department of Theology across campus." Dr. McGruder slapped his back. Oscar rose to his feet, but he only smiled. He knew who got him that score. And he wasn't about to apologize for giving thanks.

"Hey, Dr. McGruder," Oscar said. "I really enjoyed your litigation class this semester."

"Well, I enjoyed your participation," Dr. McGruder said. "You know, we get a lot of students fresh out of undergrad. No life experience. And, well . . . some of their comments reflect it."

They shared a knowing grin. "Yeah, kids are funny that way. They know everything until one thing blows away their whole understanding of life."

"You know, one thing I don't understand is why you didn't apply for an internship with me at Higgins, Riley and Smith in D.C."

"Yeah, well, the beauty of being one of those kids is that they don't have to worry about a wife and four kids."

"Four kids?"

"Yes, sir."

"Wow. Well, I can see how your calendar would be a little full."

"Yeah, my day job is babysitting for the next three years while I'm in school."

"What does your wife do?"

"She's an attorney for Legal Aid."

"Those poor children." Dr. McGruder laughed. "They'll never get away with anything."

"You'd be amazed."

"Well, I won't lie to you and tell you I'm not disappointed. You would have been a tremendous asset in some of the projects we have planned for this summer."

"Well, you never know what the future holds."

"What if I told you I had a place you could stay free of charge? With the money you were making you would have more than enough to take care of your family for the summer."

"I don't know." Oscar fought the urge to scream "yes." This was his favorite professor asking for him to work in one of the biggest corporate firms in D.C. But Adrienne had already borne the brunt of being the sole breadwinner this past year. He couldn't ask her to uproot her life for a lousy summer.

"I'll be honest. If you say you will go I'll stop looking for applicants. I believe the experience just may change your life. Just think about it and e-mail me if you have a change of heart."

"I will seriously considerate it, sir."

"That's all I ask." Dr. McGruder slapped Oscar's back and moseyed down the hall.

Oscar resisted the urge to dance down the hall until it struck him that he had aced all his exams and had been offered the most prestigious internship advertised on campus. "What the hell?" Oscar gyrated his hips and moved his neck as he glided down the hall. A couple of young women giggled as he passed by, but nothing could ruin his high.

Adrienne sat at her desk behind the couch, crunching numbers on her calculator. Oscar leaned against the edge of the table watching her work. He was always amazed at her analytical mind. How could she calculate all the bills while cooking dinner for the kids? He could barely keep the checkbook balanced within five bucks. He watched as her cleavage rose slightly while her hand tapped the keypad. In her low-cut shirt the skin on the tops of her breasts protruded just enough to turn him on. He moved behind her and began kissing her neck and fondling her breasts.

"I know you're ecstatic right now." She kissed his arms and continued clacking away. "But we have to stay focused." Her passive defiance steamed his insides. He cracked a smile and tried to lift her out of the chair.

"Oscar." She turned to kiss him. She pulled back a little, but he knew she would cave. They kissed and fondled one another until she finally wiggled free of his grasp.

"Okay, we need to have a serious talk."

George K. Jordan

"Okay."

"I'm serious, keep it in check."

He moved in and kissed her again. "That's the last one I swear."

She smirked and turned back to the long piece of tape that flowed from the calculator. She ripped it against the steel teeth behind the plastic cover and turned to Oscar.

"Okay, the bad news," she said. "Even if we rented out this home, which I don't want to do, and I cashed in some of our investments, it would be a stretch to afford us all living in D.C. for the entire summer, with just your income."

"I figured it was a long shot." He kneeled next to her chair.

"Hold your horses." She threw her hand in the air. "I have a proposition for you."

"Oh Lord." He smiled, knowing his wife's "propositions" always cost him something. "What?"

"I can't leave my job while you are in school. That's non-negotiable. We need the money. But the kids have the whole summer off and would love a summer away from Atlanta."

"You're going to stick me with all those monsters? Hell no."

"Nice to know how you really feel about the children, but no." She grabbed him.

"What then?"

"Just take the boys," she said. "They are pretty self-sufficient right now and could be in a youth program during the day and then you all could have some real bonding time for the summer."

"You really think they are old enough for that?"

"They are eight. I think they are old enough to appreciate it."

"But I'll be at work all day. What about when I have to stay late?"

"Here is the other part of my idea."

"I knew it," Oscar said. He could see her mind clicking behind her big brown eyes.

"Take Q with you."

"What?"

"He is twelve now and can babysit for a couple of hours until you get back. He loves the boys and we both trust him."

"Yeah, but he isn't my son."

"No," Adrienne said. "But Maria said it's been hard talking to him lately. He's distant, and she thinks he misses his father."

"I can understand that, but a whole summer?"

"He could really use a male role model. And that is why you suggested they live here, right?"

Oscar walked over to the couch and collapsed in the soft pillows. "Man, what about Damon?"

"What about him?"

"I think I should at least tell him what I am doing. I mean, I know he loves his son."

"Well, you have been avoiding visiting him for about a year. It may be a good time to get some closure on that."

"I know. I just don't know what to say."

"Tell him you are looking out for his prize possession, his family. Tell him you love him and that you are his friend no matter if he accepts you or not. Tell him Q needs a man in his life, and you would like to fill in the gaps wherever you can."

"I don't know if he is gonna take that well."

"Frankly, I don't give a shit."

"Come on, Adrienne."

She walked over to him and crossed her arms in proper genie position. The lecture was about to begin. "Come on nothing," Adrienne said. "You have been trying to make peace with this boy for too long. He made his decisions and now he has to live with them. But his son is smart and vulnerable and deserves a chance to have the life Damon willingly gave away.

"Yeah, you're right." He pushed himself off the couch's cushions and looked at Adrienne. "So you think Maria would be cool with it?"

"She needs help, Oscar. Q is right at that crossroads period. If you don't help direct him, I'm pretty damn sure someone will."

"You've already talked with her, haven't you?"

"I may have mentioned it."

"So I really don't have a say in this marriage thing, do I?"

"On paper only, baby."

He rose slowly. "Well, I am about to invoke one of my husbandly rights." He crept closer, hands out to grab her.

"No, Oscar," Adrienne pleaded. "The kids will be home any minute."

"I only need a minute."

"I've been meaning to talk to you about that."

Oscar let out a growl and chased Adrienne, giggling, up the stairs.

Oscar watched through the kitchen window as Q threw a baseball high in the air and stuck his glove out to catch it. Oscar smiled as he heard the familiar soft thud of leather hitting leather. He walked outside and watched the boy for a few more minutes. He looked so much like Damon now, it was scary. The brown deep-set eyes against long lashes. A prominent jawline squared his baby face. Even his bony frame reminded Oscar of Damon years ago.

"Hey, buddy, you mind if I play?"

"I guess."

Oscar walked up the hill that slanted against the fence. "Let's see that arm."

"You don't have a glove."

"I'll be all right."

Q hunched his shoulders and then stood still. He stared at Oscar for a moment, then slowly bent his torso forward. His hands hid behind his back. Suddenly he cocked his shoulders back, lifted his right arm, and released the ball. It took a second for the burn to set in after the ball slapped against Oscar's hands.

"Sh–hoot." Oscar shook his throbbing hands. "That is some fastball."

Q smiled. "I want to join the baseball team next year."

"You should." Oscar threw the ball back.

"Yeah, but all the eighth grade kids are huge and I don't know if I'm good enough." He threw the ball again and Oscar winced from the pain.

"If you keep practicing, I know you'll make the team. I could practice with you this summer if you'd like."

"That'd be cool."

"Speaking of this summer, did your mom tell you I was going to D.C. for an internship?"

"Yeah, she said you were taking Tre and Terrance. That's cool."

"Have you ever been out of Atlanta?"

"Nope."

"Would you like to go?"

"Really?" Q's face brightened as he looked across the yard at Oscar.

"Yeah, it would be fun. Just the boys."

Q beamed for a moment, and then the smile eroded like a hill of sand under a menacing wind.

"I better not," he said. "I don't want to leave my mom alone."

"I think she would be okay with it."

"But then she would be here unprotected."

"Well, Adrienne would be here."

"Yeah, but she wouldn't be able to stop him if he came to get her."

"Who?" Oscar asked.

"My dad."

"Buddy, your dad's in jail." Oscar walked toward Q. "And besides, he loves you guys. He wouldn't hurt you."

"But he has hurt us," Q shouted. "All he does is hurt us over and over again. I won't let him come and hurt us anymore. If he comes here I'll be ready for him."

Oscar looked at the boy, a bundle of anger and fear trapped in a twelve-year-old's body.

"Your dad is not coming to get your mom or you." Oscar put his hand over Q's shoulder. "In fact, I am going to visit him to make sure he's cool with you going."

"Really? Can I go?"

"Uh." Oscar had not planned on reuniting father and son on his trip. "Are you sure you want to see him right now?"

"Yeah."

"Okay, we'll go." Oscar said. "You still want to throw the ball?"

"'Kay."

"Just one thing," Oscar said. "I gotta grab my glove, 'cause you're killing my hand." They both laughed and tossed the ball until the aroma of dinner cooled their enthusiasm."

Chapter XXXV

Damon took to praying and reading his Bible early in the mornings before the sunlight poked through the iron bars and before he could hear the sounds of stirring souls moving around in their cells. He pulled the book from under his pillow and jumped down from his bed. It was awkward, at first, kneeling in prayer. His family had never been the churchgoing type, and he couldn't remember ever attending a service. But something about the peace that covered Xavier whenever he read or quoted from it made Damon want to give respect to the book.

The first couple of times his knees cracked and the cold concrete made his body shiver. He asked Pastor Jeffries, who ran the church ministry every Thursday and Sunday, how to pray.

"It's a rather personal process," Jeffries said, smiling at Damon as they sat in the empty front row of the makeshift church in the cafeteria.

"I just want to make sure I'm doing it right, Pastor," Damon said, his voice shaking.

"Just talk as if you were having a conversation with God. He is not only your father, he is your counselor and friend."

After a few misfires and stunted prayers that sounded like "Thank you for my food, uh, amen," Damon forced himself to talk to God.

With his fingers interlaced and his elbows pressed against the mattress, propping himself up, Damon closed his eyes and talked to his new friend.

"Ay, uh, what's up, God? This is Damon here. I know you really don't know me because I really don't know you. But you sent this old cat down here who was my only friend and then you took him back. But he left his Bible for me, so I figure that's a sign I need to get my shit, uh, oh, sorry . . . my stuff together. The problem is I just don't know how. I mean, all I was trying to do was make a way for my family. I mean, I know I wasn't supposed to rob nobody, but what else was I supposed to do? I mean, wasn't nobody checking on gettin' no nigga a job or a chance. So I had to make my way. Why you got to make it so hard anyway? I see plenty of cats with Benzes and houses an' shi—stuff. You be making it easy for them. But my family got to suffer. Why is that?"

He continued: "I didn't mean to hurt that woman or her baby or that other cat. It was a mistake and I am sorry. But what the hell do you want me to do? I got a son I need to take care of and I am stuck in this prison. What do you want me to do? How am I supposed to make a difference and I am stuck in prison? How am I supposed to be a better person when anything and everything I ever cared for was taken away?

"Do you hate me for not coming to church?" Damon asked. "Man, I didn't even know about you. My mom never took us to church and my father left us when I was five. But you know that. Hell, you probably planned for him to leave. So what you expect me to be, some whack Christian, and all you've ever given me is pain?"

Damon felt his closest friend, anger, creeping down his arms, causing his hands to tremble. In a rage he grabbed the mattress and flung it across the tiny room. He kicked the metal frame until it bent in the middle. The spring croaked in pain as Damon drew back his bloody foot. He tossed the stack of magazines that had been gathered in a heap next to the bed.

He ripped the sheets and threw his stick of deodorant and tube of toothpaste, watching as they exploded against the wall. He finally slumped to the floor in a heap, his energy spent as he looked at his mess.

He quickly and politely began cleaning up his meltdown. When everything was in seemingly good order he searched for his Bible and found it lying on the floor next to the urinal. The pages were open. Damon slowly glanced over at the book and picked it up. He glanced at the words, so confusing and lost to him. Suddenly his eyes focused on a verse:

We do not want you to be uninformed, brothers, about the hardships we suffered in the province of Asia. We were under great pressure, far beyond our ability to endure, so that we despaired even of life. Indeed, in our hearts we felt the sentence of death. But this happened that we might not rely on ourselves but on God, who raises the dead. He has delivered us from such a deadly peril, and he will deliver us. On him we have set our hope that he will continue to deliver us.

Damon's eyes searched to find the chapter—2 Corinthians 2:8–10. He moved back to his bed and read the passage over and over again.

The next day Damon kneeled to pray, but instead of trashing his room he whispered, "What am I supposed to do, Lord?" He turned the pages in his Bible. His heart placed his fingers in between the pages.

Love the Lord your God with all your heart and with all your soul and with your entire mind and with all your strength. The second is this: Love your neighbor as yourself. There is no commandment greater than these.

His eyes fixed on Mark 12:30–31.

He followed his scripture reading pattern for weeks until he finally found the strength to approach Pastor Jeffries after service.

"So, Pastor, can I ask you a question?" Damon pushed his tone down so the other inmates couldn't hear him. "What happens once I'm saved?"

"What do you mean what happens?" Jeffries curled his bushy eyebrows.

Damon hated his eyebrows. "I mean, once I'm saved am I getting to heaven?"

"Once you accept Jesus as your personal savior, yes, you see him in the Kingdom of Heaven."

"Even after all the shit I did?"

"God is not fickle and mean-spirited like us. He loves you despite your mistakes."

"What if I got out and robbed another bank?"

"If you love the Lord you will try to live in his image. Robbing banks is not in his image."

"Will this pain inside go away?"

"If you surrender it to Jesus, and let him take it on."

"Hmm," Damon answered and walked away. He sat in the back during the next month of church services, making sure not to catch the pastor's eye. Finally one Sunday, the pain inside him hurt so much, he had to let it go.

"The doors of the church are now open." Jeffries held his hand in the air. Damon felt his legs betray him and they stood him up. He moved slowly down the aisle past the aluminum seats and the sprinkling of churchgoers.

His knees gave when he reached the pastor and he collapsed at the altar. He felt a hand massaging his head.

"Son," Pastor Jeffries said as Damon bawled on the floor, "you made the Lord very happy today." He chuckled as he helped Damon to his feet, then added, "And the devil very mad."

* * *

Damon clung to his Bible as he watched Oscar and Q sit at the table across from him. He gulped back saliva as Q scooted his chair close to Oscar. Damon wanted to grab his son and hold him in his arms, but he saw the anger in Q's eyes. It was like peering into a mirror. Q sucked in his teeth as Damon nodded to him.

"Hey, man, you're looking good," Oscar said to Damon.

"I am blessed."

"Yeah." Oscar leaned over and tapped Damon's Bible. "I see you been reading the word. That's good."

"You go to church?"

"Every now and again, but yo, I believe in God, though. For sure."

Damon rolled his eyes at Oscar and turned to his son. "And what's with you, little man?"

"Fine."

Damon could feel the chill ooze off Q's words. "You don't sound fine."

"It was a long drive up here, man." Oscar tried to justify Q's attitude.

"I ain't talking to you, Oscar." Damon slammed his hand on the table. Immediately he felt pangs of guilt. Was this what being a Christian meant? Feeling guilty for releasing the only thing that gave him relief in this world—his anger? "I apologize. I really was just speaking to my son."

"I ain't your son," Q blurted. "And you ain't my father."

"Come on now, Q," Oscar said.

"No, let him speak." Damon held his hand up. "Go on, little man, speak your mind."

"You hurt all those people, you tried to hurt Mom, you left me all alone. I had to spend a year in a foster home. All because you didn't want to get a real job like Oscar, you just wanted to be a hustler."

"I made some mistakes, but I am trying to make them right. I am a Christian now. I am taking night classes. They say when I get out I can go to school. I don't know what I'd take, but I am thinking about it."

"That's good, man," Oscar interjected.

"I don't care," Q shouted. "Do you know what it's like to go to school and have kids call you names 'cause your father was on the news for robbing a bank? Do you know what it's like to have people feel sorry for you 'cause you don't have a home you can go to for Christmas and Thanksgiving? I wanted to be you when I was growing up. But now I am grown up and I realize you ain't nothing but a thug and a loser. And I never want to see you again." Q got up and walked to the gate. The guard let him out.

"I'll talk to him, Damon," Oscar said.

"Haven't you done enough?"

"What?"

"Not only did you destroy my life, you have to steal my son. Do you have to take everything?" Damon asked.

"Slow your roll there, buddy. I didn't take your son. You made choices in this shit."

"So now I gotta watch you be his father."

"You are his father, Damon, but you haven't acted like a father in a long time."

"Fuck you," Damon spat out.

"Real nice with the Bible in your hand."

"Why'd you bring him here . . . to gloat? I already know he's staying with you. Hell, he practically looks like you now. Did you just finally want to see me crack?" A flood of tears pressed at the corners of his eyes.

"Damon, he wanted to come here to say what he had to say. He's angry right now. But if he didn't love you he wouldn't even do that. We're going to D.C. this summer for my job. I'll talk to him, maybe—"

"Wait a minute." Damon rose from his chair. "You're taking my son away to another state and you didn't even ask me how I felt about it?"

"Well, Maria liked the idea of a male figure in his life, and since I was taking my boys I figured—"

"Get the fuck out of my face. And don't you ever fucking come back here again or I swear on this Bible I am holding I will kill you."

"Damon, aren't we a little old for threats?"

"Partna, right now this ain't no threat."

Oscar leaned back and stood. He walked away, but turned suddenly. "Damon, your son needs you to grow up now. You don't have the luxury of being an angry black man as long as you have a kid who needs you." He turned and walked out.

Damon thought about his son's words during lunch, during prayer service, during cleanup time. Even during his evening shower his mind could not escape his son. Only a light slap across his head brought him back to reality.

"Hey, pretty girl." A humongous man stood naked behind him. "Saw you crying earlier. You have a fight with your boyfriend?"

Damon turned back around and mumbled, "Nigga, I am not in the mood for no faggot shit."

"Oh, that's right, pretty girl here is saved. She done found Jesus and is praying to find a husband to marry her off so she can have his babies. Well, I got a rod and a staff to comfort you, pretty nigga."

Damon gave in to the rumbling inside him and pounced on the man. Damon had him on the floor in seconds, his fists crashing into the man's skull. He saw a tooth fly out and splashes of blood scatter. He knew for sure he would kill him right there, naked in the shower.

Suddenly a hand clamped his shoulder and a swift jab of a blade penetrated his side. He felt it again and again until he fell off the man. Then a barrage of spit and kicks against his legs, testicles, and head sent his mind reeling. He knew he would be beaten, possibly raped, mostly likely killed. He had nothing left to fight with anymore, so he surrendered to the only thing he knew would help him: God.

Chapter XXXVI

Fifteen freelance articles, fourteen months, and one boyfriend later, I thought my life was pretty much on track. I managed to secure a small condo just outside the perimeter in Stone Mountain. It was quaint with arching ceilings and top-to-bottom windows for maximum light exposure. Carlos, my official unofficial boyfriend, had put up all the artwork. I had been quite comfortable writing my little articles about Atlanta and was starting to get some buzz for a piece I did on police brutality. Carlos stayed up all night with me as I celebrated and cringed in fear at my first anonymous death threat.

But I would never imagine I would be sitting in the Human Resources Department of CNN, waiting for Delia Wilson to walk through the door. I knew about her from back in school when I ran the college newspaper. She had run it ten years before I arrived. She covered international news for the Associated Press and then wound right back in Atlanta as an anchor, then executive producer, for CNN. The fact that she even knew my name was a mystery, let alone how she got a hold of my clips. When she walked through the door I felt the first pangs of fear press against my heart. I swallowed hard and rose as she extended her hand.

"Ms. West, a pleasure to finally meet you." Her shake was firm and focused. Just two pumps and she was done.

"You too," I countered. "I heard so much about you at Spelman. You are like a legend there."

"Oh God, I hope not." She giggled. "Usually legend is a nice word for has-beens and dead people."

I chuckled lightly, not really knowing by her brash tone if I had offended her.

"Let's get out of this boring place and have lunch. I'm starving." Delia swung the door open and positioned her hand out to direct me out of the office.

My heart sank. I didn't really count on a lunch interview. In my experience those are not good for the interviewee. You try to recant the highlights of your resume while pieces of asparagus dangle from your teeth. Or worse, you asphyxiate your future boss with the deadly combination of garlic and onion breath. I instinctively ran my tongue over my teeth to check for refugee food particles holding out from breakfast.

The moment we walked through the front entrance of the small bistro she had chosen, I felt like I was in an old episode of *Cheers*.

"Hey, Delia," the staff rang in unison as she waved at them and bypassed the hostess to find a corner booth away from the rest of the diners.

"Would you like to start off with your usual?" a waitress asked, materializing out of thin air like a vampire.

"You got it, and keep them coming. I'm not shy around guests," Delia said. "You want a drink, sweetie? I'm having vodka and cranberry."

"Oh, uh." I fumbled at my drink menu. A drinking lunch interview was the worst kind of situation. If I didn't drink I would be a prude. But if she was a regular, which the staff's response seemed to corroborate, no doubt she was gonna get sloshed. "Red wine, please."

"Don't be so prissy." Delia sighed. "She'll have the same

as me. Just bring us the bottle and put it on my tab," she told the waitress.

I decided the only way to maneuver through this situation was to handle the business before one of us fell off our chairs. "So, I'm amazed that you read my clips."

"Oh yeah, you're an amazing writer, I have to say. It usually takes several years to get to the caliber I have seen in your articles. How long have you been a journalist?"

"Actually I was in PR for several years, and then I—"

"Oh yes." Delia snapped her fingers. "You did all those hip-hoppity parties. And then that thing with the robbery and your kid. Sorry about that, sweetie. But hell, kids are just money-grubbers anyway. You're better off."

Okay, it's official. This bitch was crazy. I clenched my teeth and took that blow for the team and because I had the opportunity to write for a world-renowned news organization.

"Yeah, well, I just fell in love with doing enterprising pieces about our community. There are so many stories right here in Atlanta."

The waitress dropped a bottle of vodka on the table and a bottle of cranberry juice. She mixed the two in a long silver cylinder and then poured them into our separate glasses. She ran off as quickly as she came.

"Well, here's to new beginnings." Delia raised her glass, and I clinked mine against hers. She downed her drink before mine hit my lips. "So, let me just be frank here, Jackie." Delia poured another drink. "Can I call you Jackie?"

"Everyone just calls me J.C. for short."

"Yeah, Jackie, whatever, the reason I called you is that I need a strong team of writers for my new eleven o'clock news program. We are getting our asses kicked by other news programs because we don't have fresh young thinkers on our staff. Half our staff has been around since Nixon, and the other half barely graduated from college and can barely shit on their own."

"Wow, okay," I said. I mean, what else would I say to that?

"You're pretty freakin' old for ingénue status, sweetie. But hell, compared to me you're a freakin' newborn. I mean, I don't read the Bible. I translate scrolls. That's how old I am."

We laughed and I reached for a refill.

"So I need a writer who's old enough to not still be enamored with the power of her own breasts, if you know what I mean. But still young enough to know they still work."

"I'm sorry but I don't follow." I downed another drink, hoping I might pass out and wake up to find this was some sick sketch on Mad TV.

"Look, sweetie, you can write and you're talented. But this is a man's world and you're still easy on the eyes. Believe it or not, even behind the camera they care about that shit. Do you think they would have tolerated my loud black ass if I didn't turn a few heads back in the day?"

Delia was, in fact, still beautiful with full lips, prominent cheekbones, and doe eyes. I'm sure she could grab any man's attention if her eyes weren't bloodshot from inhaling drinks like a salmon jumping upstream.

"I need a fellow sister warrior who is aware of all the bullshit but not in it. That's how you make news, sweetie. So what do you say?"

Normally I would PR my way through this situation and speed as fast as I possibly could back to the suburbs, never to see this nut again. But the job intrigued me. Okay, I had to endure one crazy person to get the bomb job, so what? There would be crazy people if I worked at Kinko's too. And it wasn't like I hadn't been in crazy situations the last couple of years. But in all power plays you have to be a good negotiator and show you aren't desperate. Besides, this chick needed to be checked.

"I say my name is J.C., not Jackie. I say you're a desperate old bird praying that new blood comes in and proves that you still have the right touch to run a newsroom, and I say I don't walk through the door for anything less than forty-two thousand."

"You haven't worked in journalism long." Delia laughed and chugged her third or fifth drink. I couldn't be sure which because I had blinked a few times. "You start at thirty-seven thousand and if you tell anyone, I will scalp your ass myself."

"It's a deal." We clinked glasses again and after an hour more of drinking and laughing I had landed a job and a hangover. I caught a taxi home."

I fell asleep on the couch, a victim of a mind-gouging headache. When I woke up the sun had descended, and only flickering light filled the room. I rose from the couch and considered the garden of candles that were planted around the room. The familiar smell of sautéed salmon eased through the air.

I sauntered into the kitchen ready to thank my considerate boyfriend.

"It already smells great. I can't wait to . . ." I fell back against the banister as I spotted David tolling over my stove.

"How did you get in here?"

"You're going to have to use a little more imagination when hiding your spare key." He laughed. "Everyone knows the fake rock under the bush bit."

"Can I help you with something?"

"I was getting desperate." He turned and smiled at me. "I have called you every day for months, written you letters, sent you flowers, sat in front of your door as you've walked right past me. I decided I may need to work from the inside out."

"So you break into my house."

"I don't mean that." He smiled and turned to the food. He poked at a piece of fish and turned back to me. "Taste this for me. I think it may be too salty."

"I'm not tasting anything," I shouted. "Now get the hell out of here."

"J.C., I may have done you wrong but you know I don't pose any type of physical threat. So can you turn down the Lifetime drama act for me?"

My lips curled and I wanted to laugh, but I refused to give him the satisfaction.

"Why are you here now?" I asked. "I have moved on with my life. I have a new home, a new boyfriend, and a new job. Our time is gone. Why can't you understand that?"

"I believe our time is gone." David grabbed plates from the cupboard and spread the fish and vegetables over them. "It's gone. But I am renewed. J.C., I have been going to church and thinking about all the things I did wrong with us. And I know I can't change all that, but I would just like one night with you. Just one night to plead my case."

"There is no case, David."

"Look, just sit over there. Eat the fish, drink the wine—"

"No more wine," I protested.

"Fine. Drink the water and hear me out. If you don't like what you hear, there is a document over there I am sure you would like instead."

I moved over to the table and spotted the divorce papers I had sent to him over six months before. He had signed his name in all the appropriate places.

"All I have to do is sit for dinner and then you're out of my life?"

"If that is what you want, yes."

"Fine." I sat down. "Bring it on."

He brought over my favorite dish of salmon and asparagus with brown rice and soup. I was in heaven. It was the perfect topper to my day, but I couldn't let on. I grimaced through the first course.

"Okay, I cheated on you and betrayed every sense of trust we ever had. But that was not my only sin. I was really self-ish when our child died. I just wanted to hurry and have an-other one and couldn't understand all the pain you were going through. I just wanted to get past it, and when you couldn't I needed someone to help me get past it. Nicole was—"

"Please do not say that heffa's name in my house."

"She was a huge mistake I made because I could not deal with my emotions and the loss of my child. And for that I apologize."

"Apology accepted. Move on."

"Okay." David smiled as I nibbled on my food. "When you left I went into a depression not because I missed you but because of all the things I missed you doing for me. Doing the budget, cooking dinner, finding places for us to eat. But as time went on I started missing the friend I could tell secrets to, and the laughs we shared when I would trip over the ottoman every morning when I got out of bed. I missed making love to you in every inch of our house. I missed the way you smelled when you first got out of the shower. It was like heaven coming out of the bathroom."

"You really should have been a poet," I said, slicing a piece of cheesecake.

"Can I finish?" David moaned. "I love you so much that it physically hurt to move for a few months. But when I started going to church they told me that I had truly betrayed your trust and to prepare for the fact that you may never come back. I prayed and prayed on that, and I think I have found some peace. That's why I was able to sign the papers, 'cause I really just want you to have the best life you can. And if that means it can't include me, then so be it."

"Wow. I—"

"But I am hoping and praying that you do include me and give me a chance to be the man you fell in love with all those years ago."

"David, that is sweet, really," I said. "And I appreciate your honesty. But the fact is I am no longer the woman you fell in love with. I'm different for many different reasons. And all and all, I think I like her. Before, I was about status and being the best at everything and having everything. Then I lost it all and discovered I really didn't want any of it. I don't even honestly know if at that time I would have made a good mother."

"You would have," David protested.

"I don't know," I said. "I mean, I would have loved my child, but everything about my life before was about creating this illusion of perfection. The house, the cars, the job, the child. Now all that I have left is me and I kind of like that. I am rediscovering what it's like to be a human, not some bourgeoisie stereotype."

"Well." David rose. "I guess there is nothing left to say. If this makes you happy, then you have to go for it. I love you, J.C., more than I have ever loved or will love anyone else. But sometimes love ain't enough. So you have my papers. And I will leave you alone." David walked over and grabbed his jacket off a chair and headed for the door.

I followed and grabbed his hand. He turned around and I moved into his chest.

"Good luck, David." I kissed him and felt my hands snake around his waist. I pulled back and opened the door. "Take care."

I closed the door behind him and leaned against it. I peeked through the hole, hoping he would still be at the door. But he walked to his car, opened the door, and got in. I watched as the headlights in the peephole backed away and slipped out of view. I walked back to the table and sat down. I grabbed the divorce papers and clutched them in my hands. It is amazing how everything can seem so right on the outside, while on the inside the turmoil has just begun.

Chapter XXXVII

Christopher ran into the hospital room, pushing open the metal doors separating him from his father. Alonzo was reclining in a bed that lifted his torso almost to the sitting position. Camille lounged at the end of the bed next to him, holding his hand. A tall, plump doctor was scanning Alonzo's medical records, which were on his steel clipboard.

"Hey, Dad." Christopher eased close to his father. The once-powerful figure looked defeated, wrapped in tubes and clothed in a skimpy hospital gown.

"I'm all right." Alonzo's voice quivered as Christopher relived the all-encompassing fear he had wrestled with as he lay in the hospital bed all those months ago. The scar barely visible on Christopher's chest began pulsating violently. He cleared his throat and pushed on.

"You look so tired."

"He is exactly that," the doctor interrupted, placing the metal clipboard at his side. "He had a rough night."

"Mmmph," Camille mumbled.

Christopher resisted giving her an evil stare. "So what happened?"

"It's very common." The doctor turned to Christopher. "Dr.

Milpatrick. You must be his son. He has been talking about you all night. He refused to talk to me until you arrived."

A smile broke across Christopher's face. "What is it?"

"A broken heart."

"Excuse me?" Christopher moved in close so he could hear the doctor better.

"It's basically a form of anxiety attack, but it very closely resembles a heart attack."

"Wow." Christopher's eyes couldn't help but follow Camille as she suddenly rose and headed to the window. She stared at the street below with her arms crossed. "Well, what usually causes a broken heart?"

"Just ask my wife, she broke mine several times." The doctor offered a hollow chuckle, and then cleared his throat. "Sorry, bad joke. Actually it is usually caused by heavy stress."

"Dad, you think you may be working too many hours driving the truck?"

"Well, actually—"

"Hell naw." Camille whipped around. "He's just upset because I'm pregnant."

"Huh?" Christopher wanted to beg Camille to repeat herself. But he didn't want to agitate her any further. Her eyes had narrowed and her lips pouted. He knew it was only a matter of time before she blew.

"Pregnant," Camille yelled. "And this nigga don't even have the decency to make an honest woman of me."

Christopher recalled the two of them naked on his rug, and thought the time to regain her "honesty" had long since passed. He turned to his father instead.

"I'll be making rounds if you need me." Dr. Milpatrick was already pulling the door open and slipping out, quicker than a thief who'd discovered he'd triggered a silent alarm.

Christopher tipped back toward the door hoping to escape

before it clicked back into the locked position. "Well, this is a private conversation. I don't want to—"

"You need to talk to that man. If he can stick his—"

"Camille, watch yourself." Alonzo gave her the patented "don't go too far" look he was famous for. It wasn't so much an angry look, but with thinned-out lips and eyes barely glancing her way, he almost made an additional statement with the spaces between his words.

"This is my family," Alonzo whispered. "We can discuss this later."

"Hell," Camille shouted. "I am your family now. This baby is your family."

"Uh, Dad, if you're okay I think I'll just catch up with you later."

"No, you stay." Camille marched over to Christopher and grabbed his arm. She looked at Alonzo. "You tell your son in his face. Tell him in his face that you refused to marry me."

"I didn't say I wouldn't marry you, Camille." Alonzo pushed himself off the pillows. "I just said I don't know if this is the right time."

"With niggas like you, it's never the right time."

"What did I tell you about using that tone with me? I ain't your daddy. You can't pitch a fit and expect me to cradle you in my arms like a child."

"I don't need a father. I need an honorable Christian man who will handle his business."

"You weren't looking for no Christian man when we was laying up. You was looking for someone to get your hair fixed. Get your nails done. Buy you nice clothes. Hell, I did all that. I wear ten-year-old jeans and live with my son while you drive an Accord and switch in three-hundred-dollar shoes. But I say I need a minute to think and you go acting like you're on Ricki Lake or something."

"I am a twenty-eight-year-old woman." Camille's eyes began to water. "Christopher, will you tell this fool that a woman my age just can't walk back into church pregnant without at least a husband? Besides, it's not like we don't love each other. You do still love me, right?"

"Of course I do, Camille. Now, don't go starting that." Alonzo looked at Christopher. The bags under Alonzo's eyes sagged, making him look even more tired and frail. He hunched his shoulders up. "Boy, will you explain to this woman that it's a little hard to think about marriage and a kid when I live with my son?"

"Well, I'm sure Christopher wouldn't mind us staying there until we get on our feet." Camille said. "I have some money saved and if we keep saving we can get a little house before the baby is born."

"I just had a heart attack. Can you give me a chance to get my head together?"

"You didn't have no heart attack. You're just scared to be an old man and have a baby," Camille said.

"So maybe I am. I done lived my life. I'm entitled to mull over a few things before I start over. Now, if you don't mind I would like to talk to my son alone for a few minutes."

"Fine by me." Camille swiped her purse and sweater off the windowsill. "Call me when you grow the hell up." She stormed out, making sure to slam the door shut. Both Alonzo and Christopher exhaled slowly, their sighs amplified in the small room.

"Well, looks like I done messed up again," Alonzo said as Christopher inched closer. "You can feel free to let me have it."

"Why on earth would I do that?"

"Well, I was never there for you as a kid. Now I'm going to have this kid and do the same thing. I know that's what you're thinking."

"Dad," Christopher said. "These months with you have saved me. I was so used to being by myself and being independent that I had cut off everyone from getting close to me.

But when you came it forced me to open up, to face up to the fact that me being alone is all my doing."

"Well, as long as I'm around you're never alone, Son," Alonzo said. "I've realized a lot living with you, too. Like how much I missed watching you grow up. Now you're all grown and I think your mama did a better job of raising you alone than I ever could. The only thing I ever gave you were them good looks." They both giggled and Christopher sat on the bed.

"I'm just afraid that I will make the same mistakes that I did with you," Alonzo continued.

"You don't have to repeat anything, Dad," Christopher said. "Just try your best and that child will be lucky to have you in its life."

"Yeah. I may be able to handle being a daddy, but I don't know about being a husband."

"The real question is, are you in love with her?"

"That woman is pure hellfire." Alonzo laughed. "But the truth is when I look in her eyes, I thank God I have another day to see her."

"Then I think you know what you have to do."

"Yeah. I'm just too damn old for all this."

"You're never too old for love."

"Hey, buddy, I could say the same about you."

"What do you mean?"

"I mean you're too young to be sitting at home watching movies all weekend. You need to live a little. Love a little."

"It's a little more complicated than that."

"No, it's not. Love is love. We just complicate things. I did with Camille. But the bottom line is she is the love of my life. Now, if my old ass still has a chance for love, then I know you do."

"Well, I'll think about it."

"Thank you."

"By the way," Christopher said, placing his hand on his

father's knee, "if you need to stay at the house to get stuff together you can, you know."

"I appreciate that."

"No problem," Christopher said. "Now let's get you dressed and out of here before they make up something wrong with you."

Tim sat across the table, a soft cotton blazer hanging elegantly off his broad shoulders. His locks were pulled back into a ponytail. His wide-framed sunglasses accentuated the sharp angles of his face.

"I was afraid you wouldn't call," Tim said.

"I was too."

"Well, lunch is definitely a positive step." Tim laughed. "It was a safe move, though."

"Safe?" Christopher felt his heart thumping hard against his chest.

"Yeah, safe," Tim protested. "You picked lunch 'cause you could control the situation. You knew there would be less sexual tension, and we'd both be pressed to get back to our kids."

"Maybe just a little." Christopher smiled and looked around the room, hoping to find anything to divert his eyes.

"So how long will it take?"

"Excuse me?"

"More water?" A waiter poured water into Tim's half-empty glass.

"Uh, can I have another Coke please?" Christopher asked. He felt a moment of relief, then again felt the awful churning that kneaded his stomach as he sat across from Tim. "I'm sorry. You were saying?"

"How long will it take for us to be together? I mean, we are both intelligent, busy men. We know what we want, and I definitely want you. But instead we go through all that dating get-to-know-you crap, asking the stupid dating questions that only end up in arguments. Then there is the first sexual experience. The honeymoon period, the boredom, and finally ending up in the sweet comfort of finding love with that special someone. Let's drop all that bull and just go straight to the love."

"It's more . . ." Christopher caught himself and smiled.

"What?"

"Look, I am a work in progress on this relationship stuff, so can you just bear with me and finish lunch? Then we can work on our domestic partnership documents."

"I will pace myself. But I really do think I am falling for you."

"Hmm." Christopher smiled and raised the menu over his face. He knew he was too.

Chapter XXXVIII

"Baby, this is a once-in-a-lifetime opportunity," Andre said, hunching closer to Maria in the huge leather booth they shared. "God is moving me."

Maria sat quietly, her hands cupped under his, wondering why she always picked men who would eventually leave her.

"HP Records is a major label with all kinds of rappers under them." Andre's smile radiated as he talked. His perfect white teeth peeked out from under his lips whenever he grinned. Maria didn't realize how much she loved him until she saw him smiling at this moment.

"So they want me to move out to their headquarters in L.A. Can you believe that?"

"Actually I can," Maria said, and meant her statement. Of course this was the second time in her life she had opened up to someone who would leave her behind. Of course it would force her to buck up and survive heartache and pain again.

"You're real talented, Andre, and I am very happy for you. If you let me visit you I will come see you any time you like."

Andre pulled back with a puzzled expression dropping on his face. "Visit," he said. "I don't want you to visit me anywhere." He let go of her hands and slid out of the booth. For a brief moment the pain of desertion was too much for Maria to bear. She wiped her watering eyes and gulped down tears. But when Andre got to his feet he immediately fell to his knees. His hands slipped into his pocket and returned with a tiny black box.

"No," Maria squealed so loudly that everyone in the restaurant turned to face her direction.

"Can I ask the question before you answer?" Andre laughed. He extended his hand and when she grabbed it he pulled her out of the booth. She stood before him, knees knocking and head reeling, as he grabbed her left hand.

"Maria Christina Adee, I loved you the first time I saw you smile at McDonald's. You turned my time in hell into a preview of heaven. I want to make sure I spend my whole life repaying you for the happiness you bring me every day you breathe." A chorus of women said "aww" and he opened the black box. "Will you make me the happiest man on earth and marry me?"

They were the words she had wanted to hear for so long from Damon. But hearing them come out of Andre's mouth felt like the most natural occurrence in her life.

"Yes, of course." She cupped her mouth as he slipped the ring on her slim finger.

"She said yes, everybody." Andre jumped up and hugged Maria. She held him in her arms until the roaring applause dulled behind them and there was only his soft kiss on her ample lips to think about.

God obviously had the sharpest sense of humor of anyone Maria knew. Why, when she gave her heart to only the second man in her entire life, would she receive a call that the first man she loved lay dying in a hospital? She didn't want to go at first but when the physician at the prison explained Damon's internal organs were not recovering from a fight he had more than a year ago, she knew it was serious. Why else would she surrender her purse to the correction officer as she squeamishly walked through the metal detectors? How could anyone else explain her looming over the man she swore never to see again, standing in the place she promised herself never to set foot in again?

Maria smiled to herself as she studied Damon lying in the hospital bed. For a moment she became lost in the rhythmic beeping of the life-support machine. She fondled her engagement ring as he stirred himself awake.

"My angel," he whispered. His gravelly voice sounded worse with the clear tubes jutting out of his nose.

"You look awful."

"Feel awful."

"Does it hurt?" Her hand lightly traced the red bruises that tattooed his arms.

"I don't feel too much with the morphine."

"That's good."

"How's Q?"

"He called yesterday." Maria sat next to him in the nearby chair. "He says he really likes D.C."

"Really?"

"Says it's just like Atlanta, just not as hot." Damon tried to laugh but succumbed to a coughing spell.

"Are you sure you're all right?"

"I ain't gone lie, Maria. They got me pretty bad. The doctors haven't exactly been too positive about my future."

"Oh my God." Maria grabbed his hand. "You're not going to die, are you?"

"I don't know."

"You can't. Q will be crushed."

"Q doesn't much like his daddy right now."

"He's mad, Damon. Doesn't mean he doesn't love you. You really hurt him. You hurt us. But he can get over the hurt. But if you die . . . I just don't know if he can take that."

"I don't want to give it to him, either." Damon smiled. One

of his front teeth was missing and there was a small black space in its place.

"He needs you to survive this," Maria said. "I need you to survive."

"Looks like you're getting along fine without me." Damon eased his right hand on Maria's left, fingering her engagement ring. "Anyone I know?"

"No." Maria retrieved her hand and placed it on her chest. "His name is Andre. He's an entertainer. He's a good man."

"Do you love him?"

"Yes."

"Are you in love with him?"

Maria rolled her eyes and braced herself. "Yes."

"Then I am happy for you."

"Are you sure you didn't die already?"

"Maybe a part of me did. I really don't feel like I did before. All that anger I had. The need to destroy anything or anyone that insulted me or refused me, or just got in my way—I just don't carry it anymore."

"Wow." Maria smiled. "This is too scary."

"Maria, I want you to know I am so sorry for all the shi— stuff I put you through." Damon sighed hard as he talked, as if he were fighting to retain every breath. "I never should have put my hands on you. You are so beautiful. I never wanted to touch you. I was just scared of you leaving me. And I'm sorry for dragging you into this robbery mess. I know you never wanted to get involved, but I forced you. I pray you can forgive me in time."

Maria scanned her memory for any moment she recalled of Damon apologizing. She couldn't think of a single mental entry. Suddenly the seriousness of the moment hit her. Her hands shook and she pushed away from him.

"I have to go, Damon," she said. "I can't do this. I can't watch you die."

"I need you to do me a couple of favors."

"Damon, I can't do this."

"Maria, I won't keep you but a few more minutes. Can you please stay with me for five more minutes, please?"

Maria returned to her seat.

"I actually only want you to do three things for me," Damon said. "Do you promise me you'll do them?"

"Yeah."

"You have to promise, Maria."

"I promise."

"All right." Damon grabbed her hand and drew her close to his face. "First, I want you to make sure you tell my son every day that I love him. He's a little man and he is already going to go through a lot of stuff. He has a temper like his old man and the last thing he needs is you telling him I didn't give a . . . that I didn't love him with all I had, with every piece of my flesh."

"He knows that, Damon."

"Just humor me and promise to remind him every day."

"I will."

"Secondly, I want you to go to the place I first told you I love you. My sins are there. You do whatever you need to do to make it right."

"Huh?" Maria questioned.

"Just go there and God will tell you what to do."

"Uh, okay."

"Now the last and most important thing I want you to do."

"Anything."

"I want a good-bye kiss."

"Damon . . ." Maria fought the tears as he smiled.

"Just one more kiss so I can let you go."

Maria grabbed her hair and pulled it behind her sweater. She bent over and caressed his chin with her hand and pressed her lips to his. He raised his arm and ran his fingers through her hair. For a moment Maria got lost in the emotion. She felt herself press into his flesh, rubbing his eyebrows with her fingers. Then the

Chapter XXXIX

Higgins, Riley & Smith was an abyss of marble, mahogany and $2,200 suits. The secretary was flanked behind a gold-trimmed desk with wood thicker than most walls. Each door was stained to hide the goings-on inside. Oscar imagined he would occupy one of the smaller associate offices on the lower floor. To his surprise, his office was adjacent to Dr. Mc-Gruder's and almost as big. Expressionist paintings adorned each wall, and fresh bouquets of flowers decorated each end table. His office was bigger than his living room at home.

To make him feel worse, he had an assistant and a receptionist at his disposal. When he called one of them to ask a question it was like a race to see which one would get to his office first.

Most days Oscar answered phone calls or researched all sorts of subjects on his computer. Usually he could ignore the aching itch that rose in his throat in such large confines. But today he watched the rush of people sauntering outside the glass and he longed to escape.

"Parks." Dr. McGruder waved Oscar over from across the room. Oscar ran over to him, praying for an opportunity to run an errand. As he walked closer to his mentor Oscar felt like a child begging his mother to let him explore the neighborhood under the guise of purchasing milk at the local store.

"Yes, sir," Oscar said, pressing his fingers into Dr. McGruder's desk.

"You're coming with me," McGruder said, rising to his feet and whipping his suit jacket from its resting place on the back of the chair. "We are going to the Capitol to meet with some local lobbyists who are going to help get some tobacco legislation turned around for us."

"Okay," Oscar said. "What do you want me to do?"

"Grab all these boxes and follow me to the car."

Dr. McGruder swiped his PDA and cell phone out of their chargers and scurried to the door. Oscar grabbed a luggage cart from behind his desk, and tossed the boxes on top, before racing after his professor.

With a beep the trunk of Dr. McGruder's Mercedes slowly opened, and Oscar threw the boxes inside. He jumped in the passenger seat and they were off.

"So, how do you like it here so far?" Dr. McGruder glanced at Oscar sporadically as they whizzed down the street.

"It's interesting, sir." Oscar nodded and tried to smile.

"You hate it, don't you?" Dr. McGruder laughed and slapped the steering wheel with his hand.

"It's not that I don't like it," Oscar said. "It's just corporate law was so interesting when I was studying my books. But actually working on them . . ."

"It's like watching paint dry, isn't it?" They both fell back in their seats laughing.

"The law and the process of getting legislation passed and working through litigation is so long. I'm kind of used to having an immediate impact, you know, being a cop and all."

"Yes, the process of working with clients and lobbying is tedious, to be nice." McGruder smiled. "But that's how it gets done."

"Well, no offense, but I just don't think this is what I had in mind when I went to law school."

"What did you want to do?"

"Help people." Oscar shook his head violently. "Not that you're not helping anyone. I just . . . I don't know . . . I like how my wife is always talking and interacting with the people she deals with."

"So you want to be a P.D.?"

"Don't know. I've been thinking about it."

"Well, can I be honest?"

"Of course, Dr. McGruder."

"Austin." He smiled. "Call me Austin."

"Okay, Austin. Be honest."

"I think you want to be a lawyer 'cause you suffer from guilt," Austin said. "Guilt from having opportunities when others don't. Guilt 'cause you're blessed and smart. Guilt 'cause you killed someone in your teens, I don't know. But I do know that an attorney's job is about upholding, testing, arguing, and ultimately respecting the law. It's through that that we help people. If you go into it with this peace corps save-the-world mentality, your bleeding heart will hemorrhage to death."

"Can't help it. I actually think I do want to change the world."

"We can only change ourselves. Others may react to what we do, but we are ultimately only responsible for the mountains we climb and the valleys we fall down into."

"I know that, I just feel like I am supposed to be doing more."

"You are doing great," Dr. McGruder said. "You are raising four children. If that isn't changing the world I don't know what is."

"Well, I just feel like I have let too many people down by just thinking about myself." Oscar rapped on the window with his knuckles. "I feel this is my second chance."

Austin stared at Oscar for a moment, his smile resonating

from ear to ear. "I admire your heart, Oscar. I think that's why I brought you up here. I just hope you don't spend so much time working for others that you miss happiness for yourself."

Oscar nodded and looked back out the window. "I hope not, either."

Oscar felt his heart thumping in his ear when he spied that his hotel door was open. Instinctively he grabbed his side, but with no gun to grip he eased toward the door. He pushed the door forward and ran in.

"Daddy," all four of his children sang in unison. Oscar's mouth dropped at the sight of his daughters lined up next to his sons. He kneeled down and stretched out his arms as they ran to him. His well of joy rose back again, on hearing all his children laughing. Not that he didn't love bonding with his sons; the impromptu touch football games in the hotel courtyard were all that kept him sane before he ordered pizza and tunneled through mountains of research files.

But watching all his children huddled together teasing each other, laughing, made this nearly two months of alienation worthwhile.

"There's my man," Adrienne said, entering from the bathroom. She almost lunged for him, landing in his arms. They embraced and kissed long and hard. The couple stood locked in a silent moment of reconciliation and peace. They did not want to let go, but both knew that life would pull them back to their reality.

Oscar suddenly looked around the room. "Hey, where's Q?"

"He's in a room down the hall. Maria couldn't stand to be without him one more day, so she begged to come with us." Adrienne planted her head in Oscar's chest. He felt her soft arms around his waist. Her bosom pressed against his torso. Words couldn't express the longing he had for her, but his body responded for him.

"I missed you so much," Oscar said.

"I can tell." She smiled. "I missed you too. How have you guys been holding up?"

"The boys are fine. But it's just been so hard. I don't know what the hell I'm doing anymore or who I'm trying to please or what direction I'm taking."

"Corporate law not working out for you, huh?"

"It's not that I don't have an interest," he offered. "Just not a passion. I was so gung ho about coming to D.C., but I put you all through all this for nothing."

"No more than I put you through when I was in school," Adrienne argued. "Besides, you have another two years before you graduate. Things will work out."

"I wish I had your faith."

"I just have a husband who's always ready to catch me so I can make leaps of faith."

"Do you think we could bribe the kids to go to the arcade downstairs?"

"I don't think bribery would be necessary—just small change." They both let out quiet giggles.

"Good, 'cause I only got a couple of hours before I have to go back to studying and only one Donny Hathaway CD. So foreplay will be quick," he said.

"How did you get to be so romantic?" She laughed.

"Romance for Dummies," he joked. "Twelve dollars on eBay."

They fell back on the bed and laughed as Oscar searched his pockets for change.

By ten o'clock everyone had been lulled into sleep. The kids covered the floor in their sleeping bags, watching the TV Guide Channel roll an endless barrage of show listings in front of them. Adrienne had picked her side of the bed and was bunched in a ball, snoring lightly.

Oscar adjusted his glasses as he scanned the pages of the law book on his lap. He grinned at the thin veil of pages that stood between him and the end of his chapter. He was rubbing the edges of the last two pages when a soft rattle at the door stole his attention.

He climbed over his children and spied through the peephole. Maria was on the other side. He cracked the door open and crept outside.

"Hey," he said and they exchanged a brief hug. "What's up?"

"Is Adrienne asleep? I wanted to talk to her."

"Yeah, she knocked out about an hour ago," he said. "What's up?"

"Well, I can share it with you," she said. "You're like the brother I never had."

Oscar smiled. He never knew how Maria took him, considering he had turned in her husband. His eyes lit up. "Thank you." He beamed. "I appreciate that."

"Well, I just wanted to let y'all know that Andre asked me to marry him, and I accepted."

"That's great." Oscar hugged her again. "He really seems like a good man, and is working hard on that music thing. Congratulations."

"Thank you." She placed her hands over her face. "He has been working hard to set up a foundation for us. And . . . well, he got signed to a major deal a couple of weeks ago."

"Are you serious?"

"Yeah. He already moved out to L.A. where the label is and wants us to meet him out there."

"That's a big move." Oscar folded his arms and leaned back on the doorpost. "How does Q feel about this?"

"He's okay." She ran her fingers through her hair. "He was pretty quiet when I asked him if he wanted to go. But he said he wanted whatever made me happy."

"And are you . . . happy?"

"Yeah," Maria said, and the tears fell. "I am happy. It's

just . . . I'm so not used to it. I'm waiting for the other shoe to drop, you know? Like Andre will beat me or leave me out there, or our plane will crash, or something else."

"You don't feel you deserve happiness?"

"I hurt a lot of people getting to this point, Oscar," she said. "I just don't feel worthy of such a blessing."

"My understanding of the Bible is rusty, but I thought you never deserved a blessing in the first place. Weren't you blessed because God loved you so much?"

"I don't know." Maria wiped her face dry. "I just wish there was some way to know if I was making the right decision."

"What does this tell you?" He pointed to her heart.

"It says for the first time I can wake up and not be afraid that love could hurt me both physically and emotionally. For the first time I feel like I can fall and not get stomped in the ground for being weak. For the first time I have friends and family who care about me rather than what drugs or money my boyfriend has access to. I feel like I could have a future."

"Then what's the problem?"

"I am afraid my past will come back to haunt me."

"Maria." Oscar took her hand. "The past you are talking about could come back looking for you. But do you know what they will find? They'll find a new person who is a responsible adult, a hard worker, and a good friend. Those moments in our lives are in our past to shape us, not rule over us."

"So you're okay with everything you have done in the past?"

"Maria, I've made a lot of mistakes. But the one thing I will say is when I go back into this room and see my kids and wife lying there, I have to move forward. Not just for me but for them. We owe it to the people we love to keep on hoping for the happy ending."

"I'm gonna have a happy ending." Her tone was both a statement and a question.

"You're going to have a happy ending."

Chapter XL

Then Jesus said, "Did I not tell you that if you believed, you would see the glory of God?" So they took away the stone. Then Jesus looked up and said, "Father, I thank you that you have heard me. I knew that you always hear me, but I said this for the benefit of the people standing here, that they may believe that you sent me." When he had said this, Jesus called in a loud voice, "Lazarus, come out!" The dead man came out, his hands and feet wrapped with strips of linen, and a cloth around his face. Jesus said to them, "Take off the grave clothes and let him go." John 11:40–44.

There was no blinding light in death. Damon just saw darkness. An all-encompassing, all-consuming black encircled him. It was the familiar place he hid all his anger. It was home to the myriad of sins he inflicted on himself and others. He could see right through it, yet couldn't make out anything beyond it. His fists were no good here. He could spit acid all he wanted; no one would hear him. He couldn't even see himself, though he knew he was there, floating in a heap of feelings, emotions, and the shit that had become his life. He tried to move but couldn't get a foothold on anything solid around him. He yelled out, but only through his mind's eyes winced from the treble in his voice. He heard no sound.

Suddenly he longed to escape the dark hole of existence. He shook and jumped and swung his arms out, but remained in the same spot. He prayed for some pictorial slide show of his life, like in the movies, to flash across his face so he could at least see where he had been. But the deafening white noise of silence was all he had. He stayed there for what seemed like forever. Then his mind wandered to the idea of eternity.

Was this it, a lifetime of darkness? This was worse than hell, not because the abyss was unknown, but because it was all too familiar. He had lived his life walking in complete darkness, swinging at anything that made noise, got in his way, or slowed him down. But for all his wandering, where had he ended up? Back in the very spot he left. The black hole of his soul, and he had enough.

He screamed in his mind, "I am sorry, Lord. Forgive me!" Suddenly, like a pair of sharp scissors poking through a black canvas, a sliver of light opened up his world. He could hear himself screaming as beams of light burned through the darkness till he could see clearly in front of him.

Damon watched as a pile of doctors worked feverishly over a man. His feet jolted and kicked as 5,000 volts surged through his body. With each shock, a searing pain stabbed at Damon and he felt himself falling back away from the darkness, until finally he disappeared from the black completely.

He blinked his eyes open to see his pastor clutching his Bible and mumbling prayers to himself. A doctor dabbed at Damon's face with a towel, soaking up the beads of sweat that gathered in between the lines in his forehead.

"I think we got him back," the doctor said. The wrinkles around his eyes lifted and Damon could see his red cheeks under the mask. "Mr. Harvey, can you hear me?"

"Yeah," Damon mumbled, his eyes trying to stay open. He did not want to return to the darkness under his eyelids.

"We thought you were a goner for a second there, son." The doctor grabbed his shoulder and pulled off his facial mask. "I think he is fine now, Officer."

Damon didn't see the corrections officer standing guard behind the bed. Before he could get his bearings, the guard was on him and had clicked a metal handcuff on his wrist and clamped it onto the bedpost.

"What?" Damon could barely move before a nurse pricked him with her magical needle. The room expanded to three times its size and Damon felt his mouth curl into a slow grin. He kept it there as the pastor bent over to his ear.

"You are truly blessed," the pastor said. "For a second I thought we would be calling your mother, telling her to buy a black dress."

"Can you stay a little longer?" Damon pleaded sheepishly. "Maybe read a few more verses?"

"Of course." Pastor Jeffries settled into a nearby chair, cracked his book open, and softly read until only the words floated in Damon's head.

After a few weeks of rest in the prison hospital, Damon was transported back into the general population. The second he found free time he searched for Pastor Jefferies. Damon found him in the cafeteria, sweeping the floor with a sad, wilted broom with barely enough straw bristles to move any dirt.

"Hey, Pastor Jefferies." Damon waved as he slowly walked toward him.

"Well, someone is feeling much better." Jeffries let the broom fall to the floor as he pulled Damon into his arms. "I'm glad to see you back."

"That's the thing, Pastor." Damon scratched his head. "I ain't coming back. I can't."

"Why not?"

"You saw how I reacted when I saw my son. I bugged out and almost killed that dude in the shower. No matter what I do, I disappoint everyone. I can't do that to God."

"Everyone has setbacks, Damon." Pastor Jeffries chuckled. "There have been many times I wanted to crush some skulls like you did."

"But you didn't."

"Not now, but we all have our pasts." Pastor Jeffries extended his hand toward a chair and they both sat down. "The important thing is asking for forgiveness and then moving forward. Moving forward doesn't mean doing the same thing, but trying to approach life in a different way, in the renewed spirit of Jesus."

"I don't know if I can control my anger."

"I never thought you could," Pastor Jeffries said. "That's why you are surrendering it to God."

"Oh," Damon said. "Pastor, do you think God will ever let me see my kid again? Do you think I will ever be able to be someone God or anybody would be proud of?"

"The word says 'seek ye the kingdom first and everything else will be taken care of.'"

"How do you do that?"

"You're on the right path. You're reading your Bible, going to church. Why don't you work on a ministry, help someone else?"

"How the fu . . . heck am I supposed to help anyone else when I don't know anything myself?"

"We all have spiritual and material gifts that can be used to glorify God. We have a computer ministry, a prayer ministry, even a literacy ministry, all going on every week."

"I used to always read to my kid. And I was pretty good in school till I dropped out."

"Well, there you go. Why don't you try tutoring some of the other prisoners? Get immersed in service and let God handle your problems."

"I'll think about it."

"While you're thinking," Pastor Jeffries said, slapping the broom with his foot and sliding it over in Damon's direction, "make yourself useful."

"Man, how I supposed to sweep with this thing? It's only got like three bristles."

Pastor Jeffries smiled and patted Damon's back. "Approach it like your ministry. Start small and sooner or later you'll look back and see everything you've accomplished."

"Don't play me, Pastor." Damon smiled. "You just want me to sweep the floor."

"I always knew you were a quick study." Pastor Jefferies saluted him and walked out, leaving Damon alone in the room making small circles on the ground with the broom.

Damon didn't realize how hard his new ministry would be until he heard his first tutoree read one of his favorite books that he had read to Q.

"I d-d-d-d-d-do l-l-lo-love ga-greeeeen . . ." The young prisoner looked up, his fingers still following the sentence on the page. "Hey, what is this word?"

"Eggs." Damon kept his expression even. He didn't want to smirk or throw the book like he wanted to. Q used to read this book in five minutes. This man, twenty-five years of muscle and cockiness, couldn't even get through the first page in their hour session. Damon said a silent prayer and managed a smile. "You're doing good."

"This shit is bullshit." The man leaned back from his chair. "I hate reading and when I get out I never have to do it anyway."

"Do you drive? Don't you want to know which direction you're going on the freeway?"

"I got a brand-new Range Rover sitting at home waiting for me," the man said. "It don't matter which way I go. Everyone is following me." Damon stared at the man for a moment. They were bonded together not only by location but by mentality. This man saw his materialism as his badge, his proof of being a worthy member of society, when everyone else spat on him. Would learning to read Dr. Seuss really transform his mentality into believing he was more than the money he made and the pimping lifestyle he maintained?

"Yeah, this stuff all seems stupid right now," Damon said. "But I have to sit here with you 'cause I want my kid to know that I didn't spend my whole dang life messing up people's lives, not trying to do the right thing."

"How old's your son?"

"He's twelve now." Damon winced. He had missed three years of his son's life.

"I got two boys, ten and seven."

"Really?"

"Yeah, man. I kind of wish I would have been there for them, helped them with their homework, all that good stuff. But it's too late now."

"It's never too late, man."

"You really believe that?"

"If I didn't, I wouldn't be here sitting next to you." Damon smiled. "Now, if we can get through this Dr. Seuss book I promise you I will find you something more interesting to read."

As soon as his session was over, Damon went to the library and set out to compile a reading list for his students. He scanned all the beginner books and then moved up to Harry Potter novels. He even found some Donald Goines and James Baldwin, though he had only heard about them, and never read their work. He decided to read each book before he recommended them to his students.

By the end of his first year tutoring, he had twelve students and had read forty-five books. When he was bored with books he perused old newspapers and microfiche. As he was researching an article about Jermaine Dupri in the *Atlanta Journal-Constitution*, he came across a startling article. MAN ROBS BANK, NEARLY KILLS TWO. Framing the headline was a picture of a man he hardly recognized. A young man stared blankly ahead, his lips pressed against each other, his eyes small dugouts of light. His brow carried the weight of years of anger. Under the picture, like a yearbook photo, was a familiar name: Suspect Damon Harvey.

Damon pressed PRINT on the machine and pulled the still-hot page from the tray. He gathered the rest of his books and went back to his room. He stared at the picture and article for what seemed like hours. He debated tossing them in the trash or burning them. But instead he folded the picture and article nicely at the corners and stuck them in his Bible. He could no longer carry the weight of his crimes, no longer punish himself for his past. So he gave it up to someone who could handle his problems. Damon looked at his watch and hurried to his next tutoring session. He had two more students to teach that day, and a small moment in time to learn as much about life as possible."

Epilogue

I sat in the food court area of the CNN center watching people whiz past me by the dozens. My eyes tried to focus in on a pair of eyes, a shoulder blade, anything that resembled my guests of honor. But no one showed up. I fumbled through the entire paper and had started gathering my belongings when a pair of hands covered my eyes.

"Guess who," the creamy baritone moaned behind me. I could tell from the faint aroma of cocoa butter on his hands that it was Carlos. I grabbed his hands and turned around.

"Hey." I pecked his cheek.

"I was beginning to think you were avoiding me." Carlos smiled and I had to steady my legs against the table. God, he was fine.

"No just thinking." I pried myself from his grip.

"Uh-oh." Carlos raised his hands in the air as if he were getting arrested. "I don't know if I can handle you thinking."

"Cute," I said. "Look, I invited you and another person because I wanted to explain something and I . . ."

"Am I too late for the party?" David stepped up to us in a sandpaper-colored suit that made him look like he had stepped off a European runway. I gulped. Why was I doing this again?

"This is the other person you invited?" Carlos questioned.

"Yes." Carlos rolled his eyes and I placed a soft hand on his chest. "Just wait a second, have a seat."

"And I suppose you want me on your left side." David snickered.

"Think you missed that opportunity," Carlos mumbled.

"Young cat," David said, turning to Carlos, "this ain't no campus open house. We don't need any class clowns here."

"Do you need me to show you I'm a grown man?"

"Before this turns into a cockfight, I just have a few things to say." I offered David a seat. He stared at me and Carlos and then sat in the chair next to me.

"Well?" Carlos said.

"The floor's yours," David added.

"I invited you both here because you both need to hear what I have to say," I said. "Look, I was lucky enough to have a husband who loved me and cared for me and we grew up quick. And our bond is something that will never leave. And then I found a man who helped me rediscover what tenderness meant. What a caress and a kiss felt like all over again. You are my past and my present and I want to truly thank you both." I steadied my trembling hands and pressed on. "But the only way I can have a future is to really take time for me. Not because of circumstance or because I was hurt. But really taking time to figure out who I am. And I can't do that with either one of you as my man."

"So you don't want to see either of us?" David said.

"I am asking you to be my friends," I said. "That's all I can give right now."

"I'm sorry." Carlos got up. "You know I love you and would do anything for you. But I thought we had something . . . and I am looking for a wife. I got enough friends."

"I understand," I said as I closed in on Carlos and put my arms around him. Carlos looked at me with his huge brown eyes, hesitating under my embrace.

"I gotta go." He gave a hard stare to David and then marched off. I looked at my ex, half expecting him to follow.

"You can leave too, you know. I'll understand."

"If being your friend will keep me in your life, that's what I'll do."

"I am not interested in anything other than friendship."

"There was a time when I was your best friend." He stood up. "I miss that."

"Me too." I looked at my watch. I had only had this job for a day and I was already running late. "I gotta go."

"Hey, good luck with your new job and your new life. I'm proud of you."

"Thank you." I hugged him and felt the warmth in his arms I used to feel. "I appreciate you supporting me."

"So, can a friend take you out for dinner?"

"Someday." I smiled. "But right now I need to enjoy my own company for a while." I waved, walked to the elevator bank, and pushed the UP button. I didn't know what would happen once I got upstairs to my new life. But I knew I was ready to tackle anything.

The sky was painted the kind of blue that inspired birds to glide across it all afternoon. Under the shade of the small gazebo in the back of Christopher's house, the preacher stretched his collar as he read from the Bible. Alonzo stood just in front of Christopher, sweat dripping down the back of his neck.

"I now pronounce you man and wife." The preacher smiled. "You may now kiss the bride."

Alonzo turned and lifted the veil that covered Camille's immaculate face. A single tear fell from her face. It strategically ran down the back of her cheek, and stopped just short of her chin.

The couple turned and the small crowd of twenty or so

family and friends roared into a crescendo of applause. Christopher held his new brother, Michael, in his arms, and pressed the baby's tiny hands together as Alonzo and Camille walked past them.

"That's Daddy and Mama, buddy." Christopher laughed as Michael gurgled in amazement at the fingers in front of him.

The guests sifted free from the block of chairs that sat around the makeshift altar, and headed for the reception area held under a large tent toward the edge of the property.

Within seconds the spread of food was devoured, leaving only a handful of pastries and a smattering of soft drinks.

Christopher found his father taking a break from the barrage of photos. The photographer struggled to juggle changing the batteries in his camera while eating off a plate of chicken wings on his lap.

"You did it, Dad." Christopher patted his father with one hand while holding on to his brother with the other. "I'm so proud of you."

"Son, if you had not forgiven me for my mistakes and taken me in, I don't think I ever would have had this new chance for happiness."

"Well, we're proud of you, Dad," Christopher said. "Both of us." Michael held his hands out when he saw his father.

Alonzo grabbed him and held him in his arms. "God, am I too old to be a daddy again?"

"Yes." Deborah strolled down the aisle, approaching her son and ex-husband.

"Deborah." Alonzo's voice trembled. "What are you doing here?"

"Your new wife sent me an invitation. And despite our differences I am here to support my son. For whatever reason he seems to believe in you. Don't let him down."

"I won't."

"Okay, I'm done being a bitch. Now let me see that baby."

Deborah extended her arms and swiped Michael from Alonzo. The baby smiled as Deborah cooed at him.

"Thank God he doesn't look like you, either." Deborah smiled and walked away.

"Wow. What was I thinking when I married that one?"

"Hey, she was a good mother." Christopher smiled. "Like you're a good father. And to answer your question, you're never too old to love, Pop."

"I hope you're right." Alonzo smiled.

"All right, let's get the whole family together," the photographer said. Alonzo grabbed Christopher's hand and led him to his wife. They all arranged themselves around her.

"You look beautiful," Christopher whispered in Camille's ear. She faced him and gave a smile that would inspire artists.

"Thank you for treating me like family," she said.

"You are family."

"Hey, don't forget this one," Deborah yelled as she walked over with Michael.

"I got him." Christopher took the baby from his mother and then held him in his arms. "Thanks for being here, Mom."

"I'll always be here for you whenever you need me. Just say the word. Now go on with your other family."

"Thank you." Christopher dabbed at tears hitting the corners of his eyes.

"All right, Roberts family, say cheese." The photographer snapped the picture, and for the first time Christopher felt like he belonged, not only with his family but in life. He endured the photo session and then stepped back to watch his new family do the electric slide to Frankie Beverly and Maze.

"What, you're not going to dance?" Christopher turned to see Tim standing in front of him in a dark gray suit that framed his beautiful physique perfectly.

"Hey, what are you doing here?"

"I was at work and I knew how important this day was to you, so I left early and here I am."

"Wow, thank you. But you didn't have to do it. I mean, we've only been going out a little while."

"Hey, if it's important to you it's important to me."

"You're important to me," Christopher said. Suddenly he was very aware of the beads of sweat trickling down his neck and torso. Tim sat down next to him and grabbed his hand under the table.

"I'm just going to say it before I lose my nerve." Tim exhaled and inched his way closer to Christopher until his lips tickled his ear. "I love you, Chris."

"I love you too." They both smiled as Tim gripped his hand tighter. "Now what?"

"Now we just enjoy the moment while we have it," Tim said, and the couple watched the Roberts family shimmy and shake until the sun came down.

"Oscar Parks." The announcer called Oscar's name, and he rose, holding his cap to keep it from slipping off his now-bald head. He walked past the podium, shook the dean's hand, smiled for the camera, and was back at his seat in less than two minutes. *A hundred and twenty thousand dollars for this?* he thought. It wasn't until his family joined him outside the hall and he had caressed his leather diploma case that the moment felt real.

"I graduated from law school." He grinned at Adrienne, who held his face and kissed him.

"Yep," she said softly. "You have been my husband and friend, but seeing all you went through for this moment you are truly my hero."

"What are you talking about? You already have your law degree."

"That was before we had kids and all our responsibilities. We were Bohemians then. Not real adults. You went and did the damn thing."

"Thank you, baby." He laughed. "But I couldn't have done it without my sugar mama."

"Yeah, and you will be paying me back tonight," she said as they both giggled.

"Daddy, we have a gift for you," Joy said, standing slightly in front of the other children. "Okay."

"They all grabbed on to a banner and pulled it out. It stretched a couple of feet and read BEST LAWYER DADDY IN THE WORLD and had a hand-drawn picture of Oscar, his head encompassing half the banner. His stick arms held big red books that said LAW BOOKS on them.

"Oh my gosh." Oscar laughed.

"So, Mr. big-time lawyer, what are you going to do now with that fancy degree?" Adrienne asked, while caressing his neck.

"I'm going to Disney World!" Oscar shouted as all the kids cried "yeah" in unison.

"We're already in debt." Oscar hunched his shoulders. They walked outside and felt the remnants of the spring sun beating down on their faces as they went to their car.

Damon had known God was a miracle worker when he was sent to his warden's office two weeks ago. He sat silently, waiting for the warden to enter his office. The slightly small man hunched over at the shoulders dispensed with niceties and plopped in his chair.

"We're offering you a weekend pass."

"Huh?" Damon gulped back salvia caught in his throat.

"We recognize what you have been doing with our literacy program," the warden said. "It has gotten a lot of recognition both locally and nationally. And we understand you have a son who is moving out of town. We want to offer you a chance to say good-bye."

Damon sat stunned. It had been so long since people had been nice to him. It felt strange to have someone, let alone the prison system, do something nice for him. He held his Bible and prayed a silent prayer, and then said, "Thank you, Warden."

"Keep it up, Harvey," the warden said.

Now as Damon sat boxing CDs and lamp shades, he felt ashamed his transformation had taken so long. He watched his son move crates outside to the car, careful to avoid eye contact with him. When Q was safely outside, Damon moved to Maria.

"He won't talk to me. This was a mistake coming here," Damon whined.

"He loves you, Damon," Maria insisted. "He's just mad and hurt and scared."

"Well, so am I," Damon said.

"I know." Maria rose from her seat. "Luckily it's not about you, though. It's about him."

"I know." Damon pursed his lips.

"Then get out there." She pointed to the door, and Damon trudged outside. The sun was reclining behind the Georgia mountains and a red line stretched across the horizon.

"You all ready for the big move?" Damon stood by the steps as Q stuffed boxes in the back of a U-Haul truck.

"I guess," Q said, not looking at his dad.

"I hear you can get great seats at Lakers games."

"Yeah," Q muttered.

"And the women there are fine. You'll have you a girlfriend in no time."

"Whatever."

"Q." Damon walked over to his son and put his hands on his shoulders. He felt his son's body stiffen under his palms.

"Look, buddy, I'm sorry, okay? I know I messed you over and I left you here alone, and I am sorry." He could see his son's eyes clouding with tears and his body trembling. "I asked God to forgive me for everything I ever did to you and everyone else. And God did. And then I had to forgive myself so I could move on. Don't you think it's time you give me a break too?"

Q stood for a moment, his lanky arms moving slowly back and forth, until finally they wrapped around his father. "I don't want to leave you, Daddy."

"You are not leaving me, Son, you are just moving on with your life," Damon said. "But I will always be here for you, in prayer and in spirit, until I can be with you for real."

"I missed you so much," Q said, his body shaking in his father's arms.

"I missed you too." Damon turned his son around. "Here, look at this sunset. See how big it is? The one you'll see in L.A. will be the same one I see here. So we aren't that far away."

"I know, but—" Q interrupted.

"Shhh." Damon hugged his son. "Let's share our sunset together." They both watched as the sun finally dipped out of sight, leaving Damon and Q basking under the last strip of light that they had together.